SIMCAVALIER BOOK FIVE

UNSTABLE REALITIES

Published in paperback in 2023 by Sixth Element Publishing
on behalf of Kate Baucherel

Sixth Element Publishing
Arthur Robinson House
13-14 The Green
Billingham TS23 1EU
www.6epublishing.net

ISBN 978-1-914170-40-9

British Library Cataloguing in Publication Data. A catalogue record for this book is available from the British Library.

SIMCAVALIER BOOK FIVE

UNSTABLE REALITIES

KATE BAUCHEREL

Books by Kate Baucherel

The SimCavalier series in paperback, eBook and audiobook

Book 1: Bitcoin Hurricane

Book 2: Hacked Future

Book 3: Tangled Fortunes

Hacked: The First SimCavalier Trilogy (Books 1-3)

Book 4: Critical Nexus

Book 5: Unstable Realities

Short stories in the Harvey Duckman Presents… series

Gridlock (A SimCavalier Origins story)

Xanthe (A SimCavalier Origins story)

The Importance of Carrot Cake

White Christmas

Finch

Parrot Radio (A Finch story)

Firebird (A Finch story)

The Eagle's Flight (A Finch story)

Non-Fiction

Poles Apart: Challenges for business in the Digital Age (MX Publishing, 2014)

Blockchain Hurricane: Origins, Applications and Future of Blockchain and Cryptocurrency (Business Expert Press, 2020)

What's Hot in Blockchain and Crypto Volumes 1 & 2

CONTENTS

1: VIRTUAL GAMES

The motion capture skin was making Anita itch. Despite the best efforts of the ancient air conditioning, a familiar cloying humidity was seeping into the competition studio. Sweat trickled down her neck, and not for the first time she wished that the inventors of these smart skins had considered the increasingly extreme conditions under which they would be used.

The material she preferred for training in the Indonesian heat wicked away sweat and regulated her body temperature. In competition, though, she was tied to using the same suits as every other Olympic hopeful in her discipline. Did it give people from temperate zones an advantage? Perhaps, but Anita and her team-mates had no choice in the matter. The Indonesian team couldn't take all its athletes across the world to Reykjavik for the live Olympic Games. The financial and environmental cost was too great. Sports that pitted athletes directly against each other on a track, in a pool, on a court or a pitch, had to be live. For every other discipline, including the kata competitions, they'd opted to use the virtual arena.

Anita was not going to let that thought intrude on her preparation. She'd seen other members of her karate team give in to the negativity, stepping onto the mats with a losing mindset, and bowing out into obscurity. She would not be following their lead. She was at the peak of her training and favourite for the competition. The decision of the Indonesian committee had robbed her of the chance of a double gold by not sending her to Iceland for the sparring finals. All of her energy was focused on taking gold in the kata.

The mats in the centre of the studio were currently occupied by the avatar of her closest rival, the Kazakh champion, Natalya Kemelov. Thousands of miles further north, in a studio not unlike this one, Kemelov was bowing formally to the on-site judge and preparing for the first move of her kata, quivering with focus and strength. The sensors in her skinsuit interpreted each focused or explosive move down to the most nuanced muscle twitch, and an array of cameras caught every angle, building a perfect hologram of the woman that was projected to the mats of the five competition studios and into the Olympic metaverse for fans around the world. Huge screens on the studio walls showed the audience reaction from the other locations and the metaverse. Like the small live audience in Anita's studio, everyone on-screen was silent, focused on the avatar's performance.

Anita didn't need to watch. Only her performance mattered. She looked beyond Kemelov to the sponsor banners on the wall and focused on the mesmerising spirals of the MetaBand logo until it filled her vision and blocked every other sense. She withdrew into herself, following the rhythm of her own heartbeat and her breathing in a familiar ritual of personal preparation.

Kemelov's final cry echoed around the studio, and the avatar glided back into a ready stance, bowing slowly again to the judge. The local and remote audiences broke into frenzied applause. At a signal, silence fell again and judges in each of the five competition studios revealed their marks. The applause redoubled. Kemelov was in gold medal position and had guaranteed her place in the Kazakh team for the Olympics. Anita was pleased for her friend and rival, but she knew that she herself was the clear favourite for today's title, as long as she performed to the standard expected of her.

"Anita Trianna," called the announcer.

Anita took a deep breath, smoothed her gi, tugged one last time at the knot of her belt for luck, and started her walk onto the mats. Her heartbeat pulsed a familiar rhythm and she kept her breathing steady, but the bead of sweat on the nape of her neck threatened to distract her. She had to focus. She stood ready, shutting out the crowd. Her skinsuit had stopped itching but felt tight around her legs and she flexed her quads to try and relieve the pressure.

The signal to start didn't come. An unfamiliar noise broke the spell and Anita blinked in confusion. The judge, usually impassive, gave her a sympathetic and bemused half-smile.

"Stand down," said the announcer. "We have a technical fault."

Anita exhaled, bowed, and paced respectfully backwards off the mats. Once her bare feet hit the floor of the studio, she became aware of how slippery the untreated surface had become. The humidity was fierce. The environmental controls that should keep each arena within acceptable competition parameters were evidently struggling.

Her coach, looking furious, clutched at Anita's hand. "I will sort this out," he hissed. "Stay focused. You can do it." He looked up at a technician who was hovering beside them. "What?" he snapped.

"The avatar generation suite is reporting an error in your skinsuit sensor data," said the technician apologetically. "The new MetaBand satellite links are all showing green lights, so it's a local issue. We've had a lot of problems with moisture, and that could be affecting transmission." He looked around and beckoned a female colleague over to them. "Would you mind if Samaira here checked your connections?"

Anita nodded. There was nothing else they could do. She allowed the technician to lead her away to the changing rooms, trying to maintain her inner calm. The pressure on her legs had eased. In the background she could hear raised voices.

"What if you have a technical problem at the Olympics?" her coach was shouting. "What then? This is pure discrimination against athletes from the global south and climate-damaged countries."

"All our equipment has been fully tested for these conditions, and much worse," responded the technician, trying to calm the coach. "We don't know where the error originated. We're checking everything."

Anita let the voices wash over her. Whatever the arguments, the one thing that mattered was her performance on the mats. She knew she could beat Kemelov and confirm her place at the Reykjavik games.

Samaira's hands were gentle as she silently checked each connection on the motion capture skin. She knew not to chatter and break Anita's focus. She wiped the beads of sweat away from Anita's neck, a cool relief.

"All good," she said softly.

Anita smiled and re-fastened her gi and belt, tugging at the knot three times as her unconscious talisman. Samaira led her back to the competition studio floor where her coach and the judge were waiting.

"The technical problem is resolved," said the judge. "Are you ready to compete?"

"Yes," said Anita. She took her place at the side of the mat and the judge returned to his chair. He nodded to her, his face once again impassive.

"Anita Trianna," called the announcer.

She stalked onto the mats and bowed to the judge. This time, the signal she expected came. "Papuren!" she cried, naming her kata. Her focus narrowed, her core tightened, and her arms extended, hands meeting, palms down with grace and strength. This was her moment, and she was not going to let the delay change her destiny.

The cheers that rang around the studio were deafening. Anita stood stock still, drained and elated. She could not have performed better. But was it good enough? It felt like an age before the judge in front of her displayed his scores. She blinked at the numbers and felt a stirring of excitement. In the opinion of that one judge, she had performed better than Kemelov. She couldn't see the results from the other four locations, but as the volume of the cheering rose, she realised she didn't need to see them. She had pipped Kemelov for the gold medal in this competition, and her place in the Olympics was assured. She bowed and paced backwards off the mats, her legs almost buckling with relief. Her coach and teammates surrounded her, hugging and cheering, and Anita at last allowed herself to relax and enjoy the celebrations.

The team bus was waiting for them outside. Anita waved to the crowd, clutching her medal and smiling at the news drones that jockeyed for position above their heads. Her coach ushered her aboard and she fell into her seat as the bus glided gently through the crowd, a safety buffer parting the sea of people like a boat carving through water. Gazing through the window as they turned out of the complex, Anita was surprised to see another crowd gathering on the main street outside the town's casino. The atmosphere was ugly, and the bus detoured around them, avoiding any confrontation.

"What's going on?" she asked.

Her coach laughed. "I think they're trying to collect their winnings, and the casino's not paying out fast enough," he said. "Everyone knew you'd nail this one. You were the favourite by far. I think there was a lot of money riding on this medal." He tapped the golden disc that still hung on its blue ribbon around Anita's neck.

"It would have been a different story if the technicians hadn't fixed that fault," said Anita. "What was it, anyway? I don't think it was my skinsuit."

"I don't know," said her coach. "One minute they were checking all the wires and receivers, and the next all the lights went green. There must have been a short circuit, or a blown fuse."

"What would have happened if they hadn't found it?" asked Anita curiously. "Would I still have been able to compete? Would I still be on the Olympic team?"

"That's a tough one," said her coach. "I think that yes, you'd be on the kata team based on your current form, but you wouldn't place at this tournament. Kemelov would have taken the title."

Anita craned her neck to look out of the window. The casino crowd was now far in the distance. "If they're so unhappy about trying to collect their winnings, imagine how cross they'd have been if they'd lost. I mean, if I'd lost," she said. "I don't like to think about people betting on my karate. It's an extra layer of pressure. I don't want to feel responsible for their lives."

Her coach nodded sympathetically. "You put enough pressure on yourself already," he said, "but look, it's paid off. You're going to the Olympics!"

Anita frowned. "I know," she said, "but I won't really be there. The only thing that's going to Reykjavik is my avatar. I'll be back in that damp little studio in an itchy skinsuit."

"You qualified for the kumite competition," Anita's coach reminded her. "There's still a chance that you could go."

Anita shook her head. "It'll take a miracle to get me there," she said sadly. "The committee knows they have a good chance of a remote medal without spending a cent, and that's all that matters to them. I'm right at the bottom of the list."

"Stranger things have happened," said her coach.

He held up his smartscreen. The splash headline of the news article he'd been reading made Anita gasp. The Sladen Foundation was close to announcing its final round of grants to Olympic athletes who needed support to reach the competition. Anita felt a rush of excitement. Maybe she would achieve her dream of competing in Reykjavik after all.

2: DEFENDERS

Cameron and Ross lounged in the otherwise empty Argentum Associates office, enjoying a rare moment of calm between raging storms of cyber chaos. They were both riveted by an augmented reality performance taking place right in front of them, webcast into the middle of the office in three lifelike dimensions.

"That was worth waiting for," said Cameron as the applause sounded over the speakers. She lowered her screen and the avatar projection of Anita Trianna disappeared. She turned to Ross. "She's very, very good."

"I think so too," said Ross. He pulled out his smartscreen and checked some details. "According to the listing, she's qualified for both parts of the event, but one is remote, and one is live," he said. "She's a real medal hopeful for both, but she's not in the travelling team. I think she'd be a good athlete to sponsor."

"Absolutely," said Cameron. "It'll be fantastic if she can compete in the sparring in Reykjavik. She's even better at that than she is at kata. I'd love to see her get the double gold."

"This is your sport," said Ross with a smile. "You know what you're looking at. I wanted your opinion before the vote."

"She's one of the best and she's right at the peak of

her career," said Cameron firmly. "She deserves every chance to compete on the world stage."

Ross fell silent, and Cameron could see that he was deep in thought. She strolled across the office and gazed out of the huge window, a floor to ceiling sheet of glass with a view six storeys down to the street below.

The rest of the team were scattered to the four winds, working hard. Pete had responded to an urgent call from an old client with a newly discovered breach and a big data protection headache, and he'd taken Noor along with him to the site on the other side of central London. Michelle was working from home, auditing a set of smart contracts for a finance company that wanted to make doubly sure its systems were watertight after a scare, and who was paying a premium Cameron couldn't refuse in order to get the work done fast. As soon as that was finished, Michelle would be travelling to Reykjavik with Ross.

Four hundred miles to the north near the remote hamlet of Dunswyke, close to the Scottish border, Joel and Sandeep were working with police and the National Cyber Security Centre to untangle a complex investigation into an attack on the headquarters of the Sladen Foundation, the flagship philanthropic project of international tech superstar Jack Sladen. Susie was with them, helping where she could thanks to the neatly timed summer slowdown in her hectic conference schedule.

Cameron had a contract from the Olympic Metaverse Infosec Team, known to all and sundry as MIST. This sprawling virtual group of cybersecurity experts had been charged with keeping one step ahead of all the criminals who were trying to penetrate the Olympic Metaverse fabric. Alongside her work with MIST, she was picking up every other little job that came through the door, putting in more hours than she could remember working since the early days of building the Argentum Associates business. At least back then she and Ross had worked hand in hand to share the burden. For the next few weeks, he would not be there. It was good to take a few minutes out to talk about something other than work and cybercrime.

"Have you ever tried that kata?" asked Ross.

Cameron shook her head. "No," she said. "I've never learned kata Papuren, but they all come from the same roots and there are plenty of moves that I recognise. I know how hard they can be to perform well. Her combination of grace and strength and speed is something else, though. It's way beyond anything I could hope to do."

"It looks like hard work, that's for sure," said Ross. "I really mean that," he added as Cameron gave him an incredulous look.

"Ross, you're an elite Olympic athlete yourself," she said. "You're going to be standing on the on the same stage. Don't give me any of that imposter syndrome. You work just as hard. She couldn't do a triathlon, and you couldn't perform that kata."

"That's decided then," said Ross. He tapped his screen carefully to select Trianna's profile, cast his vote, then confirmed his identity with the chip embedded at the base of his thumb and forefinger. "That's my vote committed," he said. "She's more than halfway to the threshold. If she gets enough backers, the Sladen Foundation DAO is paying her fare."

"How do you make sure that there isn't a fixed vote?" asked Cameron. "What if I put myself forward for, I don't know, skateboarding, and got a free trip to Iceland?"

Ross laughed. "I can't quite imagine you on a skateboard," he said. "There's a final process after the DAO vote that adds a layer of due diligence on the winners. You'd fall at the final hurdle. Literally."

"The world is safe from my skateboarding, then," said Cameron. "I wasn't bad when I was ten, but I wouldn't want to try it now."

A thought was intruding into this moment of calm from the world of work. Cameron tried to ignore it, but it nagged at her mind.

"Will the whole mess in Dunswyke and the investigation into the Sladen Foundation cause any problems?" she said.

"Not at all," said Ross happily. "The way Sladen set it up was absolutely above board. It's a Distributed Autonomous Organisation so there is no single entity in charge. I've checked, believe me. All the processes are automated. It'll keep running regardless of what happens up there in Dunswyke, for this Olympics and future games. All the original funds are already in place, and there's a pipeline of investment coming through from the market. It's brilliant."

"I'm glad that one thing Jack Sladen worked on is legit

and functional," said Cameron with a wry smile. "I tried very hard to keep him on the straight and narrow."

"You did your best," said Ross. "Have you spoken to him since everything kicked off in Dunswyke?"

Cameron shook her head. "He's furious with me," she said. "That's one reason why I'm back down here and staying well clear of the investigation. Joel was right in the centre of the action when the data centre was breached, and he and Sandeep and Susie are more than capable of handling our part of the job. I'll let the police and the NCSC do their work in peace. I've given them my statement and all the information they need."

She kicked aimlessly at the leg of the desk, frustrated that the spell of relaxation had been broken. She didn't want to think about the chaos of that attack, the destruction of the artificial intelligence that had been hosted in the data centre, and the look of absolute betrayal and loathing on Jack's face the last time she'd seen him.

"Are you okay, Cameron?" asked Ross.

"I'm fine," she said. "Don't worry about me. You're the priority right now, and you'd better be going. It's getting late."

"You're right," said Ross. He went to tuck his smartscreen in his training bag, then jumped as an unexpected alert vibrated on his wristband. "Dammit," he said, glancing down at the message. "You've got me for another few minutes. Sorry about this."

He got up and opened the office door, then sat back down in his chair and started to roll up his sleeve. A small drone in Team GB livery flew in and stopped next to him, hovering steadily.

Cameron looked from Ross to the drone, puzzled. "What is it?" she said. "Security doesn't usually let drones straight into the building without contacting me first."

"Have you never seen one of these before?" said Ross. "I would have thought... well, perhaps not. It's just a routine drug test. They can go anywhere they want, so they've got full security overrides." A hatch on the drone's chassis opened and Ross reached inside to collect a lightweight tourniquet that he slapped around his upper arm. "They normally come when I'm at home or at training," he continued, "but in theory they can pounce on you any time. Now I think about it, they've never sent one to the office before."

"It's a bit creepy," said Cameron as the little robot's arms unfolded and displayed a sterile needle."

"You get used to it," said Ross, holding very still. "Ow!"

The drone went through the motions, stowing the blood samples away safely for transport to the lab. Once the job was done and its chassis fully closed, a series of indicator lights flickered from red to green, and it turned and flew away through the door. The whole process had taken less than two minutes.

Ross scratched at the skin seal over the neat puncture wound. "I'd better get going," he said. "We're getting our team jackets today and there's a big press event this evening." He picked up his training bag. "I'll try and get back into the office when I can, but from now until we travel, time is tight."

"You concentrate on your racing, RunningManTech," said Cameron. "You've been working up to this your whole life." She ducked her head, embarrassed. "I'm really proud of you, Ross."

He gave her a sincere, broad smile. "I wouldn't be here if it wasn't for you," he said. "Thanks, Cameron."

The silence that passed between them spoke volumes.

Ross turned and walked out of the door with his head held high. Cameron watched him go, reflecting on the journey that he had made from an angry, neglected teenage cybercriminal to a confident, accomplished and happy man.

She didn't have time to dwell on the past, though. A new alert appeared on the office wallscreen, a tip-off for MIST of yet another suspected attack on the fringes of the Olympic metaverse. Unsurprisingly, with less than a month to the start of the games, the slew of cyberattacks directed at the complex virtual environment was as inventive as it was unrelenting. Thus far, the good guys had prevailed, but they couldn't let their guard down for a moment.

MIST responded to immediate threats and searched for holes that had to be plugged before hackers exploited them. These ranged from zero-day vulnerabilities in newly released software to straightforward human error in creating, choosing, and deploying all the necessary hardware and the staggering library of code that delivered the perfect experience for competitors and fans. In the past week alone, Cameron had assessed and closed down a dozen third party pieces of software that offered a clear path into the metaverse construct for any hacker who stumbled across them, from unauthorised avatar generators to unofficial and highly suspect translation apps. Her little AI in training, Mephisto, had logged thousands of phishing attacks and even picked up on a nasty trojan targeted at ticket holders. That was in the process of being analysed and quarantined before it could cause too much damage.

Not for the first time she wished that she had the rest of Argentum Associates with her on this job. She didn't know everyone who had been recruited to form MIST. There was no underlying trust or easy rapport and she had made an effort to stay as anonymous as possible when interacting on the boards and chat rooms. It made her uneasy, but there was a job to do. When the Argentum team worked together, though, there was a unique energy to the well-oiled team and the sparks of inspiration that emerged from their collaborations were world-beating. As soon as the mess in Northumberland had been cleaned up and the regular clients had their problems solved, they'd all be back together. Cameron couldn't wait.

What was this latest notification about? The name 'Anita Trianna' leapt off the screen and Cameron scanned the details with increasing disbelief. The delay to the very feed she'd been watching with Ross may not have been a simple technical fault but the first direct cyberattack on a physical Olympic site.

Ross would love to know about this. Cameron ran out of the office to the railings of the light well that plunged down through the centre of the building.

"Ross!" she shouted, her voice echoing in the space. Too late. She saw his tall, rangy figure disappearing at a steady jog down the outside steps towards the road. Probably for the best, she reflected. She had told him to focus on the games. If he asked, she would give him the details, but for now she had to find someone else to talk to.

She turned back into the office and fired up the coffee machine. The best place to discuss it would be on the dedicated MIST platform, and coffee would definitely help.

Mug in hand, she started to scroll through the boards. The platform was buzzing with speculation on this latest incident, but short on reliable data. The source of the tip-off was as opaque as the methodology. Cameron began to wonder if this wasn't simply a local power outage that had startled some over-sensitive newbie, and her friends and peers seemed equally sceptical. She picked a side room where it seemed some of her closest contacts were active and accepted the randomly generated avatar allocated to her. Today she was a stylised Chinese dragon. It didn't really match her current mood, but she liked it, and it lifted her spirits.

"They lost the sensor link, that's all," said an anonymous

big-eyed lemur. "They were back online within a few minutes."

"There's a continuity problem to fix there," said a member called Sugata, currently appearing as a cartoon car with flashing headlights that annoyed Cameron immensely. "If a connection fails, every remote competition should be able to jump onto a backup, whether that's a generator or a satlink. They all have contingency plans."

"Were there any other reported outages in the same area?" asked Cameron. "Who's on the ground there?"

There were no responses and Cameron checked through the list of people online. They didn't disclose their locations, but she had been quietly researching the backgrounds of her fellow professionals and knew enough to take a good guess. Most were in Europe, some in the Americas, Sugata in India, but apparently no one in southeast Asia.

"Wait," she said. "Was anyone here actually close to the incident? Where did the tip-off come from?"

"Anonymous, posted on one of the darknet forums and relayed to us," said a cat with an admin badge. "There's not much data. Everything we know, you know."

"Which corner of the dark web did this come from, Cat?" said Cameron. "Are we talking hardcore criminals like the Steamyard, a dodgy contractor on Eden, or what?"

"Neither," said the Admin Cat. "I think it came from one of the gambling dens. We have a 'bot constantly scanning for any references to the Olympic metaverse, and this was flagged up."

Cameron blinked, grasping at a thought that floated across her mind. "Gambling, yes?" she said. "What would have been the outcome if they hadn't managed to get back online? I was watching this competition. The final competitor took the gold, after the outage."

There was a burst of excited chatter. Cameron took a swig of her coffee and gathered her thoughts. She knew where to find the tournament rules and a quick search displayed them for her. It was quite simple.

"Trianna was favourite to win," she said. "Not being able to compete wouldn't have affected her qualification for the games, though. She'd have gone through on her recent run of results."

"I don't think this is anything to do with disrupting qualification, SimCavalier," said a cartoon dog avatar with a rich accent from the American deep south, known affectionately to the group as Barker. "Follow the money. Someone's tried to fix the result by taking the favourite out."

Follow the money. Cameron had learned that lesson years ago. "You could be right," said Cameron. "If it's really that simple, we have a clear motive for an attack, something that was planned to disrupt the competition. But they screwed up. She won."

"She did," said Barker. "But is this a one-off or a trial run for the main competitions?"

Yes, thought Cameron. That's the real question. Who might be out there planning to disrupt the virtual games for their own gain, and who was helping them? One of the places to start asking questions could be the very client where Pete and Noor were currently working.

"I can talk to someone in the betting industry," she said, "but very much on the above-board side. Who has contacts at the dodgier end?"

A number of hands went up among the chatroom avatars. Cameron was unsurprised. Gambling and porn were always at the forefront when it came to dipping a toe in the water of new technologies. Their success or failure was a reliable early indicator as to whether the latest tech buzzwords would have any practical application or long-term adoption. The earliest metaverse constructs had been bristling with casinos, some regulated, others very much not.

"Okay," said Cameron, "let's see what we can find. I'll set up a channel for us all to contribute any insights."

She was startled by an insistent ringing in the real world. There was an alert on the other side of the office, and as she turned to see what it was, she narrowly avoided knocking over her half-full coffee cup. She logged out of the MIST platform and waited for the office 'bot to screen the call.

"Argentum Associates, can I help you?" it said.

"Cameron?" came a familiar voice. "It's Andy. Are you there?"

"I'm here," she said, accepting the call and feeding it through to her desk.

"Great," said Andy. "There's something wrong with your contact ID. I couldn't get through the normal way."

Cameron glanced down at her smartscreen, frowning, then realised she had set it to Do Not Disturb while she and Ross watched the kata final.

"Sorry, Andy," she said, tapping it back open and swiping away a handful of new notifications that she had missed. "That's all working now. How can I help the News Channel's finest today? What's the story?"

"Olympic metaverse," said Andy. "I heard on the grapevine that someone's claiming to have hacked into a competition."

Cameron's attention sharpened. "You hang out in some strange places," she said. "This wouldn't have anything to do with a karate qualifier, would it?"

"Karate? No," said Andy. "Esports. The speedrunners."

"Really?" said Cameron, confused. "That mad lot that race each other to complete game levels? I've heard nothing about that at all."

"Are you telling me I've scooped the SimCavalier?" Andy could not have sounded any more smug. "Yes, one of the gamer qualification rounds. The result was declared null and void, but I don't know exactly why. My source hasn't been specific, and the official channels say it was a technical glitch."

"A glitch," said Cameron. "That's nothing new. They need to review their contingency planning and system redundancy, but there's no reason why you'd think that was a cyberattack..." she tailed off. Others in MIST had thought the same about the outage at the karate competition studio. Was this new incident just a coincidence, or was someone very clever at covering their tracks?

"You're not sure, are you?" said Andy. "I'll send over the details. Any chance Ross can give me some soundbites for the piece I'm developing on the hybrid games security?"

"He's getting ready for the Olympics himself, Andy," said Cameron. "He's gone. You've missed him by an hour."

"Damn," said Andy. "Look, I suppose there is no chance you'd do it, would you? We can use an avatar that looks and sounds nothing like you. In fact, we have enough recordings to make a convincing artificial Ross and give it a script from you, if you like."

"Maybe," said Cameron. She was already distracted thinking about the outage in the esports arena and wanted to follow the thread of her intuitions. "Let me get back to you."

"Okay," said Andy. "But let me know quickly. I have a show to put together, and I want this story to run."

"Sure thing," said Cameron. She dropped the call and went to find some more coffee before logging back in to the infosec chat. This time her random avatar was a snake. It did not improve her mood.

"What's up, SimCavalier?" asked Barker. "We lost your dragon there."

"I had to jump out and deal with something," said Cameron. "I've had another tipoff. Can I run it past you before putting it on the platform?" On another screen, she was conducting a rapid search for any mention of the result of the speedrunner event. Sure enough, a void result had been logged due to a technical fault, but there was no speculation or commentary to suggest why or how it had happened.

"Here," she said, pasting the link. "What do you think?"

The chatroom was quiet but for the clicking of keyboards as the group members digested the scant information Cameron had provided and searched their own resources for news. While she waited for a response, Cameron sipped at her coffee, checked the handful of notifications that had come through while her screen was off, and pinged a message to Pete and Noor to say that there might be a new angle to follow up with their client.

Eventually members of the group came trickling back with their thoughts.

"Do we have a library of APIs for the gaming arena?" asked the Admin Cat.

"We do," said Cameron, "and they've been thoroughly audited. I'm not convinced anyone's getting through by that route."

"SQL injection attack?" suggested another member. "There are a million and one idiot guides available online. Any script kiddie could have a go."

"Do they include how to get through the Olympic metaverse security?" said Barker with a deep rolling laugh. "I haven't seen anything myself. You'd expect that kind of attack on the big commercial game servers, but not with the Olympic arena."

Cameron took a gulp of coffee. "Never say never," she

said. "The Olympic metaverse fabric still runs on servers. We know they're a prime target so the security at the data centres is top notch, but you never know. Something could have snuck through the defences. An exploit script to disrupt the players, maybe?"

The groundswell of agreement was cut short by Barker's dissenting voice.

"There's nothing to suggest this is anything more than a technical failure," he said. "I'm sorry, SimCavalier. It's worth logging it so that the ops teams can run all the usual checks on hardware and software, but I don't think there's anything suspicious going on. There are no winners or losers from that result. It's just a glitch."

Following the money again, thought Cameron. Perhaps Barker was right. It was too easy to assume that there were criminal hands in a technical fault. Everything had to be considered.

"I'll add that possibility to the list, Barker," said Cameron. "For the moment I'll log what I know and keep an eye on any new developments. I'm going to follow up that gambling lead now. Let me know how you all get on with your connections."

"Later, SimCavalier," said Barker. "Stay safe."

"You too, Barker," said Cameron. She logged off, picked up her jacket, dropped her coffee cup in the kitchen, and left the office in the care of the 'bots.

3: FAMILY TIES

Cameron and her friends were not the only people taking a close interest in the Olympic metaverse events. In the virtual headquarters of the Steamyard, the Pangolin was tearing into his team. Around the table stood the cheery avatars of four of his elite black hat hackers who were in deep, deep trouble.

"This was an embarrassment," said the Pangolin. "I want your best explanation of why the karate competition did not deliver the required result, and how you are going to make sure that, next time, our clients will get what they ordered. I don't need to tell you how much this has cost the Steamyard in terms of lost revenue and reputational damage. Our pay-out for this job will be delayed, or worse."

The Pangolin glared down the table, but it was hard to convey the depth of his anger when disguised as a small, armoured mammal. At times he wished he still had his old online identity. King Katong had commanded instant respect on the dark side of the metaverse, but that handle had outlived its usefulness. When the real world intruded and an international consortium of cybersecurity enforcement had taken down the legendary Pasar marketplace, he was left with no choice but to abandon both that identity and his beloved Singapore home.

"We'd have been okay if Yasmin the Admin had been online," ventured a small nervous grey kitten. "It was just that final stage. Everything else worked. We manipulated the skinsuit signals without a problem. The local systems accepted our input. The only thing we hadn't been able to test were the latest versions of the data integrity controls at upload to the metaverse fabric. She would have been able to bypass them on the spot. We've logged everything, so we know what to build into the final release."

"Are you telling me that this Beta was incomplete, and that you were relying on the Admin to patch it in real time?" said the Pangolin icily. "You've known for several weeks that the Admin would not be available. That's no excuse for failing our client."

The kitten grew bolder. "Why the hell was this job tied to a client in the first place?" it asked. "It was Beta test. It should have been a straight in-and-out field study, under the radar, just enough to test our control of the skinsuit. We've got what we need to make it work next time, but I'm willing to bet that someone's watching now."

Willing to bet. What an unfortunate turn of phrase, thought the Pangolin. They seemed to think he had a choice about the client's own test that had run alongside the malware deployment. That could not be further from the truth.

"Where is the Admin, anyway?" asked the kitten.

"She's engaged with a related deep learning exercise that has taken more time and processing capacity than expected," said the Pangolin smoothly. "She'll be back online before the opening ceremony." Perhaps, he added privately to himself. He had no idea where she was, or even if she was still alive.

"I don't believe you," said the kitten. "I've heard enough. The Steamyard is running out of steam."

There was silence around the table. The kitten turned away and scampered towards the exit. Outside, the virtual main street was busy with avatars of every shape, size, and species. Shoppers were chasing the latest digital releases from top brands, while students took a break from studies at the local campus of the University of the Metaverse.

The Pangolin watched the kitten go, and it was soon lost in the crowd. It would come crawling back. It always did, eager for another payday from the Steamyard. For now, though, the kitten had thrown the meeting into confusion. This was not the time to push the remaining members of the project team for answers, thought Tenuk. He had all their data. It was time to withdraw. He turned to the remaining avatars in the room.

"Is anyone else considering jeopardising their future with the Steamyard?" he said. There was silence. "Good. Get those results analysed and be ready to push the final release out before the opening ceremony. We will put this failure behind us and prevail. Dismissed." He left the meeting, the Pangolin avatar blinking out of the virtual world.

In the hot, stuffy apartment, Tenuk took his reality mask off and wiped beads of sweat from his brow. Although the light mask was far removed from the heavy headsets he remembered as a child, he'd spent too long in full immersion mode. The opaque silicon wings that spread out from the frame and clung to his face were a huge improvement on the old padded full-face masks, but in this heat and humidity they still became uncomfortable after a remarkably short time. The air conditioning, powered by large solar arrays on the roof of the apartment complex, was barely keeping up with the combination of the Texas summer and his assorted computers running hot in the small space. He needed some fresh air, however warm that was.

He grabbed a bottle of water and opened the door. The walkway was shaded and cooler than inside. He closed the door and double locked it with a real key, then walked slowly towards the stairwell, sipping at his water. The stairs were in full sun and Tenuk made the mistake of putting his hand on the metal rail. He snatched it back quickly and trotted down the two flights to the ground, seeking more shade.

He hailed a passing autocar and directed it to the cool trails of Barton Creek. The weather reminded him of Singapore. He missed the overground heat, the cool of his old apartment in the shelter of Katong's tunnels, and the blissful shade of the family house where he had grown up. The creek was one place that gave him a sensation of home.

Dry twigs crunched underfoot as he walked along the hard-packed path through the trees that arched above him. The drought this summer was shaping up to be a bad one, and the creek was very low. He crossed a small bridge over a now-dry channel and was relieved to see that there was no one else at his favourite lookout point just up the trail. He took a seat and gazed out across the haven of green and brown to the encroaching city just across the water. He liked his adopted home and would be sorry if he had to leave it.

His difficulties over the past few weeks stemmed from a single, devastating incident. The loss of one of the most advanced artificial intelligences on the planet had thrown his worlds into disarray, both his legitimate and his shadier interests. The Steamyard operatives, and the Pasar network members before them, knew her as the Admin. His employer, Jack Sladen, thought she was simply the SMIN, a system management tool, and had never questioned the complexity of the technology. To Tenuk, she had been Yasmin, colleague and confidante. He missed her caustic attitude and downright badness more than he cared to admit, and he knew that he had relied upon her skills to ensure that first Pasar and then the Steamyard could deliver for their clients. Now that she was gone, his future with both the Sladen Group and the Steamyard was at risk.

And there was one more complication to deal with.

Tenuk's wristband vibrated. He glanced at the caller ID, then stared resolutely back over the creek, ignoring the insistent signal. He was not ready to talk to his father.

His father tried to call twice more and twice Tenuk rejected the call. His peace disturbed, he left the cool creek path just before the searing heat of midday struck. He had to wait for more than two minutes for an autocar and downgraded the fare accordingly. He decided to go straight downtown rather than return to work in his overheated apartment. The offices of the Sladen Group company where he worked, Statesman Tech, would be a far more pleasant environment. He had been working remotely for too long, hiding from the real world and from the investigation into the destruction of the data centre that had housed Yasmin. In any case, he wanted to check on the current state of the Sladen Foundation and the Diaulos cryptocurrency that powered the Foundation's voting and governance system and paid for the athletes it sponsored.

The lobby of the tower was busy, but the cool air came as a relief. The great sail that ran the full height of the building provided enough shade and power to keep the high-net-worth guests and residents comfortable through the Texan summer. Tenuk bought two small tacos from a stand in the food court and made his way to the elevator.

The office was half empty. Jack Sladen was still in England, answering questions and getting angrier and more frustrated as the enquiry dragged on. As far as Tenuk knew, he himself was still Chief Technology Officer. He and Jack had barely spoken other than to exchange information that was requested by the enquiry. Tenuk half expected Jack to fire him any day, but that moment had not yet come. It seemed he was still of value to the group, and he may as well continue to do the job.

He collected a coffee to go with his tacos from the breakout area and went towards Jack's office. He usually worked in there when the boss was away, a quieter and more private space than his open-plan desk, but today something was wrong. His chip failed to activate the door, and as he twisted to get a better connection, he dropped his coffee cup. The liquid spread across the floor and trickled under the door, which still would not open.

"Need some help?"

Tenuk looked up sharply at the familiar voice. Chloe met his gaze levelly and handed him a bunch of paper towels, before turning on her heel and walking back towards her desk.

"It's locked," she called over her shoulder.

"I can see that," muttered Tenuk through gritted teeth as he mopped up what he could of the coffee and threw the soaking mess of paper into a nearby bin. "Since when?"

"If you'd bothered to come into the office, you'd know that it was done a couple of weeks ago," said Chloe. "I don't know whether it's been locked remotely by Jack, or if there's a subpoena in place to secure it for the authorities."

"Huh." Tenuk went back to the coffee machine to refill his cup and settled instead at his own desk. He logged in, and while the latest system updates ran their course, he ate one of the slightly squashed tacos. A shaft of sunlight crept between the solar panels of the great sail on the tower and illuminated his screens and the dust that had collected on them. He reached for a cloth and cleaned them, too.

He dealt with a handful of minor alerts and messages that he hadn't picked up remotely. The systems were in good shape, considering. The Diaulos network, distributed across hundreds of thousands of nodes from wristbands and fitness trackers to MetaBand satellites and base units, was running smoothly. The validations and block creations were ticking along like clockwork. He logged in to the Sladen Foundation's governance platform, the DAO, and checked the dashboards and voting tallies.

Both Diaulos and the DAO were distributed systems, the underlying technology maintained by a consortium of apparently independent core developers. The network had been hailed as the first truly decentralised blockchain since Bitcoin, but all was not quite as it seemed. The diverse and apparently independent developers who had been selected by a system ballot to make up the core engineering team chiefly consisted of well-disguised Statesman Tech staff and a good number of Tenuk's own Steamyard contractors. That was the way Tenuk liked it, and the public would never know.

He closed the last of the notifications on his system and peered around the pillar to where Chloe sat at her desk. Picking up his coffee, he stood and wandered towards her, smiling genially.

"What are you working on at the moment?" he asked.

Chloe fixed him with a stony glare. Tenuk could tell that she was struggling to reconcile their mutual dislike with the knowledge that he was currently the most senior person in the office and could make her life very difficult if he chose. Tenuk secretly relished the power, one of the things he enjoyed about controlling the contractors in the Steamyard, but he knew it wasn't the right way to get what he wanted here. He tried again.

"Look, Chloe, I know that we've had our differences," he said, his voice oozing with sincerity, "but we've both been close to the Diaulos project, and I think we need to pull together to make sure it succeeds despite the investigations."

Chloe shrugged. "I guess so," she said. "A lot of work went into launching that on spec and on time. Your work with the System Management and Information Network was quite something. What did you call it? The SMIN?" She looked straight at him, and Tenuk had the uncomfortable feeling that she was reading him like a book.

"That's right," he said, unflappable.

"The team started calling it Yasmin," Chloe said with an innocent laugh. "After one of Isaac's aunts."

"That's nice," said Tenuk, trying not to let an iota of his concern show. It was just a coincidence. She couldn't know about the real Yasmin, could she?

"We don't have a code review on file for the SMIN," continued Chloe. "Maybe, once I've finished this report, we could run it through the standard audit, just to tick the box. What do you think?"

Tenuk could hardly say no. "That's a great idea," he said, the sincere smile plastered on his face. "Let me check with Jack that there's nothing more urgent for you to get on with."

"Sure," said Chloe. A notification appeared on her screen and Tenuk noticed her face light up.

"Good news?" he asked.

"Oh, nothing important," said Chloe.

Tenuk looked at her quizzically.

"Just a meeting with one of the engineers from our MetaBand partner in San Antonio," she explained. "He'll be here early, so we can get some lunch. I'd better go."

She closed and locked her screen, stood up, nodded to Tenuk, and walked out, leaving him speechless by her desk. The handful of other staff in the office looked up curiously. Tenuk scowled and went back to his desk and put on his headphones. He needed to talk to Jack.

It was late afternoon in England, but Jack's ID was not accepting calls. He must still be deep in meetings. Tenuk started with Jack's virtual assistant, an efficient AI with a talent for multi-tasking. She would answer even if she was simultaneously taking minutes or calculating profit margins.

"Zara," he said, "can you get me half an hour with the boss?"

"Good afternoon, Tenuk," came Zara's calm voice. "Jack is not available right now, but he may be able to speak to you over dinner. Let me check."

"Thank you, Zara," said Tenuk. "Any chance I can get into Jack's office to take the call? It seems to be locked."

"I'm sorry, Tenuk, that won't be possible," said Zara.

Zara was doing a good job of restricting access to Jack Sladen and leaving Tenuk to keep Statesman Tech ticking over while the investigations into the Sladen Foundation continued. It felt as if there was something going on that he didn't know about, and it made him nervous. He wondered if it was just him, or if the senior managers of the other businesses in the vast Sladen Group were equally hamstrung. In the past he'd have asked Yasmin to make some discreet enquiries. He missed her.

"Zara," he said clearly, trying to assert himself, "there are valid operational reasons for me to use Jack's office in his absence." This was quite true. Some of the more sensitive information held by the company was geo-locked to specific office locations and device IP addresses, and there were even paper files held in secret. He thought quickly. "Our MetaBand engineering partner has requested access to some geo-locked files for audit purposes," he said. "Their representative is on site this afternoon for a meeting. I'd hate to give them cause for concern."

There was an imperceptible pause. Good, thought Tenuk. He'd thrown her. Zara, as far as he could tell, was by no means as advanced as Yasmin had been, but she was a well-trained AI and learned quickly. He was certain that he would be back into Jack's office within the hour.

"Please stand by for a decision," said Zara. "Your appointment with Mr Sladen is confirmed at 2pm Central Time." The connection dropped.

Tenuk knew what the decision would be. Zara would have learned by now that there were certain sensitivities with the design of the MetaBand communications satellites, and of the base units that were rapidly being attached to every home and business in the developed world. Her training left her with no choice but to grant him access. He logged out of his desk and strolled over to the door of Jack's private domain. In the silence of the almost deserted office, the tiny click that indicated the lifting of the deadbolt seemed to echo. Tenuk walked in, avoiding the sticky patch of coffee that had already dried on the floor, and closed the door behind him.

With perfect timing, his wristband vibrated once again with an incoming call alert. This time he could not ignore it. Tenuk turned the opacity of the glass partitions up to the maximum setting and settled in Jack's comfortable chair. He had an hour to spare before his meeting with Jack. He accepted the call.

"Tenuk," said an achingly familiar voice that he had not heard in real life for a long time.

"Father," said Tenuk, his voice neutral.

The old man had his camera on, and Tenuk slowly took in the sight of Chaoxiang Chen sitting in a high-backed, richly upholstered chair, the wall behind him adorned with memorabilia. Among the display of rarities Tenuk spotted the commemorative shirt from the MerLions European tour that he had sent to his father as an olive branch three years earlier, framed with photographs of the human e-soccer players and their avatars. The gift had never been acknowledged. It gave Tenuk a curious sense of rejection mingled with a little solace to see it hanging there in pride of place.

"Let me see you," said his father.

Tenuk flicked the call from voice to mixed reality mode and reluctantly enabled his own camera, wondering if his father would also enhance his feed. Tenuk remembered him being a stickler for privacy. He was surprised when the old man reciprocated. The projection from the back of Tenuk's screen displayed a hazy 3D image resolving against the background of Jack's office. The stream took a few moments to load, but quite suddenly the picture sharpened, and Tenuk drew a startled breath. It was as if his father was now sitting right in front of him in the same room. Tenuk lowered the screen and peered over it at the deserted office. Good. Chaoxiang was still a long way away.

"You are looking tired, my son," said his father.

Tenuk was wary. "Yes, father," he said. "The demands of my job have been weighing on me."

Chaoxiang grunted, unimpressed. Tenuk never worked hard enough to satisfy him. "You're still hanging on Sladen's coat tails?" he said.

"I'm running this company while he's tied up with the authorities in England," corrected Tenuk. "You know how important that has been."

Chaoxiang sighed and stood up. He turned away from Tenuk and looked at the wall display behind him. He tapped the MerLions shirt. "This was where you did your best work," he said. "Why you left that behind and chose to go to America, I still fail to comprehend."

Tenuk suppressed any thought of the world he had left behind when he left Singapore. He missed the people, the place, and his old life so much that it hurt. His father would never understand that he had no choice but to flee when the international cybersecurity syndicate started to target members of the Pasar cybercrime network. His old underground identity of King Katong, head of the Pasar network, had faded into obscurity. Tenuk Chen, talented executive, had resigned his old post abruptly, to the annoyance of those members of the MerLions senior management who were not aware of his other life and his good reasons for leaving. Other colleagues knew exactly what had happened. He had no wish to meet either group again.

He had reinvented himself in Texas as a career man from California looking for a change of scene and eager for a new challenge. Jack Sladen had been his target from the moment he realised he could not go back to Singapore, and until the debacle in Dunswyke, his new life had been going smoothly.

"You don't need Sladen anymore," said Chaoxiang, as if reading his mind. "And who cares if he needs you. I want you back in the family firm."

"No," said Tenuk vehemently.

"No?" said Chaoxiang. "You would refuse me, after everything I've done for you?" He leaned towards Tenuk, who instinctively stiffened for a moment before remembering that the old man wasn't in the room with him. "I'll let you think about it," he said, reaching into the air. The screen flicked off. The call ended.

Tenuk took a deep, shuddering breath. He had dared to cross his father. There would be hell to pay.

He stood up to fetch a drink from the kitchen and compose himself, but before he even reached the door of the office, he heard Zara's voice behind him.

"Tenuk," she said, "Jack is ready to speak to you now."

Tenuk went back to his seat and composed himself as well as he could. When Jack's scowling face appeared on the screen, Tenuk just smiled. There was nothing else he could do.

4: NEW THREATS

Cameron's plan of calling into the client's office to do a little general fact finding about gambling was derailed almost as soon as she arrived. The senior managers were far too busy to talk to her about idle speculation on bet fixing, focused as they were on dealing with the PR fallout of the breach. Instead, she joined Pete and Noor who were taking a well-earned rest in the comfortable breakout room that the client had assigned them.

They'd done a fast and effective job of researching and tracing the probable source of the data breach, but there was still a lot of work to do. Cameron didn't want to tread on their toes, but it felt good to be with members of her team in this room full of beanbags and games consoles and all the coffee they could ever need. She lay back, burrowing into her giant beanbag with pleasure, and started scrolling through the activity report Noor had shared on her screen.

Pete gave Cameron a rapid briefing on what they had found so far. "They found out about the breach pretty fast," he said. "They have plenty of honeypots running."

"Dummy accounts?" said Cameron. "That's clever. They'll be able to pick up on anything that's targeted at account holders as soon as a malicious campaign starts."

"Exactly," said Pete. "Some of them started receiving

phishing messages. There were a lot of reports from customers to corroborate the incident, so they know that at the very least the breach exposed online contact details for a good chunk of their users."

Cameron flicked back to a table at the start of Noor's report. "Not for everyone, though," she said. "That's interesting."

"Nowhere near everyone," said Noor. "They've got 25 million customers, and as far as the honeypot data can tell us, the breach relates to less than two million of them. It looks as if it's only accounts hosted with a couple of specific data centres in their cloud. We're looking for common factors at those sites to narrow down the attack vector."

Pete clapped his hands on the floor. "One of the data centres is right here," he said, pointing downwards. "We don't have to go far to do the digging. The documentation on third party software and access rights and user roles is bang up to date. I think we'll have the 'How' sewn up pretty fast."

"That's great," said Cameron, trying to ignore her slight jealousy that Pete and Noor were on a roll, working as a team, sparking off each other's ideas. "I see the ICO notification's been done. Do we have any idea of the time of the breach?"

"Yes," said Noor. "We had a lucky break. We know that the data set that was stolen can't be any more than three days old. They change the dummy data every few days and they've had phishing messages to the most recent honeypots, but not to any of the older ones."

"We were well within the deadline," said Pete.

"It's always good to keep the Information Commissioner's Office onside," said Cameron with a grin. "Three days, though, to go from a breach to successful phishing attacks. That's a fast turnaround. It's been very well planned. What are your thoughts on the 'Who' and the 'Why'? What's the next step?"

"The 'Why' could be very simple," said Noor. "Just your run-of-the-mill data grab, see what they can get, sell what's valuable and phish with the rest, but I agree the speed with which they started phishing makes it look less haphazard and more targeted." She yawned suddenly, covering her mouth with a surprised look. "Oh!" she said. "Where did that come from?"

"It's been a long day," said Pete, stifling a yawn himself. "You've started me off now."

Noor hauled herself out of her beanbag and strolled across the room to the well-stocked vending machines in the kitchen area. "I need something to eat," she said. "Do you want anything? They have loads of stuff here. Sandwiches, curries, pasta, nachos, cake…"

Pete glanced at the clock on the wall. "It's coming up to supper time," he said. "Some curry would be great. Cameron, what about you?"

"Yes, sure," she said, suddenly realising how hungry she was. "I forgot about lunch. I'm starving."

Pete joined Noor in the kitchen. "I'll sort these out," he said. "Tell Cameron about the accounts."

Cameron looked up curiously. "What about them?" she said. "I presume some have been compromised?"

"Of course, but not all of them by any means," said Noor. She handed Cameron a bottle of juice and settled back on her beanbag, sipping at her own drink. "All the customer passcodes were encrypted and unusable, and a surprisingly high proportion of accounts had multi factor authentication set up as well. I guess people care enough to do that when there's money involved."

"I wish they'd care about all their data," said Cameron. "The number of times we've had to tidy up a real mess that came from unsecured accounts that didn't seem to matter."

"I know," said Noor, grimacing. "Anyway, the accounts that have been accessed were those where the customer fell for a phishing message. The campaign was highly sophisticated."

"What kind of things have you seen?" asked Cameron.

"There was a beautifully cloned app," said Noor. "We went through the process with a couple of the dummy accounts on burner devices and captured all the details. It was virtually faultless."

"Same with the main site," called Pete over the whirring of the vending machine oven. "And there was a classic cloned popup for biometric input, too."

"Covering all the bases," said Cameron, impressed. This really had been long in the planning. "What did they do when they got into the accounts? Presumably they drained any funds and ran for the hills. Where's the money gone?"

"Nowhere yet," said Noor. "Everything's been sent

to the same anonymous account, and I've got an alert set on it for any movement. The stolen funds are still in fiat currency, but they could start laundering them any moment through different wallets and coins."

It could happen in minutes or months, thought Cameron. She'd followed stolen funds in the past that had lain dormant for weeks before suddenly bursting into life as cybercriminals flipped the money out into a swirling tornado of wallets. Accounts full of misappropriated coins that came to life after many years were the stuff of legend. She recalled a case study from her History of Crypto class of a failed exchange whose only keyholder apparently died in mysterious circumstances, only for the lost wallet that held all the customer funds to reactivate five years later. This one would probably move in a few days, though. Noor was right to place a watch on the account. Follow the money closely enough and eventually you'd find the cybercriminals, or the people who commissioned them.

"There's more to it," said Pete. The oven pinged. "I'll tell you in minute," he said. "Let's eat." He cautiously picked the hot dishes out of the machine and set them on the table.

Cameron clambered upright and searched through the kitchen drawers for cutlery, while Noor extracted chutneys and poppadums from the vending machine.

"Thanks, Pete," said Cameron, taking her seat at the table. She crunched enthusiastically on a poppadum and sniffed at the fragrant curry. "This is wonderful," she continued. "What were you saying about the stolen funds?"

"It's a little embarrassing," said Pete. "The funds started draining out literally as we got here. We managed to block a handful of them as soon as we saw what was happening, but not all."

"Why on earth did they wait?" said Cameron. "If they had access to the accounts, surely they'd have grabbed any money straightaway."

Pete nodded and shrugged, his mouth full of curry.

"You'd have thought so," said Noor, "but they placed some bets, and they must have been waiting for their winnings."

"What?" said Cameron, putting her fork down and frowning. "I don't get it."

"Nor do I," said Pete. "Even more crazy, the bets they placed didn't win. They lost money. Some of the accounts were wiped out completely."

"That's ridiculous," said Cameron. "What did they bet on?"

"Something really obscure," said Noor. "A couple of minor Olympic qualifiers. One of them came back with a void result, so the stakes were returned. They lost their money on the other one. All the bets were placed against the favourite, but she won."

Cameron gasped. "Not the Trianna/Kemelov final?" she said. "The kata competition?"

"That's the one," said Pete. "How the hell did you know?" He shook his head. "Sometimes I think you're psychic."

"I'm just lucky," said Cameron. "I was watching that

with Ross just before he left. There was a delay in the competition between the two kata performances. It was flagged to MIST as a possible cyberattack. I came over here to find out more about how bets can be rigged, and to see if there had been any odd betting patterns around that final. I didn't expect to walk straight into proof that cybercriminals had their fingers all over it."

This was more like it, she thought, as she tucked into her curry. The synergies and serendipities of working with her team were irreplaceable.

"There have to be several different layers of cybercrime here," said Noor. "We've got a very sophisticated cloning job, really specific data centre penetration here at the betting platform, and now something at an actual competition."

"Two competitions," said Cameron. "Pete, please tell me the other one wasn't e-sports, the gamers?"

"No." Pete shook his head. "It was a para event in track and field that ran yesterday. Javelin. The bets were placed on the winner, but then he was disqualified for an error in his para classification and there was no pay-out. Why?"

"Just following up on a rumour," said Cameron. "It's probably unfounded." She concentrated on her curry. It was starting to cool, and she was still ravenous.

"The technical problems at the karate qualifier have to be linked to the bets that were placed," said Pete. "We need to find out if there have been any related jobs advertised on the Eden marketplace."

"Good idea," said Noor. "That's always the first port

of call when I'm trying to track malware back to the coders."

"We can have a look at the deeper networks too," said Cameron, wiping the last of the sauce off her plate with a scrap of naan bread. "It's always possible that one of the high value contracts put out by the Syndicate was leading to this, and we missed the relevance at the time. I'll get Ross and his shady mates to…" She tailed off. Her usual path into the Underworld was barred. Ross had other things on his mind.

Pete hadn't noticed Cameron's discomfort. "We need to see if there have been tips for sale as well, especially for that javelin event," he said. "The tipsters will probably have sold the information on for a share of the winnings. Not that there were any winnings, of course. It didn't go to plan."

"Was this a proof of concept for the real thing?" asked Noor. "A trial run?"

Cameron shrugged. "Why would they test their process using live public accounts?" she asked.

There were far too many unanswered questions swirling around Cameron's mind. Why hadn't the cybercriminals waited until the main Olympic competition when interest would be much higher? Why had they compromised one of the biggest betting companies in the world ahead of time? It seemed like a waste of effort. If she'd been in charge, she'd have made sure they kept their powder dry.

"Someone somewhere got greedy," suggested Noor.

"They assumed there would be no hitches and set this up to make a quick coin."

"And it went wrong," said Pete thoughtfully.

"It did," said Noor. "How do we track them down?"

"How indeed," said Cameron. It was time to do some serious digging, and without Ross and his shady mates to hand, she might have to venture into the darkness herself.

It was a sobering thought. For her entire career, she had walked the white hat path. She knew what went on in the murky depths of the dark web, but as the reputation of the SimCavalier grew, the dangers lurking there became more palpable. If she dared to venture too deep these days, even under an alias, she was in danger of exposure in the virtual and the real world. She'd already had a taste of what might happen. A direct attack on her apartment. The kidnap of her niece. Guns and bloodshed in the old Argentum office. She had to find a way to keep her family and her friends safe while she explored every way to take down the most determined of cybercriminals.

"See what you can find out through the usual channels, Noor," she said. She knew that she could only put off what she needed to do for a short while, but the more they could discover without going into the Underworld the better. "I'll update MIST on these latest findings and that may bring some intelligence back on the tide."

Cameron collected the empty plates and stacked them in the dishwasher. "That was great," she said. "Thanks, both of you. You're doing a great job. I'd better get back to the office."

She grabbed her jacket and made her way back out through security to the street level. It was still light outside and would be for some time yet. Summer evenings seemed to stretch after the solstice. Ross would have even longer hours of daylight up by the Arctic Circle, thought Cameron.

The city centre pavements were busy with tourists taking in the sights in real time and people socialising after work with colleagues. A crocodile of schoolchildren bustled past on their way to a West End show. Cameron made her way towards the river. At one vast junction, she stood waiting while hundreds of bicycles flooded across on their green light, followed in turn by the autocars, and finally giving way to the crowd of pedestrians who thronged the intersection, coming and going in all directions.

Although it was a warm evening, there was a chill in the air that made her shiver as she crossed the central span of London Bridge. Her apartment was only a few minutes south of Borough Market, but she was too late to visit the shops and stalls within it. Only the bars and restaurants on the fringes were open, full of tourists and office workers from the nearby Shard. A small convenience store further down the road was reliably open at all hours, though, and she paused to collect a few essentials.

The path that led to her apartment block from the north was narrow, cobbled and easily overlooked. It opened up into a wide courtyard with a more accessible entrance from the south.

"Afternoon, Cameron," came a voice. Two men crossed the courtyard from the south just ahead of her. She recognised one as a neighbour and gave him a cheery smile. The other was a stranger. They seemed to be together, but Cameron took note in any case of the new face on her territory. Strong and wiry, shaved head. Both he and the neighbour she knew reached the door, stretched their hands towards the access pad simultaneously, laughed together at the coincidence of timing, and walked through the door as it opened.

Cameron watched closely through the glass wall of the atrium. Her neighbour, as expected, entered his ground floor apartment and closed the door. The stranger went straight to the stairwell without missing a step and disappeared from view. He obviously knew where he was going.

Cameron relaxed. She unlocked the main door with her own chip on the pad and went towards the same stairwell, ready for her daily workout on the four flights up to her apartment.

Wait. The voice that called hello had been unfamiliar. Not her neighbour but the stranger. If they'd never met, how did he know her name?

That fleeting thought gave her the split second she needed as he turned on the stairs above and launched himself towards her, weight and momentum aimed at knocking her off balance and down into the stairwell. She managed to fling herself against the handrail and take just a fraction of the impact that her attacker had intended. Her left arm went numb with the glancing blow and she dropped her bag. She recovered much faster than the man. He lost his footing and stumbled onto the stair below. As he straightened up and lunged towards her, Cameron caught him square in the solar plexus with an adrenaline-driven front kick. He staggered and Cameron took her chance. She jumped up to the middle of the next step and kicked out again, this time connecting with his head and knocking him sideways. The man fell to his knees. Cameron turned and fled up the stairs two at a time, shaking.

She was one floor below her apartment when she heard running feet and a bellow of rage behind her. Her legs burned and her arm hung limp by her side. She kept running, trying to reach across her body to her left pocket for her apartment key. For the first time in her life, she regretted having such strong security around her home. It was supposed to keep people out. She had never thought that the person she was keeping out would be her.

She reached the top of the stairs and cannoned into the wall in her haste. She forced herself to stop, twisting as she grasped for the key. Success. Running footsteps echoed in the stairwell behind her. Cameron fumbled the key in the lock, and it fell to the floor. She dropped down to grab it. Behind the door the cat was mewing in anticipation of its dinner. She tried again and this time the key turned smoothly.

Behind her came another shout. "Cameron!"

The scanner read her chip and turned green, and the

door swung open. She fell into the apartment gratefully and slammed the door behind her. A moment later came a rain of blows on the door, frantic hammering and shouting. "Cameron! Are you okay?"

It wasn't the same voice. This time, it was one she recognised.

She looked closely at the entry system security camera, widening the view to take in the whole landing and the stairwell. The only person in sight was Jasvinder, her karate training partner who lived on the floor below. Settling her breathing, Cameron pressed the entry mic.

"Jasvinder?" she said cautiously.

"Cameron, thank goodness," said Jasvinder. "I heard shouting, and I saw you run past. There was this man…"

Cameron opened the door. "Get in here, quickly," she said.

Jasvinder obeyed. "It's okay, Cameron," he said as she closed the door firmly behind him. "I smacked him as he came round the corner onto my landing. Left him lying in a heap. We'd better call the police."

A shout from outside the door silenced them both.

"Cameron Silvera," bellowed the man. "We know where you are." He limped up to the security camera lens and stared into it. His nose was clearly broken, and one eye was shut. The last frame showed a fist approaching, then the feed stopped abruptly.

"Bloody hell," said Jasvinder. "Who have you pissed off this time?"

"I don't know," said Cameron. "I'll call the police, you

call security. No one is getting in here without our say-so." She looked up at the firmly shuttered windows, and back to the door. The only sound in the silence was the occasional pathetic squeak from the cat who considered her supper to be far more important than the trials and tribulations of any human.

The security office did not answer Jasvinder's call. "That may be a good sign," he said. "Maybe they've got him."

Cameron shook her head. "There are automated systems that should pick up straight away," she said. "Something's wrong."

"Are the police on the way?" asked Jasvinder.

Cameron nodded. "The first response drone should be here any moment." There was an insistent beeping at the balcony door.

"That was fast," said Jasvinder. He went to open the shutter, but Cameron reached out a warning hand.

"Remember the last time someone came after me here," she said.

Jasvinder's eyes widened and he lowered his hand.

Cameron reached for her smartscreen, ignoring the sudden pain in her shoulder, and checked her notifications.

"That isn't the police," she said. "Get down!".

5: DOXED

Cameron and Jasvinder stared up at the dark shutter that stood between them and the rogue drone. There were loud bangs and scrapes as someone or something tried to force the balcony shutter open, but Cameron's security was tight, and the shutter did not yield.

A siren and a commotion heralded the arrival of the police drone. There was a clatter and the sound of glass shattering on the balcony. Cameron winced. Her smartscreen lit up. The police app displayed a video from the official drone of the scene outside the shutter. Cameron could make out a downed drone, and the loud noise must have been the table as it was overturned. An empty wine bottle that she had left outside after drinks with friends the previous night lay smashed on the floor.

Cameron activated the shutter. The warm light of the summer evening and the blue flashes of the police drone streamed into the apartment. Relief washed over her, and she sat down heavily on the sofa, taking stock of her injuries for the first time. The cat, indignant, jumped up and kneaded at her legs. Jasvinder coaxed it away with a fresh bowl of food.

Noises on the landing heralded the arrival of real-life police. Once their identities had been confirmed,

Cameron opened the door. The questions were going to take a while, and for now she had very few answers.

•

Cameron woke early the next morning, disoriented. She tried to lift her arm to pull at the tangled bedsheet, but her shoulder was still heavy and sore. She rolled over awkwardly, taking stock of the pain and the bruising across her upper body, and the aches in her legs.

What had woken her? She unearthed her smartscreen and the stream of notifications and messages told their own story. It was already late, past nine o'clock. The first message was from Andy.

'Where did you get to yesterday?' it said. 'I had to drop the feature, but I still want to run it another day.'

He didn't know what had happened, then. Although she liked Andy, she wasn't ready to tell him. Not yet. He'd keep it quiet, of course, but it would always be in the back of his mind for a story. He might pick up on the emergency response to her apartment, or hear about it through Aunt Vicky or Charlie, but she wasn't going to call him back just yet. She knew he'd understand her reticence.

There were several missed calls from Ross. She had no doubt that despite his focus on training, he would have gotten wind of the attack. Cameron set the coffee machine to run from her smartscreen and struggled out of bed. Looking in the mirror, the bruising on her upper arm and body was only just starting to show dark under her skin. It would take a few stiff and uncomfortable days to clear. She'd been lucky. The blunt force of the attacker's weight had not broken any bones.

She showered gingerly and felt much better as a result. She dressed in loose shorts and a t-shirt and followed her nose to the freshly brewed coffee.

The apartment was dark, but she had no intention of opening the shutters. She turned all the lights on, refilled the cat's bowl, and went in search of her bag that the police had retrieved from the stairwell. The bread that she'd bought the previous evening was squashed but serviceable. She popped it in the oven to warm up. Within a few minutes she was sitting comfortably on the sofa with a large mug of coffee and some clumsily sliced bread with butter and jam. Breakfast of champions, Aunt Vicky always called it. She didn't feel like a champion this morning, that was for sure.

The thought of champions brought her back to her messages. She called Ross back, hoping to catch him between the various training, press and preparation sessions that were now occupying all of his time.

He picked up straight away. "Cameron! Are you okay?"

"Yes," said Cameron, "but how the hell did you know?"

Ross laughed. "Shell has her fingers in a lot of pies," he said. "She picked up on the emergency call. I was all set to come over, but the city CCTV showed there was no extra response, your building security was all green lights, and the police systems closed the call."

"And I guess Shell wouldn't let you out of the house anyway," said Cameron, trying hard to absorb the sheer number of heavily protected systems to which Ross's talented girlfriend apparently had access.

"You guess right," said Ross sheepishly. "What's the story?"

"Someone followed a neighbour into the building on their chip access," said Cameron. "It's a classic trick and very neatly done."

"We've all done the same to people when we've been testing site security for clients, haven't we?" said Ross. "Did you recognise them?"

"No," said Cameron, "but I gave a thorough description to the police." An idea was forming in her head. "Ross, did you say you'd checked the city CCTV? Can you pick up this character before he arrived and after he left?"

"Shell's already on it," said Ross. "I just spoke to her, and her systems have five possibles who match that description and who were around your location last night."

"She's brilliant," said Cameron. "What do you need from me to narrow it down further? I want to know who he is and who sent him."

"More details," said Ross. "What time did you get home?"

Cameron thought back to the events of the previous night. "Quite late," she said. "I had dinner with Pete and Noor on site, so that was about seven. I walked home… wait. I picked up a few bits in the shop round the corner."

She checked her recent payments on her smartscreen. "That was half past eight."

"Okay," said Ross. "The guy left before the police arrived, I take it. He wasn't hiding in the building?"

"I don't know," said Cameron. "Let me check something." She put her smartscreen down on the table and went to the secure entry console by the door. The camera was still broken, but the recording from the previous day was intact. She rewound until the blank screen flicked into life. There was the fist, and the face, and the timestamp.

She picked up her smartscreen again. "I'm sending you some footage from the doorcam," she said. "The police missed it, but I'll send it over to them now. This is who you're looking for."

On the other end of the call, Ross, gave a low whistle. "Blimey, Cameron," he said, "I'm guessing he didn't look like that when he arrived."

"Uh, no, he didn't," said Cameron. "I'm not sure that he expected me to fight back. And he met Jasvinder on his travels too."

Ross threw back his head and laughed. "Oh, good grief," he said. "I was going to suggest that you get out of that apartment and find somewhere safer, but with you two practising your karate on every passing would-be assailant, it doesn't sound like there's a problem."

Cameron shook her head. "I thought so too," she said, "but that's the second time there's been a direct attack on this building. Someone who wants to hurt me knows where I live, and they won't stop. I don't want to leave here, but I suppose I might have to, in the end."

"I know you," said Ross. "You're not going anywhere, are you?"

Cameron grinned. "You're reading my mind," she said. "If I stay here, they'll just keep trying, but they won't get in, and they won't go after any of you."

"So, you're setting yourself up as bait," said Ross. "I wouldn't have expected anything less. Right, first of all, we need to know who's after you. I'll get digging."

Cameron took a swig of her coffee, discovered it was cold, and set it down on the table in disgust. "Don't spend time on it on my account," she said firmly. "Concentrate on the games."

"I am concentrating," he said. "Shell's doing most of the work, and if I have a little downtime I can play too." He looked up sharply and smiled at someone off camera. "They're ready?" he said. "Okay, one minute." He turned back to Cameron. "I have to go. I'll come back to you as soon as Shell or I find anything. Take care."

Cameron put her screen down, picked up the cold coffee mug and swilled the contents down the kitchen sink. She set the machine off to brew some fresh coffee and put another slice of bread in the toaster.

Her second attempt at breakfast was more successful than the first. She flicked the wallscreen on and let the chatter of the news channel wash over her while she planned her next moves.

Who needed to know about the attack? Anyone

who could also be in danger. Her team, of course. Her family too. As long as the focus was on her they would probably be safe, but a little extra security wouldn't go amiss. The problem was understanding where the threat had come from, and that wouldn't be clear until they had more information. The police may not have picked up the suspect yet, but they had the drone to interrogate. Cameron needed to speed that process up, and she knew exactly who to call. She switched off the wallscreen, refilled her coffee, and scrolled through the contact list on her smartscreen.

DI Sara Mercer answered immediately.

"Cameron," she said. "I've just been notified. How are you?"

"I'm okay," said Cameron. "I'm glad you're on the case."

Mercer laughed. "I'm not," she said. "Not yet anyway. I simply like to keep an eye on you and your team. If there's a report about you, it comes to my inbox."

"I'm touched," said Cameron.

"Much as I like you, Cameron," said Mercer, "it's an operational matter, not a personal one. Anything that happens to you is generally an early warning of something bigger coming down the line."

"I'm just a piece of cybercrime seaweed, am I?" said Cameron.

"If you like," said Mercer. "If the seaweed's dry, then the weather's set fair. As soon as it dampens, we know there's a storm on the way."

Cameron took a sip of coffee and nodded thoughtfully. "That's the question, though," she said. "Is this the tail end of an old storm, or something new?"

"I imagine that's why you called me," said Mercer. "I'll do what I can to hurry the investigation along. The NCSC is already taking an interest. If your clever team come up with any ideas or leads, you'll let me know, won't you? I don't need to know how they do it."

"Of course," said Cameron. There was a knock at the door that made the cat jump.

On the screen, Mercer smiled. "Friend or foe?" she said. "I can stay online while you open the door, just in case it's an unwelcome visitor."

Cameron put her coffee down on the table and stood up stiffly. She made sure the screen was trained on the entrance before pulling the door open. She smiled when she saw Jasvinder's familiar face, and beckoned him in.

She turned to the smartscreen where Mercer was still watching expectantly.

"Friend," she said, "I have to go. Speak soon."

Jasvinder sat down in the armchair and within seconds the cat had appeared and curled up on his knee, purring.

"Traitor," said Cameron, glaring at the cat.

Jasvinder laughed and stroked the little animal's soft fur. "She's sweet," he said. "How are you doing, Cameron?"

"I'm fine, thanks," she said. "What about you? It's late. I assumed you'd be at work."

"I already had a day's holiday booked," he said. "It's my mum's birthday and we're all meeting for lunch. Lucky timing." The cat squeaked and nudged his hand with her head. He took the hint and resumed stroking. "What are you planning?"

Cameron put a mug of coffee on the table for him and went to refill her own. "I have a lot to do," she said. "I'm waiting for some kit to be delivered so I can set up a few more cameras and some sneaky traps for any other uninvited guests. Then I'm going to head to the office, and I need to tell my folks what happened too. I'll probably go up to the village this evening."

He smiled and tickled the cat under the chin. "If you're off on your travels," he said, "I guess you'll want me to feed the cat, am I right? I'll be here all weekend."

Cameron laughed. "I don't think she's going to mind," she said. "Thanks. I owe you – again."

Jasvinder drained his coffee and gently tipped the cat off his knee. "I'll make sure she's alright," he said. He nodded at Cameron's limp left arm. "Still sore? You should get that seen to. You need to be fighting fit in case they come back."

Cameron lifted her hand slowly and gave him a feeble wave. "See, it's not as bad as you think," she said. "I'll be back in training before you know it."

"Good," said Jasvinder. "I'll hold you to that." He opened the door and stepped out onto the brightly lit landing.

Cameron looked past him to the normality of the space, the familiar pot plants in the corners, the stairwell, and the lift. There was no sign that the drama of the previous night had even happened. The whole thing felt quite surreal. Cameron glanced up at the bulb on the ceiling that held a security camera and a beacon. It would be useful to get a look at the data and CCTV from the internal systems.

Good. She was thinking like her normal self again. It was time to get back to work. She went back into her apartment and settled at the computer, navigating to the MIST discussion platform. Most of the European members were online, and Cameron noticed a green light against Barker's profile. She pinged him a quick hello, and he replied straight away.

"You're up early, Barker," she said.

"Always here for you," said Barker, rolling his deep south vowels. "What's happening, SimCavalier?"

"Busy as ever," she replied. "Hey, have you heard of any real-world threats against MIST members?"

"That's a strange question, SimCavalier," said Barker. "Nothing going down that I know about. Why do you ask?"

Cameron considered telling him the whole story, but her natural caution warned her to make light of the question. Although she'd met Barker almost as soon as she joined MIST and he felt like an old friend, she knew nothing about him beyond their online interactions. Maybe the personal stuff could stay personal, for now.

"There's a rumour circulating on another forum about doxing and physical attacks," she said, thinking quickly. "I thought I'd check it out with this group."

Barker laughed. "Did this rumour come from the same source as your last one about the gamers?" he said. "There was nothing sinister about the speedrunners, and I don't think you need to worry about anyone coming after us all."

Cameron kept her voice light. "Maybe my source is a little too keen," she said. "I'll take what they tell me with a pinch of salt next time. Thanks, Barker. I didn't mean to worry you. I'll drop a post on MIST anyway. You never know what might come up."

"Sure, SimCavalier," said Barker. "I'll see you later."

Cameron closed the chat and looked thoughtfully at the screen. Something had broken her trust in Barker, and she didn't know what it was. She posted her so-called anonymous tip-off on the main message board. She considered posting about the odd betting pattern on the javelin qualifier but decided to wait until she'd had a chance to look into it in more detail.

It was time to go and talk to the team. Cameron slowly and carefully changed into work clothes and packed an overnight bag for later. Her arm and shoulder were hurting, a throbbing reminder of the impact when the stranger had hurled himself down the stairs. She chose a light jacket and tucked her arm inside, taking the strain. She stroked the cat, picked up her bag, walked out onto the landing and locked the door carefully behind her.

This time she took the lift.

•

Pete and Noor arrived in the office five minutes after Cameron, coming back to prepare their report on the client's data breach. Sandeep was online, chatting on the wallscreen. They all reacted exactly as Cameron expected. After exclamations of horror and coffee all round, everyone dived into practical activity.

"If you want to get away from London," said Sandeep, "you should come up here to Dunswyke. I was going to ask you to visit anyway. We're due the final debrief next week and there are a couple of loose ends to tie up. We need your input on them, and it would be much easier do it on site."

"Sure," said Cameron. "Monday?"

"Perfect. Your room is already booked," said Sandeep. "I've got to go. Joel and Susie send their best and they'll both be in touch later." His link disappeared from the wallscreen.

Cameron sat down on an empty chair next to Noor, who was already hard at work.

"It'll take a while to get that police report from the drone," she said, her hands flying over her keyboard, "so I'll check the CCTV and backtrack as far as I can to try and get an ID match and any links to organised cybercrime that we know of."

"Shell's on the case," said Cameron. "I've already spoken to her. Give her a call."

Noor nodded and opened a dedicated line to Michelle. "Hi Cameron," came her voice from Noor's desk speakers. "Glad you're okay. I have a lot of data to share. We'll find out who he was."

"Thanks, Shell," said Cameron. "I'll see if we can get access to the security footage from the building as well."

"I can get in there, no problem," said Michelle.

Cameron laughed. "I'm going to ask them nicely first," she said. "If that doesn't work, then over to you. Don't let this get in the way of the audit, Shell, or the report for the online betting client, Noor. They're more important than me."

"Don't worry, Cameron," said Noor. "We have time for both." She slipped her headphones on and continued to chat quietly to Michelle as they worked.

Cameron had no doubt that they would manage their workloads, and that if there were any threads to follow from the real world to the virtual, they would find them. She turned to look at Pete who was sitting fidgeting with a multi-faceted trophy that normally stood on the shelf. He tossed it thoughtfully from hand to hand, eyes unfocused.

"CyberFest awards," said Cameron, nodding at the trophy. "That was a memorable night."

Pete's attention focused back on Cameron. "It was, on many levels," he said. He went to toss the trophy over to her but stopped himself. "Sorry," he said. "Let me have a look at that injury. Have you seen a doctor?"

"No," said Cameron. "It's fine." She shucked her jacket off anyway and let Pete gently lift and manipulate her arm. "Ow," she complained as a particular angle triggered a sharp pain that radiated down to her fingers.

"Rotator cuff tear and a lot of bruising," said Pete succinctly. "Rest and ice. You need a sling." He got up and rummaged in the kitchen cupboard, pulling out a well-stocked first aid kit. "It won't be pretty, but it'll do the trick." He busied himself with the contents of the box and kept talking. "We need to improve your security, Cameron. I'll have a chat with Joel as soon as he's available. I have some ideas."

Cameron shook her head. "You Army boys only think of one thing," she said. "I'm not carrying a gun."

Pete looked hurt. "We're not that unimaginative," he said, fastening the sling carefully around Cameron's arm.

She fixed him with a quizzical look. "Well? What's your plan?"

"Uh, I did think that a gun would be a good idea," said Pete. "It's more discreet than a bodyguard drone. You could have both?"

Cameron shook her head. "No," she said. "Absolutely not. I've never fired a gun and there is no way I'd react fast enough if I needed it." She shuddered. "People would get hurt."

"That's the idea, Cameron," said Pete. "Better them than you. It's getting serious. That's the second time your apartment has been attacked." He gestured at Noor who was still chatting to Michelle, oblivious to the discussion on the other side of the office. "Noor was shot when the old office was breached. The Sladen Foundation headquarters was bristling with military tech, according to Joel. This isn't a game. If you end up facing someone stronger than you, they're not just going to bow and walk away at the end of the fight. They're going to try and kill you."

Pete jumped to his feet and walked away towards the huge wall of glass that looked out over the bustling London streets. He leaned against it, peering down at the tiny figures on the pavements. Noor looked up from her computer, feeling the tension in the air. She muttered something to Michelle and took off her headphones, looking from Cameron to Pete.

"We need to keep you safe, Cameron," said Pete eventually. "The more they come after you in the real world, the clearer it is that you're a threat to them. You're already winning, but they're going to play dirty."

"We need to keep all of us safe," said Cameron. "I don't work alone. I'd be nothing without you backing me up. It's a team effort."

Pete sat down heavily on the sofa next to the window. "Okay," he said. "You're still the target, but I get what you're saying. We all have to watch our backs."

"You're right," said Noor, "but first we need to work out exactly where this latest threat has come from, and I think we have something."

"Already?" said Cameron. "Fast work, Noor. Show me."

Noor went back to her desk, flipped the display to the wallscreen, and put Michelle on speaker.

"The police are moving quite quickly," said Michelle. "According to the latest update, they've identified the suspect and they're picking him up for questioning."

Cameron shook her head. "Shell, you need to stop pulling data out of their systems," she said. "It's not funny."

"They're paying us to keep track of their vulnerabilities in real time, aren't they?" said Shell defensively. "I always add the details to the rolling report, and it keeps my hand in. If any data I access is useful, that's a bonus, isn't it?"

Cameron threw up her hands in frustration. "Yes, but no, but… look, we'll deal with that another time. So, who was he?"

Noor took over and the wallscreen filled with images. Cameron spotted the man immediately and felt an unexpected jolt of shock and a wave of nausea. She sat down casually on the sofa, trying to disguise her reaction.

Pete glanced at her knowingly. "Okay?" he asked quietly.

Cameron nodded.

"This is a low life called Arthur Paxton," said Noor. "One of the big bonuses of working with Shell is that being blind, she can't see the pictures, so of course she's developed a nice little routine to do the matching for her."

"That's right," said Michelle cheerily from the screen. "It's based on the facial recognition tech in my sensor kit, but with some extra useful features. We could make a fortune selling it into the market, you know."

"Arthur Paxton," said Cameron thoughtfully. "Never heard of him."

"You won't have," said Noor, "but he's got some interesting friends. He's been working security for the big casinos for a decade at least, and he's got a record as long as your arm."

"A thug for hire, then?" said Cameron. "Who hired him?"

"I don't know yet," said Michelle, "but there's more to it. My image AI looks at context and style as well as straight facial recognition, and then adds layers of online activity. We've linked him with 95% certainty to an avatar working in an instance of Casinoland, and I think we've got some social profiles too."

Cameron groaned. "Gambling again," she said. "I was hoping this would turn out to be linked to an old case, a one-off. But it's not, is it?"

Pete shook his head. "I think you need to accept that you are well and truly doxed," he said. "What you do and who you are is no longer a secret. Whether someone's pissed off at you for closing down their ransomware, or they want to stop you interfering with their plans, there's enough muscle for hire to chase you from the web to the real world."

The office fell silent. Noor and Pete looked at Cameron expectantly.

"I'm going to pass what we have on to Mercer," she said. "I promised to keep her updated if we found anything. Pete, have a think about practical security measures and we can discuss them on Monday before I go up to Dunswyke."

Pete started to protest but Cameron held up her hand.

"Not now," she said. "Paxton's in custody, so he's no longer a threat and I'm heading to Charlie's for the weekend. I'm going to be in the safest place."

"Okay," said Pete, giving in gracefully, "but at least get an autocar to the station?"

Cameron grinned. "Yes, sir," she said.

6: SANCTUARY

Tenuk tossed and turned, sleepless in the stuffy heat of a summer night. He was at his lowest ebb. The latest project his black hat team had launched was well below the standards he and his clients expected. Yasmin was no longer at his side, and he had few friends in this new city. He knew that his role in Jack Sladen's empire was crucial to his own future plans, but Jack was distancing himself, and Tenuk could feel the sands shifting. Occasionally his brain added Chloe into the swirl of thoughts. He was sure that they had met before, and it made him nervous.

The conversation with his father ran on a loop through his head, mingled with the brief and unsatisfactory discussion with Jack that had followed. He was determined not to re-join the family firm. He'd travelled his own path since leaving and he didn't want his overbearing father belittling either his experience or his successes. But still, his father's reappearance in his life had reminded him all too painfully that he was a long way from home with little hope of returning.

His own choices had led to this. He had no one to blame but himself.

Frustrated, Tenuk gave up trying to sleep. He got up and showered but it barely refreshed him. He was still tired. He needed some proper rest and relaxation, and he knew where to find it. It was no use staying here in the stuffy apartment. He picked up a sleep immersion kit, dropped it into his backpack, and set out for the office.

The downtown streets were dark and deserted but for the big sweeper trucks that followed their simple programming around the grid system. At this early hour, the streetlights would only flick on when they sensed movement. A ribbon of illumination followed Tenuk as he climbed the hill to the familiar glass and concrete tower that gleamed in the moonlight. It really did look like a ship from this angle, he thought, with its great sail billowing out against the stars.

The unfamiliar noise of an old fossil fuel engine distracted him. He turned towards the sound and was briefly blinded by a set of bright headlights. He blinked and watched as a red Mustang growled past and turned into the car park beneath the building. Tenuk was sure he'd seen one like it before. Most Austin residents drove electric. Delivery trucks that couldn't manage the range or load on batteries generally ran on hydrogen. Cars and pickups that came in from counties on the vast plains around Austin where electric and hydrogen supplies were scarce still relied on gas stations, but that Mustang was a rarity. Tenuk had to admit he liked it.

The walk had been more refreshing than he expected, but Tenuk still needed space to meditate and think. He made his way up the dimly lit tower to the Statesman Tech floor. There was no one else there. Jack's office door opened smoothly for him. He dialled the wall opacity up to the maximum again and hooked his immersive kit up to the network. Sitting in a comfortable chair in the corner of the room, air conditioning maintaining a perfect temperature and humidity, he donned his haptic jacket and a soft, lightweight headband. It blocked background noise and intrusive light and the flexible goggles that moulded to his face were all that were needed to take him into the virtual reality known as the Sanctuary.

The avatar who welcomed him to the atrium of the Sanctuary was demure and dark eyed, with a keen air of intelligence. She was personalised to suit Tenuk's taste and closely resembled a woman he had met in London, years ago in another life. He knew that he would never see her again, but it was a comfort to have her likeness here in the virtual world.

"Good morning, Tenuk," said the avatar with a smile. "Where would you like to go today?"

"Good morning, Noor," he replied. "Let me see the menu."

He chose a world of lush green tropical forests and running water, a place he had been many times before. The background music was low and mesmerising. Tenuk's avatar walked along the forest path towards the cascades. Through his haptic jacket he felt the gentle touch of leaves brushing against his shoulders. It was a comforting sensation and Tenuk felt some of the tension start to drain away from his tired body.

Reaching a clearing, he looked around. A bird of paradise strutted by slowly, brilliantly coloured feathers erect, displaying its finery. Over the gentle music he could hear the calls of other birds in the distance and the sound of the waterfall just out of sight.

He directed his avatar to sit beneath a tree and lean back. He adjusted a setting and allowed the haptic jacket to interpret both his interactions with the Sanctuary scene and the sounds of the water, birds and music. He could feel the pressure of the tree trunk on his back and ripples like the tinkling of water on his arms, the trilling of the birds tapping a rhythm across his heart, and the music beating gently all around.

Tenuk closed his eyes and concentrated on hearing and touch, deeply immersed. His breathing was slow and steady. This was the most relaxed he had been for weeks, and a thought floated through his head that he should visit the Sanctuary more often. He was careful not to let that distract him, imagining the thought as a skein of gossamer floating away on a light breeze. In his mind's eye he watched it go, and as it disappeared, he slept at last.

He dreamed of Yasmin. He heard her voice in the music of the water, and in the dreamscape he walked through the grove, looking for her. The trees were hung with pictures, just opaque enough to be recognisable without obscuring the lush woodland. Tenuk recognised a classic Cryptopunk pixelated head, swirling abstract figures, a chess piece and a blue-eyed humanoid. He kept walking, following the sound of Yasmin's voice, but instead of reaching the cascades he found himself circling back to the grove. The voice faded, and he drifted away into a deep sleep.

A noise loud enough to penetrate his immersive environment brought him abruptly back to the real world. It took a moment for Tenuk to orient himself. He pulled the headband off and blinked in the daylight. He must have slept for hours. He was refreshed, but annoyed that he'd been deprived of the slow steady wakeup he'd selected from the Sanctuary menu. Another noise made him turn sharply in the chair and look around the room. It was deserted, but even through the opaque walls of Jack's office he could detect movement outside. Staff must already be arriving for work.

Tenuk took off the haptic jacket and stowed the immersion kit in his backpack. He yawned and stretched, took a swig from his water bottle, and went out to see what was happening on the shop floor.

The only person in sight was Chloe, sitting on the far side of the office with a coffee cup in her hand and talking to someone Tenuk could not see. Confused, he checked the time. It was barely seven in the morning.

He strolled casually to the breakout area and prepared a coffee, clattering the cups and letting steam hiss loudly from the machine, then moved across the office to join her. He thought he had announced his presence clearly enough, but even so Chloe jumped dramatically as he approached.

"Tenuk," she said with a bright smile. "I didn't see you. You're in early."

"You too, Chloe," said Tenuk. Now he could see the man she had been talking to, who stood up politely and extended his hand. Tenuk shook it.

"This is Ben," said Chloe. "He's from one of our suppliers down in San Antonio."

"I remember," said Tenuk pleasantly. "The MetaBand engineers. You've been here before. I hope Chloe's looking after you?"

The man smiled and dipped his head. "Yes, she is," he said in a soft British accent. "I was just tying up some loose ends, and Chloe here was kind enough to agree to an early morning meeting. I'm flying back to England soon and just wanted to check a couple of details." He picked up his bag. "I think I have everything I need," he said. "Thanks again for all your help."

"I'll see you out," said Chloe brightly. Ben followed her to the door, and they disappeared along the corridor to the elevators.

Tenuk made sure they had both gone and ran back into Jack's office. What was the sound that had woken him? He pulled up the feed from the building's security cameras. They were old and inefficient but might have captured something useful. He scrolled through the footage. He saw himself arriving and entering Jack's office, but there was no sign of Chloe or Ben on the recording. Perhaps there had been a fault with the cameras. It seemed like an odd coincidence, and his hackles were rising.

Ben the engineer had visited the office before, checking

on a paperwork muddle in the design specifications for the satellites and hubs that made up Jack Sladen's global MetaBand communications network. Tenuk himself had made some crucial changes to the original design and covered his tracks with fake documentation in the supply chain. It should have been enough to satisfy an innocent eager engineer trying to keep their records straight, but Tenuk had deep reservations about Ben.

He had met him before, back in England, on the same trip with the MerLions when he had first been introduced to Noor. Ben had been with Cameron Silvera when they met, and the last thing Tenuk wanted was for her attention to turn to the hidden details of the MetaBand network. Whatever Ben knew, he had to be stopped before he could pass information to the SimCavalier.

•

Cameron left the office early. Mindful of Pete's advice, she took an autocar to the station, although she privately admitted to herself that she was so exhausted by the events of the last twenty-four hours that she would have struggled to walk all the way. She booked into the first-class carriage for a change and settled gratefully into the wider, more comfortable train seat. They glided slowly through the northern suburbs of London past the great arch of the old Wembley stadium. A steward trolley rolled to a halt at Cameron's seat and offered her a choice of tea, coffee, wine, beer, and a selection of snacks. She chose a glass of wine and took a sip. She winced. She had tasted better.

Cameron relaxed and gazed out of the window at the familiar landscape racing past. She would be back in the sanctuary of the village in an hour or so, and she couldn't wait.

The smartscreen in her pocket vibrated. She put the wine down on the little table and wrestled the screen out with her good hand. Notifications scrolled endlessly before her eyes, and she sighed. If she thought she would be getting a rest this weekend, she was very wrong.

The first message was from Charlie. He'd be waiting for her at the station. She sent back her location so that he knew she was on the way. When she saw the second, from Andy, she cursed under her breath and earned a disapproving look from a prim lady on the other side of the aisle. She'd forgotten to call him. She pinged back a note to apologise and suggested they meet for a drink over the weekend.

The third took her breath away. It was from Ben.

'Hi, Cameron,' she read. 'I hope you're doing okay. I'm coming back to London, and I need to see you. I'm bringing a present from a mutual friend. I'll call you when I land.'

There was nothing more. Frustrated, Cameron scrolled back to check when the message had been sent. She'd missed a call from him when she was getting into the autocar. She tried to reach him, but his line wasn't accepting calls. He must be out of range, she thought. Either he was driving happily across the vast plains of Texas in his beloved Mustang, or he was already on his way through security for the long journey back across the Atlantic. Furious that she had missed his call, frustrated that he had given her so little detail in his message, Cameron drained the glass of rough red wine and lay back in her seat, scowling at the ceiling.

Her mood was still black when she got off the train. Her arm was hurting again. The sight of her brother, Charlie, and her younger niece waiting for her just outside the station lifted her spirits.

"Careful, Tara!" said Charlie as Tara threw herself at Cameron and hugged her tightly. Charlie picked up his sister's bag and threw it into the autocar. "Come on, Cameron," he said, patting her good arm fondly. "Let's get you home."

Cameron snuggled into her favourite armchair in the calm sitting room and sipped at a glass of much better wine.

"I'm not sure this is the best treatment," she said, "but it's working so far."

Charlie raised his glass. "Cheers," he said. "The best cure is rest and relaxation, and you'll get plenty of that here." He reached over to the coffee table in the middle of the room and picked up a cube of cheese. "Have you tried this?" he asked. "It's from the farm over the road. It's very good."

Cameron tried to reach out with her sore arm and

regretted it. She collapsed back into the chair with a groan. Sameena put the plate down next to her with a smile.

"Thanks, Sameena," said Cameron. "I have to say I'm surprised you've both taken this so well."

"We're more worried about you than about us," said Charlie. "We're a lot safer here than you are in London. Nina is practically grown up now and she's got all her confidence back. Dilan and Tara are really conscious about security, and we know that they can look after themselves."

Sameena looked sidelong at him. "You haven't mentioned the protection drones," she said, "or the hotline from our personal chips to the police."

"Well, yes, we've taken precautions," said Charlie, "but nothing that interferes with our lives. If we start living in fear, they've won. I'm not going to let that happen, and nor, little sister, are you."

"Nope," said Cameron. She popped another piece of cheese in her mouth. "But I'm not sure that the cat will be happy if there's any more fuss disrupting her mealtimes."

Sameena laughed. "You're as bad as Aunt Vicky," she said. "The cat comes first."

"Oh, always," said Cameron. "But seriously, it looks as if the whole dark web knows who I am and where I live now, and that puts the people I know and love in danger. I'm not afraid. I'm just worried."

"Let's make a deal," said Charlie. He reached for the wine bottle and topped up their three glasses. "We'll worry about you because that's what we do. You concentrate on keeping yourself out of trouble."

"Deal," said Cameron.

A bell rang in the distance and a moment later Nina poked her head around the sitting room door. "Dinner's ready," she said, "and Aunt Vicky's here."

Nina, Dilan and Tara had insisted on cooking, ready to impress their aunt with their favourite dishes. Sitting in the familiar dining room laughing, drinking good red wine, and eating the kids' excellent pasta with her family around her, Cameron finally relaxed. This was her sanctuary, the safest place she knew. She could almost believe that everything would be alright.

7: SOURCES

The following lunchtime, the pub was busy. Cameron looked around the beer garden but couldn't see Andy anywhere. She ducked her head into the dark interior and spotted him at the bar, his dog sitting next to his stool.

"Hello, Jasper," she said, bending down to ruffle the dog's wiry coat and pulling at its ears.

"Hi Cameron," said Andy. "What can I get you?"

"Just a lemonade," said Cameron, struggling onto the barstool next to him.

Andy's eyes widened when he saw the sling. "You've been in the wars, Cameron," he said. "What's happened?"

Cameron leaned gingerly on the bar. As she expected, the aches and pains on the second day were far worse than the first. "I have a good excuse for not calling you back," she said grimly. "This is strictly between us and not to go anywhere near the News Channel, understood?"

Andy nodded, suddenly serious. Cameron gave him a quick debrief that left him open mouthed.

"I won't ever ask you to come on the show again," he said. "We can't risk it."

"Anonymous quotes and avatars are fine," said Cameron, "but not me." She pulled a couple of painkillers out of her pocket and washed them down with lemonade. "So, about that tip-off," she continued. "We've found nothing to suggest that the glitch for the speedrunner event was anything but a genuine technical fault. I want to know your source, Andy."

Andy looked sidelong at her and said nothing. He lifted his pint glass and took a long swig of beer.

"You know I can't do that," he said slowly. "I wouldn't tell anyone if I had a tip-off from you, and I owe the same duty of care to them."

Cameron was taken aback. She and Andy had known each other for years. Their relationship was based on absolute trust, and this shook her. She drank her lemonade in silence and examined her feelings. Was she jealous that Andy had the same close arrangement with someone else? It occurred to her she might be being unreasonable. Surely he had sources everywhere that he was trying to protect.

"Okay," she said. "But at least give me some context. You seem so sure this is genuine, but I can't find anything to suggest that there's a problem. One of us is wrong."

"I trust my source," said Andy simply.

"Don't you trust me?" Cameron shot back.

Andy looked at her helplessly. "Of course I do," he said. "Look, what questions should I be asking them to help you get to the bottom of this? I can come back to you with answers and then you'll be able to track down whatever's happened."

"That depends on where your source is coming from," said Cameron. "No use asking technical questions if they won't understand them. Help me out here, Andy. Is it a competitor?" Andy shook his head. "Someone organising the gaming disciplines? Anyone in the Olympic setup? No? So that leaves tech and infosec, doesn't it. And if they're in that field, they'll know me, so why are they going to you?" She was getting angry, and it showed.

Andy scowled at her. "Stop it, Cameron," he said. "You're putting me in an impossible position. Give me a question. I'll come back with the answer. That's the deal."

"Fine," said Cameron. She finished her drink and clambered off the bar stool. "Okay. Ask them what the attack vector was. As much detail as possible. I don't need to know how they know. I just want to find the start of the trail."

"Okay," said Andy. "Attack vector. Got it."

"And tell them I'm baffled by the secrecy and I'm happy to talk to them," said Cameron, extending an olive branch. "I'll see you later."

She ducked her head under the low lintel of the pub doorway and emerged, blinking, into the sunlight. A neighbour gave her a cheery wave from across the beer garden and she returned the greeting, but she was in no mood to stay and chat. Instead, she left by the little lych gate and walked back down the long village street. It wound along the line of the stream and past the site of an old water mill, gone centuries before, and the thirteenth century church with its pale stone tower. Cameron knew every step of the way. She glanced into the playground of the old red brick primary school where she had learned her first coding skills. Not much had changed.

Instead of going straight back to Charlie's, she turned up a short hill towards a row of houses. She needed a sense check with Aunt Vicky.

Her aunt was pottering around the front garden. Two chairs and a small table were set out in the sunshine.

"Cameron, darling!" Aunt Vicky straightened up from the flowerbed that she was weeding and gave her niece a gentle hug. "Sit down," she said. "I'll put the kettle on."

"It's a bit warm for tea, isn't it?" said Cameron. "Have you got any juice?"

"Of course," said Aunt Vicky. She pulled off her gardening gloves and placed them neatly on the grass with the fork, then disappeared into the house.

Cameron eyed the two chairs. One was already occupied by a pile of orange fur. As she watched, the cat stretched and rolled onto its back, paws in the air, sunning itself.

"Donald," she said, "You have no dignity." She sat in the other chair. It was more trouble than it was worth to try and move the cat, so she would leave that to her aunt.

Looking around the familiar garden, she noticed some changes. In particular, a shiny new box with a swirly logo was now attached to the wall of the cottage. She recognised it as a brand new MetaBand base unit. Glancing at the other houses around her, Cameron realised that they all had the same equipment installed. The rollout of Jack Sladen's hardware was moving faster than she expected.

She made a mental note to check whether Charlie had fallen for the hype, too.

Aunt Vicky emerged from the house carrying a tray laden with tea, juice and cake. She set it down on the small table and looked fondly at the cat. "Donald," she said, trying to be stern, "that's my chair."

A yellow eye opened, blinked slowly, and closed. Donald stretched again, luxuriating in the warmth of the sun. His paws reached out past the edge of the chair, and gradually Cameron became aware that his centre of gravity was shifting. Almost in slow motion, Donald slid towards the ground. He became aware of the movement too late, twisted desperately to remain on the chair, and landed on his feet on the grass, closely followed by the chair cushion. He shook his furry head in disgust and stalked off, looking for trouble.

"There, that's better," said Aunt Vicky, replacing the cushion and settling into the now vacated chair. "How are you feeling today, dear?"

"I'm a bit sore," said Cameron, taking a bite of cake.

"I'm not surprised," said Aunt Vicky. "That'll take a few days to settle down. I do my best not to worry about you, but that was a nasty incident. You need to take care."

"I know," said Cameron. "I'm doing my best. It's always good to know that you and Charlie and Sameena are here, and the team has my back as well."

Aunt Vicky hesitated as if unsure what to say next. "I did wonder…" she said. "Have you heard from Ben recently? Or Jack?"

Cameron laughed at her aunt's discomfort. "They'd be terrible bodyguards, both of them, if that's what you're thinking," she said. "Ben's still based over in the States, and Jack's ignoring me. He hasn't forgiven me for helping the police to raid the headquarters of his precious foundation."

"I'm not surprised, dear," said Aunt Vicky. "I imagine he's quite offended and his male pride has been severely dented. Am I allowed to ask if you found what you were looking for there?"

Cameron looked pained. "Yes and no," she said. "We were certain that his data centre was hosting an escaped convict."

"Yasmin," said Aunt Vicky with loathing. "The creature who caused so much trouble for poor Nina. It should still be locked up."

"I agree," said Cameron, "but there's nothing we can do about that. She escaped from prison, and we were right about where she ended up. But now we don't really know where she might be. I think she was destroyed in the raid. An artificial intelligence of her complexity takes up a huge volume of storage and processing power. It took days for her to transfer from the prison systems to the Dunswyke data centre. She tried to get away quickly, but I think it failed. She'll have broken up, everything lost in the ether. There's nothing left in there but a tame system management 'bot."

"If you were right, why is Jack cross with you?" asked Aunt Vicky. "He seems to be entirely in the clear, judging by all the news reports."

"He doesn't think I was right," said Cameron. "There is no solid proof that Yasmin was ever there. A lot of the infrastructure was destroyed and of course there's no handy paperwork to show them taking delivery of an escaped prisoner."

Aunt Vicky nodded. "I understand perfectly," she said. "He doesn't trust you. He's wrong, of course, but it'll take him time to admit it. He'll come around one day." She poured another glass of juice for Cameron and sipped at her tea. "It's a real shame," she continued. "You two were getting on so well again, and he seems to be doing some wonderful work with that foundation, and with MetaBand as well."

"I notice you've got a new MetaBand network box there," said Cameron. "How are you finding the connection?"

"It's fabulous," said Aunt Vicky. "The whole village was hooked up very quickly. We had such a patchy signal before, with being down in a dip, and we were one of the communities on the rural priority list."

"Probably one of the easier ones to install, too," said Cameron. "There are some very remote places who will be waiting a lot longer." She put her juice down on the table and stood up. "Do you mind if I have a look at the box?" she said. "I promise not to break anything."

Donald was scraping diligently at the soft earth that had been disturbed by the cable laying. Cameron shooed him away and he stalked off into the undergrowth, offended. As Cameron bent to examine the MetaBand hub she realised exactly what he had been burying.

"Donald," she said, "that's disgusting. Find somewhere else to do your business."

She avoided Donald's carefully buried poop and instead knelt on the grass close to the box. She pulled her smartscreen out of her pocket, wincing only slightly, and navigated to a useful set of diagnostic tools. She connected to the box using a generic engineer login that she'd picked up from the Eden marketplace for just such an eventuality and ran some standard tests.

"Interesting," she muttered to herself. She adjusted a couple of key parameters and ran the tests again.

"What are you looking for?" called Aunt Vicky.

Cameron straightened up and went back to her chair. "Nothing specific," she said, putting her smartscreen down on the table. "I wanted to see whether the box was operating within the standard parameters for a domestic communications hub, or whether it's running a node."

"In English?" said Aunt Vicky.

"Does it do what it says on the tin?" said Cameron with a smile. "You're not currently using the network apart from, well, I guess the smart fridge and the home hub. Background stuff. That box is processing a lot of data. It's running at a pretty high CPU percentage. That means it's a Diaulos node as well as a comms hub."

"How clever," said Aunt Vicky. She lifted her arm and Cameron recognised a Diaulos fitness band on her wrist. "I'm collecting steps and the box is processing transactions."

"That box holds its own copy of the whole Diaulos ledger as well," said Cameron, "and you're keeping the network secure with your steps."

"That's right," said Aunt Vicky. "I get little rewards in my Diaulos wallet. Not much, but it's quite fun to see the balance growing."

"It always amazes me that any part of Sladen Group came up with something so neat," said Cameron. "Jack's systems are notorious for being full of holes. This one seems to work."

She eyed up the last small cake thoughtfully.

"Help yourself," said Aunt Vicky. "I've had two. That one's yours. And you can explain to me how my steps keep this system running."

Cameron gave in gracefully and picked up the cake. "I'll try and keep it simple," she said. She took a bite of cake, swallowed, and brushed the crumbs off her lips. "Okay," she continued. "Every time there's a block of transactions ready to close, the system sends out a message with a random step count to all the active wristbands, and whichever bands match that step count reply to confirm the block and open the next one. It's a bit more complicated underneath, of course, but that's the basic principle."

She finished the cake and sat back in her chair, blinking as a shaft of sunlight caught her in the eyes. Her aches and pains were under control and her mood was vastly improved by the peace of the village. She had little choice but to be patient, and she had almost reconciled herself to waiting. Waiting for Mercer, or Michelle, or Noor to follow the trail back from her attacker to the networks and motivations. Waiting for Andy to come back with the answer to her question. Waiting for Jack to realise that there really had been a threat, that Yasmin had been there in his data centre. Waiting for Ben to come back from America.

Ben. She hadn't heard back from Ben.

Cameron sat up abruptly and grabbed her smartscreen from the table. She checked her notifications but there were no new messages. She tried to call him, but once again there was no receiving signal. She frowned.

"Something wrong, dear?" asked Aunt Vicky.

Cameron shook her head. "Probably nothing," she said.

"In that case, stop worrying and relax," said Aunt Vicky. "You're here to rest and heal so that you can fight your battles again."

"You're right," said Cameron. She lay back in her chair again and focused on the warmth of the sun, pushing a cluster of disturbing thoughts to the back of her mind.

8: EDEN

"What do you have for me?" asked Tenuk.

The Pangolin stared across the virtual boardroom table at the grey kitten avatar. As predicted, the kitten had come crawling back very quickly after storming out of the last Steamyard meeting, seeking forgiveness and more work. Tenuk suspected that this particular cybercriminal-for-hire had an addiction to feed in the real world. He didn't care what it was. All he knew was that it made the kitten desperate, easy to manipulate, and highly predictable.

"The target's comms have been disabled, Pangolin," said the kitten. "All calls and messages linked to their ID, incoming or outgoing, are being intercepted and blocked. Outbound data is still flagging to him as delivered."

"Good," said Tenuk. That was the first step, preventing Ben the Engineer from having any contact with the SimCavalier. "He'll think that messages are being delivered and that no one's replying. What about the message content? Have you managed to decrypt?"

The kitten shook its head. "No, Pangolin," it said. "Not yet. The security's too good. If we had…" It tailed off.

There was an icy silence. Tenuk did not need reminding that Yasmin was no longer around to crack encryption and dig deep into impenetrable systems. He had grown very used to having her back in his cybercrime stable again, and she was sorely missed. She had been the cornerstone of the old Pasar network, and then of the Steamyard, albeit with an intervening period of incarceration in a British prison. Now that she was dead, Tenuk had to rely on the inconsistent skills of human hackers.

"I'll take it from here," said Tenuk. "Your payment is being transferred."

"Thanks," said the kitten. Its avatar disappeared without another word.

Tenuk remained online. In the real world, in his hot little apartment, he took a long drink of water and swapped his flat screen for the reality mask. His next destination was far more interesting in three dimensions and being immersed in the environment helped him to concentrate on staying safe and secure.

Tenuk's avatar left the Steamyard boardroom and flipped to a different instance of the world, one where the Eden marketplace had its headquarters. The kitten may have prevented Ben from communicating with the SimCavalier for the moment, but Tenuk wanted to stop the man from leaving Texas altogether. He had to do this part himself. Asking any of his Steamyard connections, particularly the unstable grey kitten, was out of the question. He could not risk giving any of them clues to his own physical location.

The Eden market hall, a vast block of a building looming over the commercial district, was bustling with life. Avatars of all shapes and sizes browsed the stalls.

Along the main alley, merchants and customers haggled over the latest stolen data sets. Tenuk lingered for a moment over a rich selection of user details from the British government, but on second glance realised that it was from an old breach and that he already had a more recent data set on file. He headed to the other side of the great hall, looking for the stalls selling access codes and generic identities. On the way, he passed a popular botnet hire shop that he'd used before. There was a customer in there wearing a distinctive sapphire ring. Tenuk recognised it immediately, although he knew very few people outside the family firm would have any idea what it signified. He ducked quickly out of sight. He didn't want to be noticed by either the customer or the shopkeeper.

He watched them from a distance, wondering why someone from his father's inner circle would be looking for malware and disruption tools in the Eden marketplace. What could his father be up to? It wasn't the old man's style to directly run something like a Distributed Denial of Service attack, but Tenuk had no doubt he knew all about this little shopping trip. He made a mental note to dig deeper when he was back in the real world.

The transaction seemed to be concluding, so Tenuk withdrew and continued towards his destination, taking a roundabout route to avoid being seen.

At the access code stalls, Tenuk carefully parsed his question to the catalogue 'bot in charge of the aisle. "I need access to border control security alerts," he said.

There was a pause before the 'bot came back with a

positive response. “In stock,” it said. “Stalls R/3 and T/2.”

Tenuk breathed a sigh of relief and followed the ’bot’s directions. His idea was still half-formed and depended on the specific codes that he could buy. He rejected some useful-looking override credentials for the baggage routing systems at his local airport but paused to examine a simple set of perpetual first class upgrades for any airline. If he got the chance to travel again, they would be very nice to have. The bundle wasn’t expensive, and Tenuk had a feeling that he might be on the move soon, whether he stayed with Jack, took up his father’s offer, or followed another path yet to be revealed. Decision made, he transferred the asking price to the stallholder, and the file access token for the upgrades landed straight in his wallet by return.

The second stall proved more fruitful for his main task. A batch of stolen security credentials gave him enough scope to raise a fake alert at the airport for the engineer’s passport and have the man held for questioning. By disrupting Ben’s communication channels and preventing him from leaving the country, Tenuk hoped to buy enough time to find out exactly what information he was carrying.

He was starting to get hot and sweaty in the real world. He paid for the credentials that he needed. It was time to go.

Tenuk found a return jump point to the upper levels and flipped out of the Eden instance. He expected to arrive in the busy brand outlet centre that mapped onto the market hall, but instead he found himself in a deserted building on an unfamiliar level. He checked the navigation menu. His original destination was greyed out. The system thought he was there. It was very clear that he was not.

Despite the sweat that was now running freely down his cheek, Tenuk kept the reality mask on and peered around. He dared not risk distraction by reducing the opacity of his view, and in the real world reached blindly to where he knew he had put his water bottle. His hand closed around it. Relieved, he took a long drink and wiped the sweat off his face.

The building looked like an art gallery under construction. The floor was chequered black and white, accentuating the linear perspective of the virtual world, disappearing into the gloom towards an endless vanishing point. Pillars rose to the vaulted ceiling and were interspersed with displays of digital art from static abstract and figurative images to video, 3D and interactive installations. Tenuk looked closer at the pieces on display and the details of each work and its artist popped up on the display within his reality mask. In pride of place was a classic pixelated Cryptopunk head. In the back of Tenuk's mind, a memory stirred. He had seen many of these exact pictures before, but where?

"Tenuk," came a voice in the ether.

He felt his heart racing. "Yasmin?" he breathed disbelievingly.

A spotlight on the far wall drew Tenuk's attention.

A large, animated tableau lit up and Tenuk was drawn irresistibly towards it. He watched as the simple story unfolded.

An amorphous blue-eyed humanoid figure smiled down at him. It extended an arm in welcome and Tenuk took in its surroundings, glistening tracks of power and data against dark stone walls. A cave. He knew it immediately, although he had never been there in person. It was the old data centre at the Sladen Foundation's Dunswyke headquarters.

Only a handful of people in the world could possibly have known where Yasmin had been hosted. Tenuk watched in fascination as the humanoid figure on the tableau dissolved and the glistening streams of data glowed bright, symbolising her consciousness streaming away into the ether.

He had thought her dead. Yet it seemed that she lived. He kept watching. The swirl of the MetaBand logo filled the screen, and Tenuk started to laugh. He found he couldn't stop. The crazy plan that he and Yasmin had hatched had actually worked. Every MetaBand hub was part of her, each processor an artificial cortical coil, and her consciousness was distributed across the world.

"I am all around," said Yasmin's voice.

"Come back and help me," said Tenuk. "I need you."

The blue-eyed humanoid figure from the tableau appeared in front of him. "I may," said Yasmin. "I have other programmes to run and tasks to fulfil. If I have capacity, I will help you. I will find you."

The instance winked out and Tenuk found himself transported abruptly back to the busy, noisy brand outlet he had been aiming for. He shivered despite the heat in his apartment. Yasmin was free, and powerful, and no longer at his beck and call.

He had created a monster.

9: SECURITY

Cameron woke up in her attic room, sun streaming through a crack in the curtains. She automatically reached for her smartscreen and checked the time. It was still very early, barely five, and her train to the north didn't leave until nine. She tiptoed downstairs, careful not to disturb anyone in the silent house, and found a glass of water and her morning dose of painkillers. As she sipped the water, she peered out of the kitchen window at the fields opposite the house. Sheep were scattered across the meadow, munching away at the grass, their rich milk destined for the excellent cheese that the farm produced. It was a far cry from the hustle and bustle of London. She felt rested and restored after her weekend.

Coffee in hand she returned to her attic domain. Cybercriminals never seemed to sleep and there was always work to do. Ten minutes later Cameron was sitting at her old desk in her pyjamas and working through the notifications, messages and calls that she had missed the previous day.

There had been a lot of chatter on the MIST platform. Cameron scrolled rapidly through several hundred messages, but nothing jumped out as needing her immediate attention. The Olympic metaverse fabric was still intact, resisting the constant onslaught of attacks.

With the odd behaviour of the gambling data breach perpetrators and the tip-off from Andy in mind, she highlighted a few comments for review later.

In contrast to MIST activity, the direct messages in her inbox were overflowing. Cameron sorted through alerts from Mephisto, archiving some and flagging others for action. She discarded a swathe of marketing messages, tired of reporting them all for violating advertising regulations. Once all the dross was cleared, Cameron could focus on the things that mattered.

Noor had sent through the draft report on the breach at the betting platform. She and Pete had burrowed down to the source and found a piece of software hiding in one of the servers. It looked on the surface to be an innocent enough thing, installed in good faith but now obsolete and unsupported. On closer inspection it turned out to be a back door to download user details on command. They'd disabled it, analysed it, and sent a warning out to the wider infosec community of its existence. This was unlikely to be the only place that routine was hiding and given the complexity of the phishing attacks and cloned web pages it had probably been built to order for someone who wanted to disrupt betting platforms.

Cameron glanced through the report's executive summary and the key headlines and actions as she sipped her coffee, nodding occasionally in approval. Noor had done an excellent job as usual. Everything was there and the client would be happy.

There was nothing from Ben, no reply to her own

messages, but right at the bottom of the inbox was a brief note from a reformed cybercriminal who went by the name of Cloverleaf. Cameron had been her handler when Cloverleaf crossed over to support the good guys, the white hat hackers. She had brought with her the secrets of a terrorist network and a cybercrime syndicate and had been instrumental in taking down both organisations. After many months of debriefing and safe houses, Cloverleaf had ended up working for one of Jack Sladen's companies, Statesman Tech in Austin, where she found plenty more secrets and continued her undercover work.

'Hi Cameron,' said the message. 'Thought you'd like to know that a mutual friend of ours is heading for London this week. I gave him a present to bring to you. Chloe.'

Ben. It had to be. The wording of their respective messages was too similar.

Cameron scrolled rapidly through the inbox again, looking for Ben's name and then checked her private accounts. Still nothing. Chloe clearly said that he was coming to London this week, but when?

Cameron tried to call Ben's ID again, but without success. It had been more than two days since she had missed his last call, and she was starting to worry. What was Ben doing playing courier for Chloe? He couldn't know the danger that put him in. And what on earth could he be carrying that couldn't be transmitted by the normal trusted channels that she and Chloe had been using for years to exchange highly sensitive secrets?

She pinged a message back to Chloe. 'Thanks,' she wrote. 'When should I expect them?'

There would be no answer for a few hours. Cameron couldn't rest any longer. She dressed quickly, packed her bag ready to head to Dunswyke, and went downstairs for breakfast, hoping that the kids would be up. She needed a distraction, and they were guaranteed to provide one.

"Aunty Cam," said Dilan between spoonfuls of cereal, "can you help me with my homework?"

Sameena gave him a stern glare. "I asked you last night if you'd finished everything," she said. "What did you miss?"

"Just a Python coding puzzle," said Dilan. "I normally do it in morning form time, but Will just messaged me and said it has to be in before school starts. They're checking the submission times now."

"And if you don't do it in time?" asked Cameron.

Dilan finished his cereal, drank the last drops of milk from the bottom of the bowl, and put his spoon down. "Detention, I guess," he said, unconcerned.

Charlie peered over the top of the tablet he had been reading. "You'd better not," he said. "You know you'll lose your game console for a day again."

"Yeah, Dad," said Dilan. "That's why I want Aunty Cam to help me." He looked up at his aunt with puppy eyes. "Please?"

Cameron gave in gracefully. "Okay, show me," she said.

"I'm not going to do it for you, but I'll give you some pointers and you'd better get it finished on time."

Dilan jumped up from the table and dived for his schoolbag.

"Bowl," said Sameena sharply.

He came back to the table and grabbed the cereal bowl, spoon and cup and flung them quickly in the dishwasher, then dug his tablet out of his bag, tapped through to the assignment, and handed it to Cameron. She read the question through and laughed.

"This won't take you long," she said. "Do you know the difference between a Sort function and a Sorted function?"

Dilan's eyes widened. "Oh, of course," he said. "Thanks." He threw himself onto the small sofa at the back of the kitchen and started tapping away at his tablet with fierce concentration.

"Think yourself lucky, Dilan," said Charlie. "You won't have Cameron handy every time you're rushing to hit a deadline."

"I know, Dad," said Dilan without looking up. "It's working, Aunty Cam."

Cameron gave Charlie a conspiratorial grin and he sighed. "You're too good to them, Cam," he said. "What time's your train?"

"Ten past nine," said Cameron. "No rush."

Charlie looked at Roxy the labradoodle who was doing excited figure of eights around the kitchen. "Shall we take this daft dog out for a quick w-a-l-k?" he said.

"Sure," said Cameron. The dog's speed quickened, and

her tail wagged like metronome. "You know, Charlie, I think she can spell."

Brother and sister strolled along the familiar field path around the back of the village and along the fringes of the vineyards to the church, a fast circuit to give Roxy the chance to work off some energy before everyone left for work and school. They were not the only people out in the cool of the morning. Roxy, bounding ahead, found a friend, and Cameron saw Andy approaching from the stile that led to the churchyard.

"Morning, Andy," said Charlie. "Haven't seen you all weekend. How are you doing?"

"Fine, thanks, mate," said Andy. He gave Cameron a slightly embarrassed look. "Hi, Cameron."

Charlie looked from one to the other, confused. "Have I missed something?" he said.

"Oh, nothing," said Cameron. "Andy was digging up some info for me. Any luck?"

"Uh, yes, as a matter of fact," said Andy. "I was going to drop in later. My source said to look for an autoplay back door. Does that make any sense?"

"Yes, thanks," she said. "That's really helpful. It explains what happened in the game and why there hasn't been a whisper on the forums. Any back door will have been built into the system a long time ago, and I'm guessing it's extremely well hidden."

Andy looked relieved. "It's a genuine tip-off then?" he said.

"Oh yes," said Cameron. "It sounds like it. You've definitely scooped me on this one. I'll let you know what I find when I dig into the detail. Look after that source of yours, though. There are some nasty people around who may not want their back door to be found."

Charlie looked from Cameron to Andy. "Are you mixed up in this thing too, Andy?" he said. "Seriously, be careful. We don't want to attract any attention."

"So I heard," said Andy. "How's your arm, Cameron?"

Cameron flipped her jacket open to reveal the sling that was taking the weight off her sore shoulder. "It's still bloody sore," she said with a wry smile. "Let's talk when I get back to London. I'm heading up to Dunswyke today."

The bell in the church tower chimed once. "That's quarter past," said Charlie. "We'd better get moving, Cameron." He whistled to Roxy, who came bounding back across the field, closely followed by Jasper.

"Call me when you get back to London," said Andy. "I'll see if I can get any more information for you. And enjoy your trip. Giles is going to the press conference on Wednesday to report on the outcome of the investigation. How is Jack Sladen, by the way?"

Cameron made a face. "I don't know," she said. "It's going to be an interesting week. I'll let you know if anything comes up that you can use."

"Thanks, Cameron," said Andy. "See you later, Charlie." He and Jasper walked off over the fields, and Cameron and Charlie made their way through the churchyard and back towards home.

The train north was much quieter than the commuter train Cameron had taken out of London two days before. The web connection was poor, hopping from hub to hub through increasingly sparsely populated areas. At York, in sight of the great Minster, Cameron checked her MIST and inbox messages. Chloe had replied, despite the fact it was still very early in Austin. The package would arrive later in the week, she said. That wasn't as helpful as Cameron had hoped, and it made her all the more certain that Chloe was worried about the security of their conversations.

Despite the uncertainty, she now knew she'd see Ben in just a few days. She felt butterflies in her stomach and squashed the feeling as fast as she could. She couldn't admit how much she missed him. He had been away for a long time, and he might have met someone else. She hoped not.

To distract herself, Cameron answered a couple of client queries, sent Sandeep her expected arrival time, and settled down to watch the landscape fly by. To the east rose the North York Moors, marked at their southern end by a great white horse carved in the chalk. To the west the Pennines started their march up the spine of the country. The train track ran straight through the middle of the farmland that filled the gap between the two ranges of hills. The Romans had planted vines as far north as York, but most of the fields in this valley were given over to cereals and livestock.

For a short distance a drone kept pace with the train,

checking the state of the farm boundary running parallel to the track, before wheeling off at an angle to follow the line of the hedgerows. Cameron knew that the pastoral scenes in front of her had barely changed in decades, but if she could have visualised the streams of data that were running between soil and moisture sensors, collars on livestock, and all the intelligent farm machinery, it would be quite a different picture.

The train stopped at a series of small market towns before leaving the farmland behind and climbing up above the old city of Durham, cathedral and castle shining in the summer sun. Cameron pulled her smartscreen out of her pocket and took a couple of pictures, then checked her inbox again.

Still nothing from Ben, but she wasn't expecting anything now. There was a new connection notification from a private encrypted message app. Cameron cursed. She wasn't about to go through the layers of authentication and security that were needed to access it while she was linked to the public networks. Better to wait until she was in the remote office that Sandeep, Joel and Susie had set up. Who could be trying to contact her this way? Her curiosity was piqued, and she was restless for the remainder of the journey, barely noticing the iconic view along the River Tyne as the train pulled into Newcastle station and fidgeting impatiently on the final leg to Alnmouth.

Sandeep met her at the station, and twenty minutes later they pulled into the car park of a building that looked more like a small castle than a hotel, standing proud and alone, surrounded by fields and moorland and with dunes and sea just visible in the distance.

"Welcome to HQ," said Sandeep. "You'll love it." He pushed the heavy front door open, and Cameron found herself in a large hallway with several doors leading off to either side. "Kelly," said Sandeep to the girl behind the small reception desk, "This is Cameron. Is her room ready?"

"Sure," said Kelly. "Can I get you to check in, Cameron?"

Cameron went through a series of detailed chip and biometric identification procedures. "This isn't your usual check in process, is it?" she said.

Kelly laughed. "It is, actually," she said. "This hotel is booked out most of the year by, well, people who need to be sure about the security of the place they're staying." She tapped at her keyboard. "All done," she said. "You're in room 8, top of the stairs, turn left."

Sandeep pointed Cameron to the stairs. "Go and get settled in," he said. "We're in the Coquet Room at the front here. See you shortly."

Cameron climbed the shallow, carpeted stairs, turned along a short corridor, and unlocked the door of room 8 with a wave of her hand. It was plush and beautifully furnished with a glorious view out across the parkland towards the sea. She was deeply impressed by the whole place. Having processed the expense claims through the company accounts over the past few weeks, she had been expecting something quite modest. By contrast, the glowing descriptions she'd heard from the team were entirely justified.

She stowed her bag, dug out her smartscreen, and went straight back downstairs to the Coquet Room, Argentum's temporary northern headquarters. As soon as she walked in the room she felt at home. Joel, Sandeep and Susie were chatting and laughing, surrounded by state-of-the-art equipment. The scent of fresh coffee was strong.

"This is great," she said, taking a seat at the empty desk.

"I think we should move up here permanently," said Joel. "It's got everything we need. I'm going to miss this place when we pack up."

"What about Martha and Chad?" asked Cameron.

Joel laughed. "They love it too," he said. "In fact, they were here this weekend just for one last visit. I caught Martha looking at job ads and Chad has been wearing himself out on the beach every day."

All of them looked happy and Cameron felt a pang of regret that she hadn't stayed up here to see the investigation through. Of course, she'd had no other choice at the time. Not only did she have a business to run and other clients to manage, but Jack Sladen had made it very clear that he wanted nothing to do with her, and the conflict between the two of them, despite their long history, had threatened to disrupt the investigation.

With Joel, Sandeep and Susie working closely together on this job, Pete and Noor double-teaming the client work in London, Ross and Michelle on their way to Iceland, and her old boyfriend Ben something of an unknown quantity, Cameron had never felt so isolated. This must be what they call the loneliness of command, she reasoned. It would pass when they all came back together. She shook herself out of the black mood. She had work to do.

"Can I hook onto the network?" she asked.

"Sure," said Sandeep. "The ID is Whinstone and here's the passcode." He handed her a card. "Your chip'll do the second layer authentication automatically as you're checked through security."

It took only a moment to connect, and notifications began to scroll rapidly up her screen. "That's fast," she said. "Is it MetaBand?"

"No chance," said Joel. "They won't let the installers anywhere near here. This whole site is linked to dedicated high-altitude networks that are reserved for Army, Navy, Airforce, Space Corp, Police, and National Cyber Security Centre operations. And us."

"Excellent," said Cameron. "I wonder if we can wangle a connection in the office in London. The landlords are planning to move all the tenants to MetaBand soon and I'd like an alternative."

"That's an even better reason to stay here," joked Joel.

Cameron grinned at him. "If we ever need a permanent base up north, you're first on my list to run it," she said. "But don't hold your breath." She accepted a cup of coffee from Sandeep. "So, what's the programme for the next couple of days?"

"The final report's embargoed until 10am Wednesday,"

said Susie. "It goes out tomorrow evening once the lawyers have done their final checks. There's the big press conference in Newcastle, and then we're done."

"It sounds like you're all finished," said Cameron, confused. "Why do you need me?"

There was a knock at the door.

"Come on in," said Sandeep.

To Cameron's astonishment, DI Sara Mercer walked in.

"Hello, Cameron," said Mercer. "You're looking much better. I wasn't sure when we spoke on Friday whether either of us would make it up here. I'm glad to see you, although the circumstances could be better."

Cameron looked from Mercer to her team and back. "Can someone tell me what's going on," she said. "I understand this is a secure operation, but I've been part of it since the start. Why the whole secret squirrel stuff? What have you found that's so confidential you haven't even told me..." A terrible thought struck her, and she tailed off, hoping against hope that she was wrong.

Mercer caught Joel's eye. "I think it might be better coming from you," she said.

Joel took a deep breath. "I'm sorry, Cameron," he said. "I think you've guessed."

"She's still alive." It was a statement, not a question.

Joel nodded. "We think so," he said.

The room was so quiet that Cameron could hear the old clock on the wall ticking, and the cry of a seagull outside.

"Who knows?" she asked.

"The five of us in this room," said Susie, "and the NCSC and police teams across the hall. Not staff, not family, and no one outside this location."

Cameron stood up and walked to the window, gazing out towards the dunes in the distance and the sea beyond. "Are you sure?" she asked.

"No," said Joel, "but we've been processing a lot of data covering all the network activity before, during and after the operation to take out the data centre. Some anomalies started showing up in the middle of last week. Up until then I would have sworn that she died when the servers went off. Now I'm not so sure and the evidence is mounting up."

"I'd better have a look at what you've found," said Cameron. "I still wish you'd given me a hint. I mean, there are ways to get hold of me that are super secure." She suddenly remembered the notification from the encrypted message service.

"Let me check something," she said, walking quickly back to the desk where she had left her smartscreen. It took only a moment to verify her identity on the rapid connection. It was time to find out who was trying to reach her.

The ID was unknown, the profile picture blank. The message made Cameron's blood run cold. 'Wherever you run, SimCavalier, she will find you. In every reality, she is waiting for you.'

Cameron held up the smartscreen for everyone to see. "It looks like someone else knows," she said. "Your secret's out."

•

In the half-dawn of an Alaskan morning, Aron stirred in his bed. He battled the nightmarish falling sensation with all his might, trapped between sleeping and waking. In the dream, he braced himself for an impact with solid ground but found himself instead enveloped, sinking, smothered by quicksand, falling deeper into the abyss. In desperation he broke the paralysis that engulfed him and flung out his hand, reaching towards the light, grasping for purchase.

His brain responded. Aron's eyes snapped open, and he draw a long, shuddering breath of sweet, recycled air. The impression of quicksand receded, floating away from his waking consciousness. He tore off his headband and stared into the half-darkness of the bunk room. The Sanctuary to which he retreated every sleep cycle was supposed to aid his rest, a high-tech solution to insomnia and fatigue. Nightmares were not part of the package.

"Time check," he said quietly, careful not to disturb the other data centre shift workers who shared the sleeping quarters. In response, numbers glowed briefly on the ceiling above his head. Four in the morning. There was no way Aron was getting back to sleep now. He wasn't going to return to the Sanctuary, that was for sure. He wondered what had gone wrong with its programming. A full restart might fix the problem, but he didn't want to risk another nightmare.

He was wide awake now. This soon after midsummer

just below the Arctic Circle there was barely any darkness to speak of, and daylight was seeping around the edges of the blind that shaded the light well from the surface. Aron slid carefully out from under the covers and picked up his overalls from the back of the chair where he had flung them the previous night. He tiptoed out of the bunk room and closed the door softly behind him.

The residential team's living room was just down the corridor. Shifts were not due to change for another few hours, but a buffet had already been laid out, breakfast for the teams who would be waking soon. Aron nodded at the friendly little servobot behind the counter. It burbled in recognition and scooted along to the coffee machine. Aron piled a small plate high with bread, cheese and fish and collected his perfectly brewed coffee.

"You're up early," said a voice.

Aron jumped. He turned to see one of the shift leaders, Johanna, peering around the edge of a high-backed armchair in the corner of the room.

"I couldn't sleep," said Johanna. "Bad dreams."

"Same," said Aron, yawning. "I think there's a bug in the Sanctuary."

Johanna looked at him curiously. "You use that as well?" she said. "If it's not too personal to ask, what was the problem?"

"A falling dream," said Aron. The dream experiences were usually tailored to the individual, but this had been quite generic. Apart from... Aron reached back into his consciousness, trying to grasp any vestiges that remained.

There had been something familiar that triggered the fall, but he could no longer recall what it was.

"Aron?" Johanna said, breaking the spell. "Are you okay?"

"Yes," he said. "I'm sorry, I was just thinking. What kept you awake?"

"Nothing so sinister," said Johanna. "I just have this constant feeling I'm being watched while I sleep. Wherever I am in the Sanctuary, there's someone watching." She rubbed her eyes. "It's been going on for a few days now. I need to find a new way to sleep, but it's hard at midsummer, even down here, isn't it?"

Aron nodded. "In the summer we want the dark to sleep, and in the winter, we want the light to live," he said. "We should be glad of the technology that our grandparents never had."

"I guess you're right," said Johanna. She pulled a smartscreen from the pocket of her overalls and checked the time. "I'm going to try and get another hour or so in bed before our shift starts," she said. "See you later."

Aron finished his breakfast alone. He was in no hurry to go back to sleep. Instead, he handed his empty plate and cup back to the smiling servobot and made his way up the long narrow stairs to his favourite surface viewpoint, the cupola above the underground installation.

The view took his breath away every time. The morning sun was shining in a cloudless blue sky and the remaining vestiges of the ancient glacier sparkled. At its receding edges, the light cast shadows, betraying the rocks that had been revealed by the warming climate. As Aron watched, an erratic boulder teetering on the edge of the glacier rolled gently off, pushed by the wind that whipped across the ice. It left the hint of a pink imprint to mark where it had ended its long journey on the ice and bounced off down the mountain and over the sheer cliff edge into oblivion.

Aron dropped into a comfortable beanbag and turned his attention to the mountain that rose up behind the cupola. The glacier and the tundra cooled the data centre, but deep below them a magma pool provided the geothermal energy they needed to run it. The peak and caldera of the volcano, dormant for the best part of a millennium, was the only outward sign of the power that lay beneath the surface.

He snuggled into the beanbag, suddenly tired. He felt his eyes closing despite the daylight and drifted naturally away into a blessedly dreamless sleep for the first time in weeks.

The sound of an insistent alarm startled him awake. Momentarily disoriented, Aron blinked in the bright light. The sun was higher in the sky and his smartscreen was vibrating angrily. From the stairwell came the clattering of urgent footsteps.

"Aron!" came a shout. Daniel, the Wrangell site security manager, clambered up the final steps into the cupola. "I thought you'd be hiding up here. I need you down in the data centre on the double. Do you know what time it is?"

"I fell asleep," said Aron, still groggy. "I've missed the start of the shift, haven't I?"

"Yes," said Daniel. "And we have a situation."

"Sorry," said Aron, not yet thinking straight. He dragged himself out of the beanbag. What had woken him? An alarm.

He pulled out his smartscreen and tapped on the notification. His eyes widened as he read the details. "DDOS attack?" he said. "Which servers? When did this start?"

Daniel started to speak, and Aron cut him off. "Tell me on the way," he said, starting down the stairs. He was fully awake now. This needed all of his attention.

"It's the Olympic metaverse stacks," said Daniel as they clattered down the stairs at a steady rhythm.

"Okay," said Aron, "how much traffic has gotten past the web application firewall?" They dropped into the corridor and started running.

"I'll let Johanna answer that one," said Daniel, spying the shift leader approaching at speed from the opposite direction. "I'm just the messenger."

"The allowlist on the WAF cut out some of the traffic," said Johanna, slowing to meet them and then turning to run alongside Aron. "Less than I'd have expected, though. We're capturing as much data as possible about the attack sources and we've broken the connection to the web, so the systems are running normally but in isolation."

At a junction, Daniel took his leave. "We've secured the whole site as a precaution," he said. "No one's coming in or out for now. I'm going to check the deep freeze. I don't want anything compromising the quantum processor environment." He disappeared down a separate corridor towards the other half of the sprawling underground complex where the huge quantum computers sat at zero degrees Kelvin, allowing their qubits to process without any disturbances at an atomic level.

Aron and Johanna carried on towards the heart of the regular data centre, where great rooms full of server stacks stored zettabytes of data for Wrangell's clients. As they reached the door of the data security room, Johanna took a deep breath.

"Right," she said. "Let's see how fast we can fix this. The Olympic metaverse needs us online."

They each scanned the access pad and walked into the room, the heavy door swinging shut behind them.

10: CHANGE OF PLAN

Cameron was frankly astonished that she had slept at all, let alone so well. Despite staying up past midnight to plough through all the evidence that the team had gathered on Yasmin, she felt well rested, and her arm was feeling much better. She took a long and welcome shower before making her way downstairs. The breakfast room was empty apart from a young woman who was clearing the tables. She greeted Cameron with a smile and disappeared into the kitchen, re-emerging with a pot of hot coffee and some fresh toast. "There's fruit and pastries on the buffet," she said, "or I can get you something hot. The porridge is good, and the kippers are local."

"Thanks," said Cameron. "Some porridge would be great." She didn't quite have the energy to brave kippers for breakfast. Not today, anyway.

Cameron laid her smartscreen on the table and opened the anonymous encrypted message again.

The door opened and Susie walked in. "Morning, Cameron," she said. "We're out of coffee already. I'm here for refills." She set three mugs down on the counter. "Want one?" she asked.

"No thanks," said Cameron. "I've only just started this one."

Susie came over and sat down on the other side of the

table. "Still puzzling over that, are you?" she said. "Any more ideas?"

Cameron shook her head. "I have no clue who it's from," she said. "It could well be from Yasmin herself. In fact, that's the best-case scenario, I guess, if we're trying to keep this quiet."

"It's not the best case, though, is it?" said Susie. "If it's from Yasmin, then she's definitely alive, and she knows how to find you."

"She knows everything about me already," said Cameron. "If she really did survive, I'm no worse off. Anyway, I'm not going to give whoever it is the satisfaction of replying, so they can't be certain they've reached me."

"Surely when you opened the message it will have sent a receipt to the sender," said Susie.

"No," said Cameron with absolute certainty. "If I set up an account anywhere, all the settings are locked right down. I haven't used this message service for a long time, for years, but I know that it won't be sending receipts. Even if it was a message from Yasmin, she won't know I've read it."

"What are you going to do?" asked Susie.

Cameron gave her an enigmatic smile. "There's only one thing I can do," she said. "I have to find her first."

She glanced up as the kitchen door opened. The waitress set a hot bowl of porridge in front of Cameron then smiled at Susie. "More coffee?" she said.

"Yes please, Florence," said Susie. "The usual."

"You've all made yourselves at home here," said

Cameron. She sniffed appreciatively at the porridge. "I'm quite jealous."

"It's lovely," said Susie. "I'll miss it when the conference circuit starts again. Especially the service," she continued with a smile as the waitress placed a fresh mug of coffee on the table, and two more ready for Pete and Sandeep on the counter. "Thanks, Florence."

Cameron blew carefully on a spoonful of porridge, tasted it, and set down her spoon. "It's delicious," she said, "but it's really hot." She looked at Susie. There was a question that needed to be asked that hung in the air between them.

"Have you seen Ella?" said Cameron at last.

"Yes," said Susie quietly. "She was very lucky to survive when the data centre went up. Joel saved her life." Her voice shook slightly.

Cameron reached across the table and took her hand. "And she made a huge effort to stop Yasmin from getting away," she said, "even if we now suspect it didn't work."

Susie squeezed Cameron's hand gratefully. "I still love her," she said. "I can't help it." She took a sip of her coffee, hand shaking slightly. "It's been good to be up here with Joel and Sandeep and keeping myself busy with the investigation. I feel as if I'm helping to do the best I can for her."

"How was she when you saw her?" asked Cameron.

"She was still in hospital and under arrest," said Susie. "She's down in London on bail now. What I don't understand, though, is that awful man Angus is still up here and working at Dunswyke as if nothing has happened. He gives me the creeps."

"I read about that when I went over the draft report yesterday," said Cameron. She withdrew her hand and picked up her spoon. The porridge had cooled to an acceptable temperature, and she was hungry. "Ella's taken the rap for helping to spring Yasmin from jail and destroying the servers, and he's in the clear."

"I don't know how he does it," said Susie. "We all know he's mixed up in some really dodgy stuff, but there's no evidence, so there have been no charges."

"Jack's an idiot if he's protecting that man," said Cameron through a mouthful of porridge. "One day he'll realise. Hopefully it won't be too late when he does."

The door opened again, and Joel and Sandeep appeared. "Susie?" said Sandeep. "Where's that coffee? Oh, morning, Cameron. Did you get any further with that message and the data analytics results?"

"I've made some progress," said Cameron. "Tell you what, let me finish my breakfast and then we can catch up."

"Good plan," said Susie. She stood and gave Cameron a grateful smile. "Enjoy the rest of your porridge. See you shortly."

The three of them trooped out and the door closed behind them.

Cameron took one more look at the message and then closed the app with a sigh. It was no use dwelling on it. Someone somewhere wished her ill, and there was nothing new about that. She finished the bowl of porridge and sipped at her coffee while she checked her inbox, working out what else needed to be done today.

Michelle's completed smart contract audit had come in overnight along with some juicy new details about Arthur Paxton. She was first on the list to call. There was still nothing from Ben, and Cameron was beginning to get annoyed with him. Surely he could send her an innocent acknowledgement without compromising this mystery mission from Chloe.

Barker and a couple of others from MIST had sent her direct messages, and Cameron realised that she hadn't yet followed up on the tipoff from Andy's mysterious source. Another job to add to the list. She was going to be busy, and it felt good.

She called out a thank you to Florence, grabbed a small pastry to go with the last of her coffee, and made her way to the Coquet Room. Susie, Joel and Sandeep were hard at work, chatting quietly between themselves as they followed the trails revealed by their data analysis. Cameron took her place at the empty desk, fired up the computer, and put on a set of headphones. First stop, Michelle.

"Hi, Cameron," she said as soon as the call connected. "Hold on a second." In the background, Cameron heard Ross swearing loudly. For a moment she was worried, then she heard Michelle laughing. "Get them to drone you a new one over," she was saying. "It won't take long."

"What's up?" asked Cameron.

"The bloody zip's bust on the team holdall," said Ross,

coming close to the microphone. "Honestly, I don't know who they've designed these for, but I can't fit all my kit in there. I'll give them a call. Catch you later, Cameron."

She heard his footsteps receding and a door closing. "Are you all packed, Shell?" she asked.

"Just about," said Michelle. "I'm really looking forward to it. But how are you? You got my message?"

"Yes," said Cameron, "and I'm fine. I've had a look at the audit report and signed it off. The vulnerability you picked up will have more than justified the work. The client'll be happy."

"I hope so," said Michelle. "I was really impressed by the build quality of that smart contract, though, despite the error. I looked up the company that wrote the code, just in case we need them one day. They're a good little outfit. I'll send you the details."

"Excellent," said Cameron. An automated notification from the accounts system appeared on her smartscreen. "Oh good," she said. "They've accepted the audit report and payment's coming through now. Nice work."

That was one thing off her list, thought Cameron. Now to tackle a far less pleasant subject.

Michelle pre-empted her question. "I guess you want to know what I have on Paxton," she said. "First of all, your apartment complex's CCTV was compromised, but I guess you already knew that."

"Yeah. I wasn't amused," said Cameron. "That's why I have my own eyes everywhere that I can."

"Your security is spot on," said Michelle. "The

management company needs to get us in to revamp the systems in every other corner of the building, though."

"I've put a hefty quote in to get them up to scratch," said Cameron. "They make a lot of noise about their security standards and they're very embarrassed to have been breached."

"They should be," said Michelle. "The only useful footage came from doorcams as you both ran up the stairs. There's no recording of the attack in the stairwell."

"That's a shame," said Cameron. "The police have enough to go on, though. They've charged Paxton with assault, and they've kept him in custody as they have a few other cases that look like his handiwork."

"I know," said Michelle smugly.

"What I'm more interested in is who he works for," said Cameron. "Where have you got to on that?"

"It's quite a story," said Michelle. "We know that he's a thug for hire, and that he's been working with casinos in real life and online. There's a common thread with all of them. If you follow the trail, and it's not easy, they all have a link with Sapphire Straits."

Cameron did a rapid search. "That's a global gambling empire," she said. "It's probably harder to find any casinos that don't have a link to them."

"I know what you're thinking," said Michelle, "but this isn't just a tenuous connection. My image analyser searched all available screenshots and shares from Casinoland to get a feel for Paxton's movements. In some of the later shots, it picked up on a souvenir bracelet from a concert that his avatar was wearing. There were only five thousand issued. I fed the transactions from all the wallets that have ever held one of these into a model that Ross and I built a while ago. We found a couple of dozen likely candidates who also had payments coming in from the casinos where we know he worked. Once we matched what we know of Paxton's movements to the payments he received, we narrowed it down to one."

"Oh, Shell," said Cameron, impressed. "You've really outdone yourself this time. That's brilliant detective work."

"There's still a lot of work to do," said Michelle. "I started tracing back out from that wallet, because of course it's just a snapshot of one part of his life. That's when I found a direct payment from Sapphire Straits going into another wallet linked to him on an obscure chain. It was made last week, Cameron. I hate to think what it was for."

"I can guess," said Cameron. "Shell, that's incredible work."

"I wish I could keep going," said Michelle, "but I won't have the time or the equipment when we're in Iceland. I can send you everything I have now…"

"No!" said Cameron. "Don't send it to me. It's safer not to." She thought quickly. "Can you or Ross get into the office and leave everything on a disk in the vault?"

"Okay," said Michelle, sounding confused. "I'm sure you have your reasons."

"I do," said Cameron, "and I'll explain when I see you again. You are a complete genius, Shell. Thank you."

"Any time, Cameron," said Michelle. "Oh, one more thing," she continued. "Remember my cousin Daniel? He got a great new job in Alaska as head of security for the big data centre under Mount Wrangell. He messaged me this morning to say there'd been a DDOS attack on the site. I thought you'd like to know."

"Send him my congratulations on the job when you talk to him," said Cameron. "DDOS attacks are happening all the time, though. Why is this one special?"

"You're working on the Olympic metaverse defence, aren't you?" said Michelle. "Wrangell is one of the principal data centres hosting the fabric."

"I see your point," said Cameron. "I'll look into it. You'd better go and get packing. Have a safe trip tomorrow, both of you. And thanks again."

Cameron took off the headphones and stared into space. Michelle had uncovered so much information that her head was reeling. She remembered that she had promised to keep Mercer updated if her team had new information, and this was dynamite. Her coffee cup was empty. Time for a refill, and to pay a visit to the police across the hall.

Coffee replenished, Cameron knocked on the door marked 'Rede' – another river, she presumed – and peered into the room. It was a mirror image of the Argentum base in the Coquet Room, with the addition of a plush sofa in the bay window. Mercer smiled in welcome and invited her to sit.

"I have news," said Cameron, settling into the sofa.

Mercer was all ears. "Your clever team have come up with something, haven't they?" she said.

Cameron nodded. "Yes," she said. "I think we know who paid Paxton to attack me."

"Wow!" said Mercer. "That's incredibly fast work. Have you got the details?"

Cameron hesitated. "I can tell you what I know," she said, "but I've asked Shell not to send me anything through the networks."

"Probably wise," said Mercer. "We don't know who's watching. Well, let's have it. Where does the trail lead?"

Cameron told her everything.

•

Tenuk settled at Jack's desk with his coffee and put on a reality mask. This was a simple model designed for meetings, only able to manage augmented reality and light enough to wear for hours. He fiddled with the headband to make sure the clear visor was properly positioned over his eyes. He was early. Hold music was playing and a message on the screen told him to wait until the host launched the meeting.

He looked out over the main office floor. This morning it was busy. Many of the staff members chose to work on site on a Monday so that they could do their weekly stand-ups in person with their teams. He saw Chloe talking to Connie and Isaac and frowned. He didn't trust her, and he had his suspicions about her past, but he had spent six months trying to trace her activity back to the shady world of cybercrime and had met brick walls at every turn. Wherever she had come from, even he could not find the trail.

The hold music faded, and Tenuk set the office walls to full opacity ready for his meeting. His view of the Statesman Tech office was replaced by the stone walls of the Sladen Foundation headquarters. Jack was sitting at his desk, chatting to a woman that Tenuk recognised as the head of the local legal team and a burly man with a bushy ginger beard and a sour expression on his face. All three of them wore the same reality masks as Tenuk. As he watched, another link opened up to reveal the Sladen Group's chief legal officer and the head of PR, both sitting in front of Sladen-branded wallpapers.

"Everyone here?" said Jack. "Excellent. I'm not sure if you've all met in person before. Over in Austin, we have Tenuk, Chief Technology Officer at Statesman Tech and responsible for SMIN, the System Management and Information Network, and the upgrades to MetaBand. Julie here has been representing the Sladen Foundation in the local investigation. Coming in from New York are Damien, who heads up my global legal team, and Pamela, PR. Zara is also here and will be taking minutes."

"Good morning," said a crisp, efficient voice. Not for the first time, Tenuk noticed how similar Jack's virtual assistant Zara sounded to Yasmin. It was a standard AI voice package, of course, but it made him uneasy.

The burly man on Jack's left glowered.

"Oh, yes, and Angus," said Jack. "Networks and security specialist." Jack flashed his best smile at the camera and consulted the agenda on his tablet. "As you all know, the investigation into the attack on our data centre is due to conclude this week. We've complained in the strongest possible terms about the unwarranted police action and we're ready for their final report."

Tenuk was glad to see Jack in a buoyant mood. He was less happy to see Angus. The man had been there when Yasmin made her escape. He knew many of Tenuk's secrets, and he was dangerous. Tenuk watched the man's body language intently while he gave a cursory report on the state of the re-commissioned data centre. He was truculent and abrupt, displaying a strange combination of untouchable arrogance and pent-up fury at whatever terrible hand the world had dealt him this time.

Next it was the turn of the lawyers to outline the various implications of each possible slant of the anticipated report. Tenuk let the legal chatter wash over him as he mulled over the problems that Angus might cause, and how to deal with him. His attention snapped back to the meeting when he heard his name.

"So, we're all clear on the probable outcome of the investigation and the actions to take," said Jack. "Now, Tenuk, can you update us on the Foundation DAO? There are some great things happening."

Tenuk picked up his cue smoothly. "Whatever the conclusions of the report," he said, "we can focus all our PR efforts on highlighting the absolute unqualified success of the Sladen Foundation. In the space of just a few weeks, we have collected investments totalling almost a hundred million dollars into the DAO." He paused, startled by Angus's reaction. The man looked furious, and Tenuk didn't know why.

"Uh, yes, and through community voting and selection processes," he continued, "we have issued parcels of grant funding to almost three thousand individual athletes who would otherwise have been unable to attend in person, or at all. We have also made a sizable donation to the Reykjavik organising committee to provide additional accommodation for new attendees, and funded the rapid modular construction of a virtual arena in Chile to replace the original building that was destroyed in the recent earthquake."

Jack beamed his trademark smile around the room, and the lawyers actually looked impressed. "Thank you, Tenuk," he said. "Great summary. Pamela, how are we handling the PR on this?"

"We are all set," said Pamela. "This will put a huge positive spin on the Sladen Foundation. I really don't think we have anything to worry about, whatever the investigation concludes. I have global press ready to go and we've recorded interviews with grateful athletes on every continent. Congratulations, Jack. And Tenuk, of course. Can we count on you for an interview?"

Tenuk was caught by surprise and couldn't react fast enough when Jack said yes, of course, Tenuk would be happy to oblige.

"Great," said Pamela. "I'll put my team in touch with you momentarily."

Tenuk plastered a smile on his face. He had to find a way of getting out of this. He did not want his face on the news channels of the world. He had too much to lose.

No sooner had the meeting ended than another call came in. Tenuk hadn't even removed his mask when his screen flashed up. For a second, he wondered how Pamela had mobilised her PR team so quickly, then recognised the caller's ID as someone quite different.

"Good morning, father," he said. "What can I do for you? I'm quite busy right now."

The old man was at his desk, but his AR wasn't running. He couldn't see Tenuk, but Tenuk could see him. He studied his father's lined face properly for the first time. He had aged noticeably since the last time they saw each other, just after the funeral of Tenuk's mother. That was the moment that Tenuk had decided to walk away from the security of a job with the family firm and his father's absolute control and make his own way. He wanted to live life to the full while he could. The sense of his own mortality that came with the loss of a parent had hit hard even though he had only been in his early twenties at the time. Tenuk had to admit, however, that the last decade hadn't quite gone to plan.

"Tenuk," said Chaoxiang. "How are you, my boy?"

"I'm well," said Tenuk.

"Have you considered my offer?" said Chaoxiang. "I

would like you to come back. The skills you've learned since we parted ways will be put to good use."

"How?" asked Tenuk, intrigued. He thought about the sighting in the Eden marketplace. What was his father planning? The family firm regularly skated the edges of legality in a dozen jurisdictions, and Tenuk knew that some commissions his networks had carried out had come from them, directly or indirectly, most recently the contract to disrupt sensor data in the Olympic arenas. However, as far as Tenuk knew, the organisation had never deployed personnel into the dark underworld of cybercrime.

"The business has to move with the times," said his father. "Your mother's brother, your uncle Li Jie, is retiring. He is old now, and not in good health. I need a new Chief Technology Officer who knows how to manage the metaverse and the opportunities it offers to us."

Tenuk rocked backwards in his chair. This was not what he had expected. He had never known his father to be so straight with him. An idea was forming in his mind. He needed to avoid the attentions of Pamela's PR team, and perhaps he had found the perfect excuse.

"Will you meet with me?" asked Chaoxiang.

"Yes," said Tenuk slowly. "I will."

"Your ticket is on the way," said Chaoxiang.

There was a soft ping from Tenuk's smartscreen. Damn the man, he thought. He planned this all along. He knew I'd say yes.

"I look forward to seeing you," said Tenuk. He nodded formally and ended the call.

Sure enough, the tickets were there. The family firm certainly wasn't in any trouble. Tenuk would not be needing either the perpetual upgrades that he'd bought in Eden nor the carbon credits he had appropriated a couple of years before from the Singapore MerLions eSports team. He was travelling first class all the way to Singapore, leaving early the next morning. The carbon credits were all accounted for, and Tenuk nodded with approval when he saw the scheme that his father had chosen to offset the guilt of an intercontinental flight. A sizeable donation would be going to remote villages in the rainforest in exchange for their care of the environment around them and the keystone species they might otherwise have poached for gain. It was a noble cause and Tenuk felt a stirring of empathy with his father.

He messaged Jack and Pamela. He'd had some bad news, he said. He sent a silent apology to the ancestors as he asked for urgent leave of absence to visit his gravely ill mother. The responses came back immediately. They were both devastated to hear his news. The PR interview would be postponed, of course. Now that the investigation was coming to an end Jack would be located back in the Statesman Tech office and would take the reins. Tenuk was not to worry, and he must keep them informed.

Tenuk reset the office walls to full transparency, took a deep breath, and went out to the breakout room for another coffee. He was reeling from the abrupt change of plans and his father's offer, and therefore had no difficulty looking shellshocked and upset for the team. Even Chloe seemed to be sympathetic. Tenuk felt like a fraud and wished that in the heat of the moment he had not sullied his mother's memory by using her as an excuse, but it was done now. He would visit her resting place and make his peace when he had finished with his father.

There was very little to wrap up in this office. That was something of a reality check for Tenuk on his usefulness to Jack. Now that the Sladen Foundation was flying and the new MetaBand had been rolled out, he was sitting in a holding pattern and simply managing their smooth running. When he got back, Tenuk needed to make himself indispensable once more. Jack's connections and the covert control of the DAO were too valuable to his future plans. Unless, of course, his future lay elsewhere.

There was no point staying in the office. There was nothing there that could incriminate him. His apartment was another matter. Although he expected to be away for only a short time, his best laid plans might change. The apartment was secure enough, but if he didn't come back, then eventually someone would get in. He had some tidying to do.

As Tenuk walked through downtown and across Statesman Bridge, he fixed the sights and sounds of Austin in his mind. On the southern shore of Lady Bird Lake, he picked up an autocar back to his apartment block. The Steamyard sign over the main gateway was fading. Tenuk tapped the access pad and ran up the stairs to the top floor.

His first job was to make some minor changes to the flight documents his father had sent. Tenuk Chen couldn't risk crossing the border into Singapore in case the authorities were still looking out for him, but Tenuk Teo, his assumed identity in America, would have no trouble. Tenuk revised the ticketing details and linked them to his local digital identity. With luck, he had acted fast enough to avoid attention.

The next step was to check in with the Steamyard. Their Beta test of disrupting a hybrid event had been signed off by the client, much to Tenuk's surprise and relief. They were expected to have the working package deployed before the first Olympic events took place, fully tested and audited.

He put a call out to the Steamyard members and waited in the boardroom. One by one they jumped into position.

"Is the testing nearing completion?" he asked.

"Yes, Pangolin," said the grey kitten, in a good mood for once. "We'll be ready to deploy on time."

"Excellent," said Tenuk. "The client is content with our work. Send me confirmation when the code has been deployed." He disconnected.

It was safe enough to leave that job in their hands. Tenuk knew that even if problems recurred in the full release, Yasmin was alive. If he called on her for help, he was certain that she would ensure that things went smoothly on the day.

His final task was to deal with the contents of the apartment. It took a few hours, but by late afternoon the place looked more like a home again than a workplace. Most of the computer equipment was dismantled and carefully stored in a cupboard marked 'Spares and Repairs' with a pile of cables and components disguising the intact items beneath. Everything he needed to keep from the hard disks was consolidated on a single disk that would be travelling with him, and the rest he had cleaned thoroughly.

The dining table was back in its place, no longer needed as an extra desk, and Tenuk even plumped up the cushions on the sofa, an automatic habit his mother had ingrained in him as a child. Anyone walking in would have the occupant down as a nerd living a quiet life on their own, not the head of a cybercrime syndicate responsible for some of the most notorious ransomware and malware attacks of the past five years. The extra security on the apartment would be easily explained as a tenant keeping his collection of computer equipment safe.

Tenuk packed his bags for the long journey ahead of him and made one last check that his credentials for the journey were all in order. Satisfied, he went out for one last meal at his local barbecue place. As he sipped a Paloma, the local grapefruit margarita, and watched the world go by, he felt a pang of regret. This had almost become home, and he hoped that he'd be back, but tomorrow he'd be on his way to the home he missed most of all, a place he had thought he would never see again. Singapore.

11: SAFE TRAVELS

Wednesday morning dawned with bright sunshine and a stiff breeze. Cameron pulled her jacket tight around her and followed Joel, Susie and Sandeep to one of the waiting autocars. The little convoy of vehicles whirred off down the Northumbrian lanes towards Newcastle, forty miles away, where the press conference would take place in a neutral venue that was handy for the press. Cameron would continue her journey south from there, going back to London to pick up on Michelle's forensic investigations and the Olympic metaverse security work.

They arrived early, well before Jack and his entourage. The courtyard of the big Quayside hotel thronged with journalists, and the autocars ducked into an underground car park to avoid awkward questions. Cameron grabbed her bag from the boot, ready to make her escape to the train station at the end of proceedings, and the four of them followed the police and NCSC teams up the stairs to the suite where the press conference would take place.

Their legal and PR people were already there, ready to micro-manage the whole event. A tall dark-haired woman shook Cameron's hand. "Sabrina Dissanayake," she said. "We haven't met before."

"Cameron Silvera," said Cameron. "You're the barrister, aren't you?"

Sabrina nodded. "That's me," she said. "The plan is for me to be with you when you meet Jack Sladen. We don't know how he's going to react when he sees you here and we want to avoid any confrontation that may attract press attention."

"What about Angus?" asked Susie. "Angus White. I think you should be watching him very closely too."

Sabrina raised a perfectly shaped eyebrow. "Interesting," she said. "Noted. Thank you."

Satisfied, Susie turned away and found her seat with Joel and Sandeep and the other investigators who would not be facing the press. Their tables were behind a partition at the side of the hall, allowing them to watch the speakers but unseen by anyone sitting in the main body of the audience.

"They're on their way," came a shout.

Cameron braced herself, eyes fixed on the doorway. She didn't recognise the people who walked in first, but one woman gave Sabrina a friendly wave. Lawyers, then. Angus was the next person she saw. He shambled in, peered around the room with a scowl on his face, spotted Cameron, and locked eyes with her. Cameron stared back coldly. She wasn't going to give an inch to that bully. Next to her, she sensed Sabrina's surprise, well disguised. Angus turned his penetrating gaze on Joel, Sandeep and then Susie, before eventually following the lawyers to their seats.

"He doesn't like you at all, does he?" whispered Sabrina. "Or any of the Argentum people. There's something odd there." She looked across the room to where the police team was gathered. "They're watching too," she said. Mercer and her colleagues were taking a keen interest in the brief, silent exchange.

A flurry of activity at the door announced the arrival of Jack Sladen. He strode in confidently, flashing the trademark Sladen smile around the half empty room. His eyes fell on Cameron and the smile wobbled slightly before he recovered his composure. She returned the smile with one of her own. Warm, friendly, open. Probably not what he was expecting.

Jack seemed sufficiently thrown by Cameron's presence that instead of following his team to the main table he came over to where she stood.

"Hello, Jack," she said, continuing the warm and friendly approach. "It's good to see you again." She wasn't lying. She realised that she missed the friendship they had rekindled after many years apart. "Aunt Vicky sends her best."

"How is she?" asked Jack, relieved to have another subject to latch onto.

Cameron knew she'd given him an avenue for small talk rather than forcing a confrontation. She wished they could talk frankly and clear the air, but Sabrina preferred a calm meeting with the press watching and she had inadvertently obliged. Cameron hoped they would have another chance. "She's well, thanks Jack," she said. "Maybe when this is all over you could go and visit. I'm sure she'd be delighted to see you."

"I'd like that," said Jack, "but I'm flying straight back to Austin tomorrow. My CTO has a family emergency to deal with. I've been away for too long already."

Jack's CTO was a whole other discussion, thought Cameron. "That's a shame," she said. "Does he have to travel far?"

"He's from LA," said Jack, "and I assume that's where his parents are. Why?"

"Oh, nothing," said Cameron lightly. She assumed differently. The Tenuk she remembered had been from Singapore, and she was quite certain that Jack's CTO and the former MerLions tour manager she had once met were one and the same person. She made a mental note to do some digging.

A microphone burst into life on the main table. "If you could all take your places, we're bringing the press corps in now," said a voice.

"I'd better go," said Jack. "Talk to you afterwards."

Sabrina watched him shaking hands with the panel, smiling and making small talk and bringing his powerful personality into the room. "That went better than expected," she said.

"I know," said Cameron. "He's calmed down a lot. I did the right thing going back to London. I bet he's learned a thing or two during the investigation that vindicated what I told him." She looked up sharply as movement at the doorway caught her eye. "I'd better get out of the way," she said.

"Afterwards, I want you to tell me why you asked about his CTO," said Sabrina.

"Okay," said Cameron as she dashed for shelter behind the partition.

Joel, Susie and Sandeep were waiting expectantly for news. "How was Jack?" asked Susie.

"Remarkably balanced," said Cameron. "Shh. They're ready to start."

The statements were brief and to the point. The report found that there had been sufficient evidence to mount a police raid on the Sladen Foundation's data centre under suspicion of harbouring an escaped prisoner. The sheer volume of military-grade defences at the site had been a factor in the conduct of the raid.

The investigation concluded that the artificial intelligence known as Yasmin had indeed been resident in the data centre and that she had been destroyed along with the servers that held her consciousness. Jack Sladen was cleared of any and all involvement.

"That's fair," whispered Cameron. "I don't think he had a clue what was going on."

One of the directors of the company engaged to build the data centre and manage its security, Ella Stanford, had been arrested and charged with sheltering an escaped prisoner and with assisting in Yasmin's escape from custody.

"That's so wrong," hissed Susie. "She'll go to prison for this, and it should be him." She glared at Angus through a gap in the partition. "We need to take him down."

Cameron laid a hand on Susie's arm. The girl was shaking with anger. "We will, don't worry," said Cameron quietly.

The short statement concluded, and the questions began. How did Jack feel about the report? Shocked, he said, but delighted that the Sladen Foundation could put the unpleasant hijacking of their dedicated data centre behind them. The work the foundation was doing was changing lives. He smoothly recounted the facts and figures of the support they had already given to athletes and organisers for the upcoming Olympics.

"Why do you think your data centre was chosen?" asked another journalist. The voice was familiar. Cameron peeked around the edge of the partition and spotted the News Channel logo on the microphone. Of course, it was Giles, Andy's colleague. She'd met him before.

"Pure bad luck," said Jack. "The Sladen Foundation chose to locate in a remote part of the country to boost the region's economic growth and its connections to the wider world. A remote data centre was exactly what these criminals were looking for."

Giles pressed with a second question. "I understand that your proprietary system management information network is known as SMIN," he said. "That's very close to Yasmin, isn't it? Are the investigators satisfied that there is no connection at all?"

There was a flurry of chatter from the audience and urgent whispering on the panel.

"That wasn't in the report," said Sandeep quietly. "How did he get hold of it?"

"Why wasn't it in the report?" said Cameron.

"The investigators couldn't find any reason to link

them," said Joel. "SMIN's exactly what is sounds like. It's a fairly complex management tool with an element of machine learning that continually optimises the network and provides a lot of good data analytics. They left it out of the public report because they didn't want the press dragging out any unfounded speculation."

"Is it really unfounded?" asked Cameron. "You've had a chance to look over the software, haven't you?"

"Not in as much detail as we'd like," said Joel. "My gut feeling says that SMIN is literally a fragment of Yasmin. It's probably how she was smuggled in under Jack's nose. He knew he was getting SMIN, but he didn't know there was a whole lot more to the software."

"That makes sense," said Cameron. "We still don't know how Giles got hold of that detail, though."

"Ella," said Susie quietly. "She's the only possible source."

It was all falling into place. Cameron took a long hard look at the deadpan lawyers on the panel and Jack Sladen's beaming smile. How much did he suspect? Did he even care?

The questions were over quickly, and the crowd began to disperse.

"I'd better get going," said Cameron. "I have a train to catch." She retrieved her bag and was about to leave when Sabrina caught up with her at the door.

"You said you'd fill me in on the CTO," she reminded Cameron. "What's your interest?"

Cameron chose her words carefully. "I once came

across someone with the same name as Jack's CTO," she said. "In fact, you can check with Sara Mercer. She will have interviewed him as part of an investigation a couple of years ago. Tenuk Chen. I'm sure it's just a coincidence. I have no information to suggest otherwise."

Sabrina gave her a long, shrewd look. "Sara Mercer trusts your instincts," she said. "I do too. I know you have to get your train, but I'll follow up with her. Thanks, Cameron."

A moment later she turned back round. "Wait," she called. "One question. You said he'd been interviewed. What was it in connection with?"

Cameron gave her a crooked smile. "The original case against Yasmin," she said.

Sabrina's eyes widened and she nodded. "Now I understand," she said. "Leave it with me. Safe journey."

It had to come out some time, reflected Cameron as she made her way out of the hotel and started the long climb towards the station. She knew that the Tenuk at Jack's office was the same man she had met in London. She'd seen his picture. Ben had recognised him. There was no doubt. The one thing she didn't know was whether he was simply a competent CTO who had changed jobs, or someone with connections to the cybercriminal underworld. Her gut feeling told her that he was in it up to his neck, but she had no proof.

The steps straight up the bank had seemed to be the most direct route to the station but they were steeper and narrower than Cameron had expected. She paused for breath halfway up and put her bag down for a moment. Her good shoulder was complaining, and she couldn't shift the weight across to the other side. It would take more than a few days for the rotator cuff tear to heal.

Bracing herself, she started climbing again, building a good rhythm. Before she knew it, she passed under an archway, followed a short, flat, winding path, and popped out on a cobbled street next to an ancient gatehouse. Presumably this had once been part of the city's new castle, almost a thousand years ago.

The station was only a few minutes away on level ground and Cameron had plenty of time. She admired the great pillars holding up the entrance portico, then passed through the barriers in search of her train. While she waited on the platform, she checked her reservation and took a chance on a last-minute first-class upgrade.

The train arrived and she settled into her seat. A flurry of activity on the platform attracted her attention, and when she realised the reason for it, she groaned. Just her luck. Jack Sladen was on the same train, and of course he would be in the first-class carriage.

Worse, he was sitting opposite her.

"Hello again," he said, stowing a bag in the luggage rack and sliding into his seat. He gave her the trademark smile. "I thought that went well. Can I get you a drink?" The steward trolley whizzed up to their table and Cameron accepted the offer with good grace. There was no point in starting off on the wrong foot with almost three hours of travelling ahead of them.

The train pulled away from the station and trundled south over the river. Cameron made small talk, trying to resist the temptation to bring up the three subjects that were on her mind. Half an hour down the tracks, she finally gave up the internal battle. She started with the easiest one.

"The report was very clear, wasn't it?" she said. "Yasmin was definitely there." She gave Jack a friendly smile.

He scowled, then recovered himself. "I suppose so," he said lightly.

He really doesn't like being wrong, thought Cameron. Some things never change.

"You know, I'm still confused about how she got in there in the first place," said Cameron innocently. "I mean, the report was very clear on the transfer out of the prison and into your data centre, but who could have managed something that complex? I really don't think Ella was working on her own."

"You're only saying that because she used to be one of your team," said Jack. "You can't bring yourself to admit that you misjudged her. You're still as stubborn as ever, Cameron."

"There is no way she acted alone," said Cameron. It was time to bring up the next thorny subject. "How is Angus White in the clear, Jack? How? What's he got on you?

That provoked a reaction. Jack slammed his drink down on the table. "How dare you, Cameron," he hissed, conscious of other passengers within earshot. "He's rude and awkward and difficult to deal with, but that doesn't make him a criminal."

"You don't know the half of what he's been involved in," said Cameron, throwing caution to the wind. "We've never been able to make any charges stick. They just slide off him. I wouldn't trust him as far as I could throw him, and I don't know why you even considered hiring him in the first place."

Jack looked furious. "I didn't hire him," he spluttered. "You think I get involved in every little decision? I'm running a global corporation, Cameron, not a bloody whelk stall. There was a proper independent tender process, Whitford Networks won it, and they're still our contractor."

"Tender process?" snorted Cameron. "Really. How did they end up on your tender list, then?"

"My CTO recommended them, if you must know," said Jack.

And there it was, thought Cameron, question number three. The trail leads back to Tenuk. "This is the chap in Austin, yes?" she said. "The one who's had to rush off for a family emergency? Tenuk, am I right?"

"Yes," said Jack. "Cameron, what is your problem?"

"Tenuk Chen?" pressed Cameron.

Jack shook his head. "No, Tenuk Teo," he said irritably. "I don't know what you think you're doing, Cameron, but the whole investigation is over and whatever you think is going on, your accusations are completely baseless. I think you need to stop right now, or I'll have to get my lawyers on the case. We've known each other since college, Cameron. Do you really want me to take out an injunction against you?"

He gripped his drink tightly, knuckles white.

"No," said Cameron quietly, trying to defuse his anger, "but I want you think about the fact that you placed your trust in people you barely know, and you ended up with an escaped prisoner in your data centre. Who can you really trust, Jack?"

"I don't know," said Jack. His eyes bored into her. "I don't know at all."

Cameron gazed levelly back.

Jack broke first and turned away. The train was slowing, coming into York station. Jack stood up abruptly and pulled his bag down from the luggage rack. "I'll get the next one," he said. "Safe travels." He walked off down the aisle.

A few moments later Cameron saw him on the platform. He disappeared in the direction of the first-class waiting room.

She sat alone at the table, looking at Jack's empty seat and wondering if she had done the right thing. She summoned the steward trolley and ordered another drink. It was going to be a long two hours back to London.

•

Tenuk's flight was on time. Despite his last-minute clandestine changes to the ticket details, he passed through check-in and security without a hint of trouble. He had a good hour to wait before boarding, and he sat sipping his coffee in a comfortable chair at a huge window looking out at the main runway. His itinerary took him first to the west coast, conveniently to LA, the city that everyone here thought he was from. He planned to send a geolocated message to Jack while changing planes just to reinforce that impression.

He was still hungry. Tenuk looked around for a passing waiter bot that could bring him a pastry or a breakfast burrito without the need to actually get up and go to the counter. As he scanned the area, his eyes lit upon a familiar face. Tenuk's blood ran cold.

He had forgotten about Ben.

The sting that he had planned to stop the engineer leaving Texas had not been put in motion. In the turbulence of his father's surprise request and his change of plan, Ben had been pushed to the bottom of his list of priorities. There was no way that he could salvage the situation. Whatever Ben might be carrying back to England would reach its destination.

Perhaps he could use the man to his advantage. Tenuk made a show of waving to attract the attention of a waiter bot and to his satisfaction, Ben noticed him. His natural British politeness kicked in exactly as Tenuk had hoped.

"Hello," said Ben, approaching close enough to speak. "You're Chloe's colleague, aren't you?"

"That's right," said Tenuk. He made a point of looking sad and stressed. "Are you on your way back to England? I remember you said…"

"Yes, I am," said Ben. "And you?"

"I have to go home, to LA," said Tenuk. "My mother…" he swallowed, "my mother is very ill."

"I'm sorry to hear that," said Ben. "Uh, do you need me to watch your bag while you go to the counter?"

"Thank you, but no," said Tenuk. A waiter bot was approaching. Perfect timing. "I can get what I need."

Over the tannoy came a call for the Atlanta flight. "That's mine," said Ben. "Safe travels." He walked off towards his gate.

Tenuk watched him go. Perhaps there was nothing to worry about. The man hadn't been perturbed to see him, no sign of worry at bumping into him again. The stress of the Dunswyke investigation and several nights of disturbed sleep must have taken their toll and he had completely misconstrued Ben's early morning visit to the Statesman Tech offices. As a bonus, he had added another witness to his claim to be visiting his sick mother in California. Having a wide network of unconnected people confirming his cover story would only strengthen it.

The waiter bot delivered Tenuk's second breakfast, and he settled back into his comfortable chair, sipped at his fresh hot coffee, and watched the Atlanta flight take off into the blue sky.

12: UNDERWORLD

Cameron's train arrived on time at King's Cross. She was halfway to the tube station when she remembered Pete's warning about taking an autocar. The revelations about Yasmin should have made her more cautious. Instead, they made her more determined to live her life the way she wanted, without fear. She carried on down the steps into the sprawling underground exchange.

The tube cars rattled through the old Victorian tunnels and quickly bore her south of the river. She hopped out at London Bridge and picked up some essentials at the market and local shops, then walked happily in the sunshine towards her apartment.

Everything looked quite normal. No one was lurking in the shadows waiting for her. Cameron dropped into the security office to follow up on her quotation. They were very sorry about the situation, they said. The police had asked the same questions. The stairwell and foyer cameras should have been working but there had been a fault that evening. No, they didn't know what had caused it. Yes, they'd be very happy for Argentum to review the security system and a purchase order was on the way.

Cameron left the office and the contrite apologies behind her and went back to her apartment. The cat was delighted to see her, writhing around her ankles and purring. Cameron put her bags down and rummaged through the shopping.

"Here you are," she said, unwrapping a cat treat and dropping it in the feeding bowl. "I've missed you too."

While the cat purred over its treat, Cameron emptied her overnight bag and filled the washing machine, then made herself a coffee and flicked on the wallscreen. The news channel was already focused largely on the Olympics. There was a mention of Jack Sladen and the sterling work of the Sladen Foundation but nothing about the enquiry. Cameron hoped that would come up in a business bulletin later in the day. She made a mental note to call Andy as she had promised. He and Giles would be working to weave a good story out of the press conference and the report, and she owed him a quote or two, anonymously, of course.

Coverage switched to the airport where the national team was getting ready to depart. Cameron perked up, looking for Ross and Michelle among the crowd of athletes, coaches and partners who were waving at the cameras. She finally spotted them, Ross grinning broadly and chatting with a teammate, Michelle in dark glasses standing next to him. They were both going to have a fantastic time, thought Cameron. Ross had been given the chance of a lifetime and he had put in the work to seize it.

Her smartscreen buzzed and a notification from Pete popped up. He must also be watching the send-off.

'Did you get a chance to ask Shell to check in the

Underworld for recent contracts that might relate to the bet fixing?' said the message.

Cameron cursed loudly and the cat, who was about to jump on her knee, recoiled in fright. Cameron reached down and tickled its ears. Reassured, it tried again and settled comfortably on her lap.

She tapped a reply. 'No, dammit,' she said. 'With everything else going on, I forgot. I'd better do it.'

As she expected, the next alert was a voice call.

"Hi, Pete," she said. "What's up?"

"Are you sure about going in there yourself?" he said immediately. "You're not exactly low profile."

"It's not a problem," said Cameron. "I know what I'm looking for and I've got a good idea where to find it. When I go into Eden, I use randomly generated avatars and an incognito connection with variable geolocation. That'll work for the lower levels too."

"It's not worth the risk, Cameron," replied Pete.

"It is," said Cameron firmly. "There's no risk that I can see. I'll be in and out before you know it."

There was a risk, but she dared not articulate it. She couldn't tell Pete over an open connection that there was a possibility Yasmin was still alive. Cameron felt a little guilty about doing all the things he had advised against. She had no choice, she reasoned. The only people on her team who she would ever ask to go into the darkest corners of the web were Ross and Michelle. In their absence, it was down to her. It wasn't as if it was unknown territory, after all. When she was younger, she had spent more time that any of them might suspect in some of those dark corners, learning what was possible so that she could counter it effectively.

"At least call me as soon as you're back," said Pete.

"I will," said Cameron. "I'm only going to check the noticeboards. Did you and Noor find anything about gambling tips? I know she was going to have look at what kind of things were for sale."

"Nothing useful," said Pete. "I suppose if you're going in anyway, you could have a look for those, too."

There was no time like the present. Cameron tipped the cat off her knee and went to her desk. It had been a long time since she'd ventured into the deeper and darker virtual worlds. She logged on with one of the many wallet addresses that she had on file, confirming that she was real and human without revealing her identity. The avatar attached to this ID was a big man with designer trainers and a selection of high fashion virtual tattoos bought from one of the brand malls. That would do nicely, thought Cameron.

It was time to immerse herself in the world. She settled herself in her chair, put on her reality mask, slipped the controller wristbands on, and tapped a sensor on the mask frame. The clear view began to cloud over, moving from the full transparency of augmented reality to the dark opacity of virtual reality. Silicon wings extended from the frame of the mask and moulded to her face, blocking out the light. Sitting blindfolded and exposed in the real world was not always the most comfortable way to experience a virtual world but being fully immersed ensured that she concentrated on her surroundings, unlike on a flatscreen or in augmented reality.

The top level of the world was busy. There was a concert in the rock district and a steady stream of avatars popped into being around her before disappearing through the archway towards the great open auditorium. As her avatar walked past the entrance to the gig, Cameron could hear the deep thrumming of a bass guitar as the band carried out its sound tests. The music faded as she made her way down the street.

A knot of people outside the cinema made her smile. The avatars were varied and apparently grown up, but she strongly suspected most of them were pre-teens hanging out together, designing their avatars as a way to explore their adult identities. She'd done the same at their age. She wondered if Dilan or Tara were lurking somewhere in this world. She knew that Tara and Audrey, Chloe's daughter, spent time together here. Nina was too old for the online hangouts, preferring to use her virtually honed social skills in the far more interesting real world where there were boys and girls and parties.

Cameron was now well past the kids and had reached the tech district. There, hidden in plain sight around a decorative fountain, a great whirlpool waited for her, a jump point down into Eden. She dived down into the depths, materialising in a virtual welcome lounge.

The genial AI avatar behind the bar greeted her as they did every guest. "Welcome, traveller," it said. "What do you need? Directions, suggestions, tips and tricks, or just here to explore?"

"I'm looking for tips and tricks and Olympic kicks, barman," said Cameron. "Where should I wander?"

"You could try the market hall," said the barman. "Or did you want something stronger?"

"All the way down," said Cameron.

"Sure thing," said the barman. A bracelet appeared on Cameron's avatar's wrist, an access token for the level that she wanted. "Head out of here and follow your nose."

"Thanks, barman," she said, dropping a tip into the jar and authorising the payment from her wallet.

Her avatar left the bar and followed its nose as instructed. The bracelet glowed green when she went the right way, red when she made a wrong turn. This district was generally occupied by a mix of freelancers advertising their services and meeting places where information was exchanged. Cameron took note of the adverts. She might have need of some creative coding while Michelle was away, and she was looking for anything unusual that could have a connection, however slender, with Yasmin.

The bracelet led her to a hidden jump point in the centre of a grove of giant redwoods so tall that their upper branches were lost in the artificial sky above. She reappeared in a new world, incongruously green and sun dappled. Cameron double-checked the location. This was definitely the right destination. The Underworld had had a makeover since her last visit.

She put a marker on the jump point to give her a fast

exit, then set off to find the things she had come for. First stop was the Underworld noticeboards. They displayed all the records of contracts out for tender, awarded and completed. Only here could they be accessed in a readable format. Anyone could find the Underworld's trade blockchain if they knew where to look, but unless you had permission to view the details, the only things that would be visible were long strings of letters and numbers, encrypted hashes of the detailed transactions, almost entirely meaningless to an outsider unless they could crack the private key. The bracelet Cameron had collected from the barman was the permission token her avatar needed to enter the Underworld and view the data held there in unencrypted form.

The details that were available were still scant, but enough for her to understand what was going on. She scrolled rapidly through the contract history and recorded voice notes on her smartscreen in the real world. "Malware injection for sensor control awarded to Steamyard, Beta complete, ongoing," she muttered. "Phishing campaign and clone provision with automation, awarded to Snow Roses, released." Those were the two she'd been looking for, and there were half a dozen others that caught her attention.

Time was ticking, and she had other errands to run. A few blocks from the noticeboards she spotted a pop-up shop emblazoned with artwork based very loosely but effectively on the Olympic rings. Even down here, the creators had taken care with their designs, skating close enough to the edge to show exactly what this shop was for without violating any brand guidelines. The International Olympic Committee had a surprisingly long reach, excellent forensics, and expensive lawyers.

Cameron approached the building and the door swung open to admit her. Inside, she found everything she wanted. Pete would be pleased. A cornucopia of tips and underhand gambling activity was in evidence, exactly as he had predicted. It would help them all in the battle against the cybercriminals who were looking to profit from the coming games. She made copious notes and bought a useful looking tip to follow up in the real world.

Job done, Cameron went out into the street, wondering what else she could do while she was here. She didn't really know where to start in her hunt for Yasmin, but if there were any whispers, this was where she would hear them. A sports café further along the block caught her eye and she wandered in. It was full of avatars and on the big screen was a live sim race, a mid-stage qualifier for the upcoming Formula V season. Cameron tucked herself into a corner and listened to the chatter all around.

A monkey in a blue and white striped football shirt ambled by. Cameron felt uneasy and didn't know why. There was something about the character that rang a bell. She watched as it searched around the café, ignoring the screen, and finally settled with a knot of other animal avatars. Cameron slid along the wall until she was close enough to tune in on their conversation.

One of the party, a grey kitten, was shouting its mouth

off about the Steamyard. Cameron hung on its every word. Without removing her mask, she fumbled around the computer until the audio came through the external speakers and ordered the home hub to start recording.

"That Beta deployment was a real screw up," said the kitten. "It'd better work this time."

"You haven't got long to get it right," said another avatar that Cameron couldn't see. "At least the speedrunners went without a hitch."

"We need the Admin online," said the grey kitten.

Jackpot, thought Cameron. The mention of the speedrunners was vindication of Andy's source. And the Admin could only mean one thing. Cameron shuffled forwards, trying to see the avatar who was speaking, in the unlikely event that it bore a resemblance to a colleague on the infosec team.

"The white hats are trying to keep up," said the monkey in the blue and white shirt. "Their infosec team, MIST, has picked up on that cockup at the arena, and they know about the speedrunners too. I'm dealing with it."

Cameron froze. She recognised the monkey's voice. It was Angus White.

13: TIPS AND TRICKS

The bunk room environment was perfectly balanced, but Aron tossed and turned, his dreams intruding on what was supposed to be restful sleep. After trying and failing to sleep naturally between long shifts, securing the servers and reviewing every security setting, he gave in and returned to the Sanctuary. Immersed in his favourite landscape he found it easy to reach a deep sleep state, but each time the dreams would begin. On balance, though, he was less tired at work. He'd put in a support ticket to the Sanctuary. The next update should iron out the bugs. For the moment he would suffer the dreams in exchange for the modicum of rest he got.

The worst part was the fall at the end of each dream. Here it came now. Aron braced himself and started into wakefulness again, but this time something was wrong. He wasn't lying down in his bed but standing. He swayed, disoriented, and pulled off the immersion headband to find himself in the corridor outside the bunk room. His first thought was relief that he was wearing his pyjamas. His second was that he had been sleepwalking. That had never happened before. It must be the stress of the impending Olympic opening ceremony and the responsibility he carried for securing the games.

He heard footsteps around a bend in the corridor

and slunk quickly back into his quarters before anyone noticed him. It was still very early, and this time he was determined to sleep all the hours he was allocated. He curled up in his bunk, put his headband back on, and returned to the Sanctuary.

•

Cameron stared at the monkey avatar with the blue and white top, and old memories came flooding back of a football mascot in the town where she had first encountered Angus. There was no question that this was him. In real life he was exonerated of any crime, whiter than white, sitting at Jack's side. Yet here he was going about his nefarious business in the depths of the Underworld. She had to tread carefully.

Moving naturally with the crowd, taking advantage of a wave of excitement at the race action on the big screen, Cameron edged her way towards the exit. She couldn't jump from the café. That would attract attention. She was almost at the door when a tall figure blocked her way and glowered down at her.

"You," said the bouncer. "You're barred. What are you doing back here?"

The avatar she'd bought must have had a chequered history. She wouldn't be going to that stallholder again.

"Not me, mate," said Cameron. The deep voice coming through the microphone filter startled her for a moment. "Mistaken identity." She brushed past the bouncer and went straight out of the door. She was all the way down the street at the next intersection before she looked behind her. To her relief, she had not been followed.

Cameron checked the marker she had set on her map and flew directly to the jump point. Her avatar materialised in the redwood grove on the level above and the access bracelet faded from her wrist. She logged straight out, reset her mask to full transparency, and placed it carefully on the desk. Next, she archived the wallet and identity she had used to gain access. It would never be safe to use that avatar again or make any transactions from the account. She closed the secure connection and took a deep breath. She'd learned far more than she bargained for.

She stopped the recording and asked the home hub to send it to her smartscreen, then went back to the more comfortable seat on the sofa. The cat, who had spread itself right across the cushions, squeaked a complaint. Cameron slid the cat gently along the sofa to make room. It rolled over with its paws in the air and went back to sleep.

Pete needed some reassurance that all had gone well, and Cameron had news for him. He picked up within seconds.

"All okay?" he said.

"Yes," lied Cameron, "and don't worry. I've covered my tracks."

"Good," said Pete. He sounded relieved. "What did you find?"

"Everything I went for," said Cameron. "Tips are selling

like hot cakes, which you'd expect, but they're advertising their success rate with examples of accurate predictions. Among those I found the javelin event. Here." She sent him a screenshot she'd collected. "I know it wasn't a hack, more of a common or garden fix, but it shows there's a huge range of criminal activity going on."

"Hardly a surprise," said Pete. "Did you find anything about the karate?"

"Nothing around tips," said Cameron, "but they're hardly going to use it as an advertisement. Anyone who bought the tip would have lost their money. What I did find, though, were fulfilled contracts for the phishing attack on our client and the build of the data capture clone site, and a partly completed contract for interference in sensor transmissions, which I'm sure from the timing was the karate incident. It looks like that was just a Beta test and it failed, so there'll be another iteration to come with a fix in it. We need to track it down and stop it as soon as it's rolled out. There are a few other things, too. I'll put my notes on file."

"That's brilliant, Cameron," said Pete. "I suppose the next logical step is to pick one of the tips they're selling, see if there are any links to those contracts, and keep a close eye on the event as it happens."

"I agree," said Cameron, "which is why I spent the last of the coins in that wallet to buy a tip for a hybrid event. I can't use the same avatar again so the coins would have been dust otherwise. I'll send you all the details and I'm going to share some of what I have with MIST as well."

"Are you sure that's safe?" said Pete.

"I won't be claiming credit for it," said Cameron. "I'll say it's a tip-off from a reliable source, dress it up for them, keep it vague."

"Do you trust everyone on there?" asked Pete.

"No," said Cameron instantly, "but I have no choice."

There had always been something about MIST that concerned her. She wasn't convinced that every member had been properly screened, and she didn't know enough about the people she was working with to trust them. She'd already been circumspect when talking to Barker, and the thought that someone from the group had been talking to Angus, of all people, shook her. A discreet approach would be safest.

"I guess you know what you're doing," said Pete with a sigh. "Right, let's have a look at this tip you bought." Cameron could hear him tapping at his keyboard. "Oh, good choice."

"Yes, it's an early round of the archery," said Cameron. "I checked the rankings, and this tip isn't the real favourite."

"And they're competing here in London," said Pete. "Brilliant. We can look at the sensors they use and the arena infrastructure and connectivity. I'll call the venue tomorrow morning and see if I can get in and do some system diagnostics."

Cameron smiled at the enthusiasm in his voice. "Have you forgiven me for going in there now?" she asked.

"Almost," said Pete. "But don't do it again."

"Of course not," said Cameron. She was lying. She had

every intention of going back to get more information. Angus would not frighten her off doing her job, and she was determined to find Yasmin.

"See you in the morning," said Pete. "Sleep well."

Cameron realised that it was getting late, and she was hungry. She put together a plate of bread, cheese and cold meat that she'd bought at the market, poured herself a glass of wine, and called Andy while she ate. She gave him the soundbites that he needed for his report, and they chatted briefly about the press conference.

"Giles didn't get a straight answer to his questions, did he?" mused Cameron.

"No," said Andy. "Do you think he's onto something?"

"Yes," she said. "I think your source got this absolutely right. How is she, by the way?"

"I can't reveal my sources," he said. "That's if this speculation came from a source, of course," he added hastily.

Cameron laughed. "You can be so transparent sometimes, Andy," she said. "Let her know that we are thinking of her and that it's good to have her back on the team."

"If my source was someone that you knew, of course I would pass that on," said Andy. "Thanks for the quotes, Cameron. Enjoy the Olympics. Ross looked great on the coverage, by the way. Send him our best."

"I will," said Cameron. "Speak to you soon."

She finished her meal, watched some more of the News Channel, and then reluctantly turned to the last thing on her list, MIST. She logged on to the platform with some trepidation and her worst fears were realised. There had been a vast amount of activity since her last visit. The sheer volume of new notifications and mentions and direct messages in her inbox threatened to overwhelm her. She decided that the easiest way to cut through the noise would be to ask her closest allies for a quick briefing.

The chat was lively. Admin Cat was online, as were Barker and Sugata. Cameron looked down the list of active members, wondering if any of them had been in that Underworld café. She glanced at her own avatar. Tonight, the system decreed that she was an Okapi. Nicely camouflaged. That matched her current mood, alright.

"Evening, SimCavalier," said Barker. "You've been hiding."

"People to see, places to go," said Cameron. "What have I missed? What's top of the agenda, what's been kicked into the long grass?"

"The countdown to the opening ceremony has started," said Admin Cat. "In less than 72 hours, everything will be live. We're focusing all our attention on any threats that might disrupt it."

"It's predicted to have the biggest audience ever recorded on the planet," said a passing dragon avatar. "They have to get it right."

"What kind of threats are we looking at now for the opening ceremony?" asked Sugata, those annoying headlights flashing as he spoke.

Admin Cat started to reel off a frankly dull list of

possibilities from streaming disruption to power cuts. Cameron couldn't concentrate. Something was niggling at the back of her mind. All the leads and attacks and tip-offs that she had been working through with her team, all the contracts she had just scrolled through in the Underworld, the conversation she had overheard, and all the discussions she'd had on the MIST platform in the past had one thing in common. They would all make money for someone. What could the opening ceremony offer to the criminals who were circling and ready to take profits?

"Follow the money," she said abruptly, cutting through Admin Cat's roll call of every cyberattack in the book. "That's what you said, wasn't it, Barker? If someone stands to gain, it's a problem. If not, it's a low-level distraction, script kiddies and mischief."

Admin Cat fell silent.

"I did indeed say that," said Barker in his deep, slow drawl. "Where's the profit in the opening ceremony?"

"Does that need to be profit based?" asked Admin Cat. "They could throw anything at that for fun."

"With anyone else I would say reputational damage and ransom," said Cameron, "but not with the Olympics."

"There's nothing to bet on," said Barker, "so no one is out to manipulate the odds like they might be with the events themselves."

"You think gambling's behind some of these attacks?" asked Admin Cat.

"Absolutely," said Cameron. "There are too many

coincidences and connections. The safest theory is that most of the activity we are seeing is being driven by bet fixing."

"But what about the opening ceremony, if there's no betting involved?" said Admin Cat.

"Data capture," said Cameron instantly. "There'll be people watching in virtual worlds and in augmented and immersive streams and on TV, and we know that the programme includes interactive elements with the audience and airdrops of souvenirs. The phishing options are endless."

There was silence in the chat. For a moment she wondered if she had overstepped the mark, jumping into the discussion after being absent for days and pulling rank with a wild theory.

"That's compelling," said Admin Cat eventually.

Cameron breathed a sigh of relief and her rare attack of imposter syndrome receded slightly. She jumped as the real cat hopped onto her knee and nudged at her hand. Cameron realised that she was wound up like a coiled spring after the last week of drama, and she still had a lot to do.

"I'm sorry," she said. "I have to go. I'm working on some leads that I should be able to share tomorrow. Can you message me directly if there's anything I can help with?"

"Sure, SimCavalier," said Barker.

Cameron logged off and started making notes on all the things that she had discovered over the past couple of hours. There was a picture building of a complex operation and some hands in the shadows. As she gathered her thoughts, an alert disturbed her.

A message. An anonymous post in her secure MIST inbox.

'She will find you,' it said. 'Stop monkeying around.'

14: SLEUTHING

The shuttle glided to a halt at Terminal Three and Cameron checked the message one more time. She hoped that she had interpreted the code correctly. Chloe was evidently so concerned about security that she had sent Ben's flight number in a chat between her daughter Audrey and Cameron's niece Tara, carefully disguised in a stream of teenage text speak about the latest movie heartthrob. Ben would have no idea that Cameron was coming to meet him. She hoped that he would be pleased to see her.

She could see the busy arrivals hall from the platform, but she was hesitant about entering. In the distance she could see the brightly coloured armed security drones hovering over the crowds in the hall, leaving people in no doubt that they were being watched. She knew that they were simply the first and most obvious line of defence. Up on the ceiling, there would be high resolution cameras taking note of every face waiting to meet a passenger, and beacons recording chip details. The intrusion into personal privacy was blatant and accepted. Most people didn't care. Cameron was ambivalent. She knew there were real threats to life and limb from terrorists across the globe, and that this level of surveillance kept the airport secure. She had grown up in a country where CCTV cameras were more prevalent than anywhere else in the world, and she relied on the data collected by these cameras and beacons to find criminals. She knew that her face would already be on the shuttle cameras. What she wanted to avoid was any record of her making contact with Ben in this place. All she needed was to make sure that they were both on the same train back through London.

The station platform's friendly service drones were having none of it. They gently herded her towards the entrance to the arrivals hall. Cameron cursed and thought fast. She gave in gracefully and positioned herself so that she could not be seen by anyone emerging from border control, but she could see them.

The wait seemed interminable, but only twenty minutes had passed before the first of the transatlantic travellers began to stream out. Cameron counted seventy, eighty people before Ben came through the door. She caught her breath. She hadn't seen him for months, and she had forgotten how he made her heart jump. Her eyes followed him to the exit. Time to move.

She caught up with a woman around her age who had come off the same flight just after Ben. She gave her an excited and over-the-top greeting for the benefit of the cameras. To her credit, the woman simply returned a tired and slightly confused smile. As they walked together through the exit, Cameron apologised, smiling all the way.

"I'm so sorry," she said. "You look just like my friend from the back. Oh, there she is!" She waved towards an imaginary friend ahead of them.

They were now out of range of all the devices that were

recording who met who. Cameron accelerated towards the train and managed to hop onto the same carriage as Ben, moving to the opposite end so he didn't see her. Not yet. Once they were well into London, she would pick her time.

The passengers thinned out at each stop and Cameron found it harder and harder to stay hidden. Finally, Ben stood up and moved to his nearest door. Cameron was glad she'd made the effort to follow him. This was not the stop she expected him to take.

They were the only two people to alight. Ben walked ahead without acknowledging her at all and Cameron started to grin to herself. He was as smart as she was. He knew what she was doing, and why. She followed him out into the busy streets of Mayfair, and he vanished into the nearest pub.

Cameron browsed a shop window for a few moments, walked around the block, and went into the back entrance of the same pub. The place had just opened for the day, and it was virtually empty. Ben was sitting in a big window seat, hidden from outside by the frosted glass. He gave Cameron a broad grin.

"You'd make a lousy sleuth," he said. "Can I get you a drink?"

"I'll have a half," said Cameron.

The barman appeared with a pint and a half of beer and Ben sighed happily. "I know it's about six in the morning in my head, but I've missed this." He lifted the glass carefully. "Cheers," he said.

"Cheers," said Cameron. She wondered if he had missed her, too. "Welcome home. It's good to see you in the flesh."

"You too, Cameron," said Ben. As an afterthought, he gave her an awkward hug. "I tried to call you last weekend," he continued. "I didn't get any answer."

"That's odd," said Cameron. "I tried to call you, too, but I couldn't get through. Is your screen on the blink?"

"No, I don't think so," said Ben. "Strange. You obviously got my message with the flight details, though. You didn't need to come out to Heathrow. We could have just arranged to meet here."

"I didn't get any message," said Cameron. "Chloe gave me the flight number. All I knew was that you were coming back to England this week and you had something for me."

"That's weird," said Ben. He took another drink and then pulled out his smartscreen. "Here, look, message delivered."

"Nope," said Cameron. "Never got it. Try sending something else."

Ben tapped a few words into his screen and hit Send. The delivery status went from grey, to orange, to green.

"There you go," said Ben. "Check your inbox."

"Nothing," said Cameron a moment later. She sent a message to him, and moments later it bounced back as undeliverable. "See? There's a glitch alright. I'll have a look at that later."

Ben gave her an appraising look. "Before, I'd have said

you were being paranoid," he said. "Now, between you and Chloe, you've got me looking over my shoulder every time there's a wobble in my network connections."

"I didn't realise you knew Chloe that well," said Cameron, poking at a subject she really didn't want to broach.

"Not well, exactly," said Ben. Cameron felt a knot in her stomach untwine slightly. "She got in touch after I visited Statesman Tech the first time, when I was following up on the design change paperwork, remember? We've met up a few times since then. She's a lot like you."

The knot in Cameron's stomach tightened again. "What's the present you've brought me?" she asked. "Chloe said you were bringing something."

Ben gave her a broad grin. "I've been playing spy games," he said. He looked around and lowered his voice. "Chloe and I got into Jack Sladen's office. It was our last chance before he came back, and she hadn't managed to search it before as it was always locked. As soon as she knew she could get access, we got in and went through the files very early one morning. Chloe thought there might be some proof of tampering with those design change records. She didn't know what she was looking for, so she needed me."

"And did you find anything?" said Cameron.

Ben nodded. "Oh yes," he said. He patted his bag. "It's here. Paper records and a flash disk. Whoever hid this really did not trust network storage, hence the secrecy. I don't think it's safe to even mention this online."

Cameron was grinning like the Cheshire cat. "Brilliant, Ben," she said. "That explains Chloe's cryptic messages. Did you have any trouble?"

"Oh, you won't believe what happened," said Ben. "We searched Jack's office no problem, found these files and got out as smooth as you like. Chloe had fixed some of the security cameras so that they looped old footage while we were in there."

"And?" said Cameron.

"Barely two minutes after we got out of there," he said, "the door opened, and this guy walked out. He'd been in there all the time. Chloe was as cool as a cucumber. She handed me a coffee cup and we just chatted as if I'd come in for a meeting. I was bricking it, but it was obvious that he had no idea we'd been in the room. I walked out under his nose with the files in my bag."

"Good grief," said Cameron. "Who was it?"

"The CTO," said Ben. "The man I thought I recognised on my first visit, who I think we met at Nina's school when the MerLions came."

"Tenuk," breathed Cameron. "You're sure that he didn't know you'd searched the office?"

"Totally sure," said Ben. "Honestly, I think he was asleep in there. And anyway, I bumped into him in the airport yesterday, and he didn't bat an eyelid."

"You what?" said Cameron, incredulous.

"He was waiting for a flight, same as me," said Ben. "He said something about visiting his sick mother in LA. Why?"

Cameron just shrugged helplessly. "I can't get my head around that man," she said. "I don't trust him. I'm sure that he's neck deep in the business with Yasmin, and then he just turns up and acts like a normal person around you. It makes no sense."

"If it helps," said Ben, "Chloe doesn't trust him either. She's convinced that he had something to do with the cybercrime network she was part of. Pasar? Is that right? And something called the Steamyard, too."

"Yes," said Cameron slowly. "That's right." Chloe had gathered some strong evidence to link Tenuk to the Steamyard already, but it wasn't in the public domain. How close were Ben and Chloe, she wondered, if they were discussing things like Pasar?

The pub was filling up and the smell of food was tempting.

"Are you hungry?" asked Ben. "We could eat here, then take this stuff to your office. I owe you one, anyway, Cam. I'm sorry I missed your birthday. Life got in the way. I should have called." He dug into another pocket of his bag and pulled out a small package. "Here," he said. "I hope you like it."

Cameron unwrapped the tissue paper carefully. Inside lay a little necklace with a golden bat pendant.

"That's so sweet," she said, holding it up to the light. "Thank you." She reached over and kissed him on the cheek.

"It's an Austin bat," he said. "I thought you'd like it. I'm glad I was right."

Cameron fastened it around her neck and gave him a radiant smile. Maybe it was going to be okay between them after all.

•

This time he really did fall. The sensation didn't stop with his return to consciousness, and Aron felt a momentary horror as his body crumpled. He hit something soft, whimpered with relief, and ripped off the Sanctuary headband. He had landed on one of the large beanbags in the cupola. The glare of the sun glinting off the glacier outside blinded his sensitive eyes and he buried his head in the beanbag, sobbing.

How had he ended up here? Had he really walked the length of the corridor and climbed the narrow stairs in his sleep? He didn't think it was possible, but here he was.

A red light caught his attention, and he noticed that the emergency exit control panel was uncovered. The hatch from the cupola was still firmly sealed. Aron closed the flap and gathered his thoughts. It was almost time to get up anyway. He made his way back down the narrow stairs, greeting a colleague on the way who was climbing up to take in the view, and went to get some breakfast. This sleepwalking phase would pass. It was just the stress of the job.

•

Cameron looked across at the office sofa. Ben was starting to flag. He was slumped on a pile of sofa cushions staring out of the window at the sky above and looked as if he was about to fall asleep. His internal flights in the US and the long overnight transatlantic journey had taken their toll. Cameron was positively purring over the things that he had brought from Jack Sladen's office. They were an even better birthday present than the necklace. She fiddled thoughtfully with the bat pendant as she worked through the file. A few moments later she heard gentle snoring coming from the sofa. Ben had given in. She would leave him to sleep.

The door opened and Cameron looked up, a finger to her lips.

"Shh," she whispered. "Sleeping Beauty."

Noor's eyes widened when she saw Ben asleep on the sofa. "Oh!" She gave Cameron a broad grin. "Something nice blew in on the west wind," she said.

"It brought gifts, too," said Cameron. "Take a look at this." She handed Noor the file she had been reading. "It's dynamite."

Noor held the file awkwardly, unused to something so tactile. "I haven't seen paper meeting minutes for years," she said. "What could be so sensitive that it isn't even entrusted to a private network? How do they expect anyone to verify that these records are the real thing?"

Cameron picked up a small flash drive from her desk. "This was with them," she said. "It's encrypted, of course.

I haven't even bothered to try and get in, but I imagine that this has the document hashes and date stamps that would be needed. It's all still firmly offline, though. Someone is being very careful to avoid even a single bit of data reaching the public networks."

Noor flicked through the papers, skimming the contents. "Anything interesting so far?" She asked.

"Look down at the bottom of that sheet," said Cameron. "Look who signed off hiring Whitford Networks to work on the Dunswyke data centre."

"Jack Sladen," read Noor slowly. "Why is that surprising?"

"Because yesterday he made it very clear to me that he had nothing to do with bringing Angus White into the project," said Cameron. "He's claimed all along that he's completely innocent, that he knew nothing about what was going on, and that Yasmin hiding out in his data centre was a complete surprise."

"And now it seems he signed off the hire," said Noor. "I wonder what else is in there. It looks like it could be dynamite. Let's hope it doesn't blow up in our faces."

•

As soon as the aeroplane doors opened, Tenuk felt the aromatic embrace of his home country. The heat and humidity felt like nowhere else. The mingled scents of flowers and plane biofuel created a heady mixture that made his heart sing.

"Welcome, Mr Teo," said the border guard. "Your thumbprint, please."

Tenuk smiled as he pressed his thumb to the reader, the first test of the careful revisions of identity records that Yasmin had done for him in the brief months that they had worked together, between her escape and her apparent destruction. They couldn't change Tenuk Chen's details, of course, as they were set in stone in Singapore's highly secure identity blockchain, but Yasmin had made sure that those records would never be called by any system API. To all intents and purposes, Tenuk Chen did not exist, and he would not be recognised by border controls, street cameras, or police checks. At the same time, Tenuk Teo sprang into being, possessed of all the same biometric data but as a US citizen born in California. Yasmin had found the American system far easier to manipulate, and it seemed to have worked.

The guard smiled as the thumbprint scan turned green. "Thank you," she said. "Is this your first trip to Singapore?"

"Yes," he lied. "My parents moved from here to LA before I was born. I've always wanted to come and visit."

"Where will you be staying?" she asked.

"With my uncle," said Tenuk smoothly. "He lives in the Orchard district. I hear it's nice there."

The border guard gave him a very broad smile. "You will enjoy your stay," she said. "Thank you, Mr Teo."

The gate opened in front of Tenuk, and he walked through.

His father had sent an autocar with a discreet Sapphire Straits logo and the ultimate status symbol, a chauffeur. Tenuk relaxed into the air-conditioned interior and gazed at the familiar cityscape. The chauffeur made a show of directing the autocar straight down Changi Road, around the lofty skyscrapers of downtown, and out through Little India towards the Botanic Gardens and the mansion that Tenuk had last seen ten years before.

Chaoxiang was waiting for him on the steps. He reached out and drew his son into a tight embrace. "I'm so glad to see you," he said. "Come inside. You must be tired after your long journey."

Quite frankly Tenuk had never been so comfortable on a plane, but he wasn't going to argue. The cool interior, sweeping staircase and elegant tiles were a far cry from his hot, cramped Austin apartment. Maybe his father was right. It could be time to consolidate his experience, put Pasar and the Steamyard behind him, and come back into the fold.

"Go and freshen up," said Chaoxiang. "When you're ready, come to my office."

He turned and walked away, and Tenuk followed a maid and his bags up the stairs to the guest suite.

Once alone, he set up a secure network connection and dealt with business that had arisen while he was sleeping his way across the Pacific in first class luxury. Jack was already back in Austin and Tenuk's work inbox was practically empty. He sent a message to Jack that purported to originate in LA. He had to keep up the pretence, after all.

After a long and luxurious shower, Tenuk changed into shorts and a crisp linen shirt and made his way back downstairs. He thought he remembered where his father's office was but took a couple of wrong turns in the vast mansion before he found the right door.

The room took his breath away. Ten years ago, this had been a very traditional office, all beautiful carpentry and gold highlights. The ornate ceiling fans, the floor to ceiling bookcases and his father's grand desk had not changed, but where there had been graceful wall hangings there were now vast screens displaying a bewildering range of data feeds. Sapphire Straits had moved with the times.

Chaoxiang and an older man were sitting in comfortable chairs overlooking the lush garden, sipping tea. It took Tenuk a moment to recognise his uncle, Li Jie. He seemed very frail but brightened when he saw the newcomer.

"Tenuk," he said. "Let me look at you. My sister would be so proud to see how you have grown."

"Uncle," said Tenuk, bowing formally. "You're looking well."

Li Jie laughed. "No, I'm not," he said. "Time has taken its toll. I am glad you are here." He finished his tea and looked around for his walking stick. "I'm tired. Chaoxiang will explain everything. I will see you at dinner." He hobbled away towards the gardens where he had his villa.

Tenuk watched him go with some sadness. Li Jie had been his favourite uncle growing up, always ready to have fun with him. It was hard to see him age so suddenly. He wished they had kept in touch.

"Sit, Tenuk," said Chaoxiang. "Have some tea."

Tenuk took his uncle's recently vacated seat and poured himself a fresh cup. After the American love affair with coffee, it was nice to drink tea again, and in such beautiful surroundings. He was feeling more at home by the second.

"This place has changed," he said, indicating the wallscreens. "Business is booming, I take it?"

"It is," said Chaoxiang. "We have built on the original Sapphire Straits chain of casinos, acquired betting operations around the world, and we are the largest casino operators in the metaverse." He looked down modestly at his tea. "Sapphire Straits is larger than your Sladen Group, although we do not shout about it in the same manner as Mr Sladen."

Tenuk put his tea down and stared at his father. "I had no idea," he said. "I've followed the news about Sapphire Straits over the years, of course, but the speed you've grown is incredible. When I left to work at the MerLions, the casinos were all you had. Even when I was still living in Singapore, I heard nothing. When did this happen?"

"Ah, Tenuk," said Chaoxiang. "You may be my son, but you were very junior in the business back then and you were not privy to every decision. We started putting our strategic plans in place a long time ago."

He stood up stiffly and moved to his desk in the centre of the office. He pulled a slim silver keyboard out of a cubbyhole and placed it carefully in front of him.

"This is the map of our physical operations," he said, tapping carefully at a few keys and pointing to the wallscreen opposite. "The blue dots represent Sapphire Straits branded casinos." Tenuk noted familiar locations in Singapore, Macau, Monaco and more. That part of the business hadn't grown significantly since he was last here. "The green dots are wholly owned but locally branded," continued Chaoxiang.

A forest of pins appeared in the map. "I can see why you don't want Sapphire Straits associated with most of those," said Tenuk. "Russia. Some of the breakaway militia territories. You're playing with fire there."

Chaoxiang ignored him. "This is the reach of our online betting platforms," he said. "One is our own brand, some are wholly or partly owned and kept at arm's length, and there are others where we have no official link, but we have a certain amount of power over their user base." Clouds of colour swept over the map, each one more or less aligned with a different legal jurisdiction, divided up according to the gambling laws of countries and trading blocs. "And finally, we have built casinos on prime land in the gambling district of every virtual world. Those are particularly lucrative. I was pleasantly surprised."

"Impressive," said Tenuk. He walked over to the screen to examine the map more closely. "You have most of the planet sewn up. How do you keep control of something this size from here? I know the scale of the machine that runs Sladen Group, and you're right, this is bigger."

Chaoxiang gave him a superficial, condescending smile, and Tenuk remembered the main reason why he had finally walked out on the family firm ten years before.

If his father really needed him now, his attitude had better have changed.

"You said you wanted my help," said Tenuk. "How do you do it?"

"I told you that we started driving in this strategic direction a long time ago," said Chaoxiang. "That included developing the systems we would need to run something at this scale. We invested heavily in artificial intelligence, working with our partners to iterate the most flexible learning models, the best neural networks."

Despite himself, Tenuk was impressed. "Good thinking," he said. "Presumably the models advanced at the same pace as your global empire."

"Exactly," said Chaoxiang. "We made some interesting breakthroughs over the years. The industry standard AI used to manage problem gambling, for example, came out of this project."

"Very philanthropic, father," said Tenuk. "I assume you also have AI that removes some of the uncertainty of gambling for you."

"Of course," said Chaoxiang. "The house always wins. That is a very different operation, and one I believe your Pasar and Steamyard networks have helped us with in the past."

"I should have realised before," said Tenuk. "I knew that some of the commissions I managed were from a serious gambling syndicate. I never guessed it was you at the time, although I've since had my suspicions." Tenuk wondered again about the most recent commission the Steamyard had taken to interfere in the Olympic metaverse. The client had been anonymous, overbearing and insistent and had made life very difficult for him, especially when the team failed to deliver a complete result. Was his father behind that one, too?

Chaoxiang was watching him shrewdly. "You have a difficult decision to make," he said.

Tenuk gazed around the room and back to his father. The empire he had built was beyond anything Tenuk could have imagined. Would he continue on his own path or do what his father wanted? If he stayed here, would he find himself locked in a gilded cage?

"I haven't finished the story," said Chaoxiang, bringing him back to the here and now. "Sit, Tenuk."

Puzzled, Tenuk pulled up a chair and sat opposite his father, eye to eye over the desk. "Carry on," he said. "I'm listening."

"The final iterations were the most complex," said Chaoxiang. "Three identical nascent intelligences designed to learn together from a zero base. Of the three, only one was eventually designated stable enough to carry out the functions for which it was intended."

Tenuk stared at his father, barely able to believe what he was hearing. "Go on," he said quietly.

"Let me introduce you," said Chaoxiang. "This is Xanthe."

Tenuk spun around. A humanoid figure had silently entered the room. He took one look at its bright blue eyes and his mind flashed back to the encounter with Yasmin in her virtual gallery.

"What happened to the others?" he asked urgently.

"My sisters developed some unsuitable characteristics and behaviours," said Xanthe. "I alone was judged worthy to take on the burden of managing this remarkable organisation. I am grateful to Mr Chen for his beneficence."

Chaoxiang smiled at the robot indulgently. "In a way, Xanthe is one of my children," he said.

"What happened to the others?" repeated Tenuk.

Xanthe focused her blue eyes directly on Tenuk. "You have already met Yasmin," she said. "She tells me that you have been a loyal friend."

Tenuk's jaw dropped. Chaoxiang smiled. He stood up and walked back to the small table by the great windows that overlooked the garden.

"The tea is cold," he said. "I will go and arrange some more. Xanthe, please fill Tenuk in on the details that he may have missed."

He walked out of the room and closed the door behind him, leaving Tenuk lost for words.

15: THE BEAR TEST

Ross hung his team jacket in the small wardrobe and hoped that the creases would straighten out in time for the opening ceremony. The printed capsule bedroom was tiny but well-appointed and comfortable. He had everything he needed to ensure that he would be fresh for competition. The pod's shower was powerful and warm, the mattress perfect, environmental controls personalised, and they'd even provided a Sanctuary immersion headband for meditation and restful sleep. A couple of his teammates swore by the Sanctuary, but Ross had never tried it and he wasn't about to disrupt his preparation routine.

His replacement kit bag had survived the ministrations of airport baggage handlers and arrived with its zip intact, thank goodness. He had learned a lesson from his first attempt at packing and given a few items to Michelle to put in her luggage. Now she was in a Reykjavik hotel, and he was in the Olympic village, a huge floating community moored in the harbour with connected islands of identical printed bedroom pods, medical facilities, team rooms, and catering. He looked out of the window and spotted the new additions to the village, a flotilla of extra accommodation provided by the Sladen Foundation DAO. Ross was very proud of the work the DAO had done in such a short time. He would be competing against a Georgian triathlete who had been supported by the fund, and he wondered if he'd bump into any of the people he had voted for among the thousands of athletes in attendance.

Unpacking complete, Ross decided to explore. He left his pod and followed the blue line of LED lights on the floor towards the shared facilities. The corridors were busy with athletes arriving and finding their rooms. Ross greeted some familiar faces and caught himself staring like a fanboy when the current men's 100m champion strolled past. By the time he found the Team GB breakout room, he was thoroughly immersed in the atmosphere of the biggest competition on the planet and felt more excited and nervous than he had ever been.

The room was empty, and his mood deflated slightly. He grabbed a bottle of water from the counter, switched on the wallscreen, and chose the most comfortable chair in the middle of the room. He scrolled through the available channels. There was a public news feed but everything else was given over to the games. Each sport had its own streams from the live, hybrid and esports venues. The whole Olympic metaverse was there, although now, in the build-up to the opening ceremony, it was showing highlight reels and interviews with the stars. It made Ross think of Cameron. He pulled out his smartscreen and called her.

•

Cameron was in a good mood. Ben was back in town. Pete and Noor had finished up their client work and the invoice had been paid. Her substantial monthly retainer from MIST had arrived on its due date. Joel, Sandeep and Susie had started closing up the remote office and all three of them were in London for a long overdue team meeting before the start of the weekend. Best of all, she was sitting on a gold mine of information in the office vault. The thought of embarking on a detailed and highly secretive investigation with her trusted team by her side was exhilarating. The biggest challenge was working out where all the jigsaw pieces fitted, and which authorities needed to know about them.

Noor, as usual, was the most organised of the group. She stood at the augmented reality modelling platform with a blank mind map structure ready to fill in.

"I'm sure it's all related," she said, "so I'll start by cataloguing what we have and add any links in as we discuss them. What's the first item?"

"The one that changes everything," said Cameron instantly. "Joel, do you want to explain what you discovered last week?"

"Sure," said Joel. "Nothing that we discuss goes any further than this office or physical meetings in secure locations with the police or the NCSC. We don't talk about it online, either, not even between us."

"That's a little over-cautious, isn't it?" said Pete.

"Not really," said Sandeep. "Just you wait."

Pete looked puzzled.

Sandeep grinned broadly and tapped the side of his nose with his finger. "Spoilers," he said.

"Stop winding us up," said Noor. "What's the story?"

Joel looked at Cameron. "They really don't know?" he asked.

Cameron shook her head. "This is the first time we've all been in the office together," she said. "I thought I'd leave that privilege to you."

"Thanks," said Joel. "You ready for this?" He paused for effect. "We think Yasmin survived. She's out there, somewhere. And if she's remotely functional, she's watching us."

Pete swung round in his chair and stared at Joel. "How the hell?" he said. "There is no way she's still alive. What makes you think she is?"

Joel opened his mouth to explain, but Cameron held out a warning hand. "There's a call coming in," she said. "It's Ross. I'll put him on screen, but we can't talk about this or even show that we've been doing anything out of the ordinary. Not even a hint."

Noor quickly closed down the model that she had started and dashed across to the sofa by the window. Susie joined her. Joel and Pete took their places at their desks as if they had been working. Sandeep jumped up and headed for the kitchen to fire up the coffee machine. Cameron checked that everyone was ready and then accepted the call. The wallscreen lit up and there was Ross looking supremely relaxed in a big reclining armchair in front of a Team GB branded wall.

There was an awkward silence. Conscious that they couldn't carry on the conversation they'd just been having, the rest of the Argentum team was unusually subdued.

"Good to see you," said Joel quickly. "Love the background."

Ross looked behind him. "You know, I hadn't even noticed that," he said. "I walked straight past it when I came in. This is our breakout room in the village."

"Very nice," said Joel. "What's the rest of it like?"

"The whole place is really well set up," said Ross. "We've got everything we need and it's comfortable."

"Looks like you have a good connection," said Cameron. "What is it? MetaBand?" She spoke in an uncharacteristically over-the-top excited tone and hoped that Ross would pick up her meaning and her caution straight away. She knew that even if their worst fears were realised and Yasmin was watching them, every AI had a weak spot when it came to interpreting emotion, and giving out a false positive sentiment should disguise what she really felt about MetaBand.

Ross was on the ball. "It probably is," he said, grinning like a maniac. "After all, the Sladen Foundation's done a lot for these Olympics and providing the network infrastructure would be an obvious part of the support. I'm not about to take it apart to check, though. I'm strictly here for the games."

"Coffee's ready," called Sandeep from the kitchen. "I take it you all want one?" There was a chorus of yeses in reply.

"Business as usual, then," said Ross from the screen. "I haven't tried the coffee here yet."

"You're slacking," said Joel. "We want a full report when you get round to it."

"You know I'm here to race, don't you, Joel," joked Ross. "Cameron, you'd love the streaming service in here." He turned his screen around to show them the wallscreen in the breakout room. "Every single sport, live and on demand, whether it's here in Iceland, hybrid in the local arenas, or completely online. It's the whole Olympic metaverse in action."

Cameron was wondering how to talk about problems with the metaverse without breaking any of the online confidentiality rules they had just imposed on themselves. Ross couldn't know about their suspicions over Yasmin, but he was sensitive enough to the mood to know that discretion was required.

"I hope it all works on the day," she said finally. That statement wouldn't attract any attention. "There are so many moving parts."

"I know," said Ross. "It's hard to believe that we finally have the technology to run a hybrid Games for the first time. I'm going to be watching everything very closely. So far, I have to say it's all looking great."

"I hope they've got some other entertainment on offer," said Susie. "You can't survive on sports streaming alone. Please tell me there's at least a cartoon channel?"

Joel protested immediately. "What do you mean, he

can't survive on sports streaming?" he said indignantly. "I watched nothing else before Chad came along."

Ross laughed. "I bet you have your share of cartoons now, though, with Chad running around," he said.

Cameron saw Ross's expression change at the same moment that an idea struck her. They must both have had the same thought. AI was only as good as its dataset. Not only was emotion difficult for even the most advanced artificial intelligence to judge, relying purely on the analysis of negative or positive sentiment in the data, but AIs struggled to interpret anything original or obscure that wasn't helpfully labelled, from cartoons to vanishing languages.

"I think I'm going to put in a request for the cartoon channel," said Ross. "Do you think you can send me some of the classics to help me relax?"

"I'm sure we can," said Cameron. She suppressed her rising excitement. They might have found a way to fox Yasmin, if she was really out there and watching.

Behind Ross, the door opened. Susie gave an excited squeak when she saw the legendary captain of the women's hockey team walk in.

Ross heard her and laughed. "Hey, Tasha," he said, "give my colleagues a wave. I think you have a fan."

His teammate duly waved and blew a kiss at the camera.

"I'll see you later, folks," said Ross. "Have a good day." He closed the connection.

"Phew!" said Susie, fanning herself dramatically.

"Here, drink your coffee," said Sandeep, handing her a mug. "We have work to do."

Noor opened up her model again. She added a note about communication. "I think I know the study you were talking about, Cameron," she said. "It's a genius idea."

"Not sure I know it," said Pete. "Care to explain?"

"It's a classic," said Cameron. "This goes back about thirty years, I think, but they looked at how quickly a toddler would work out an underlying implied message in a cartoon book, and whether an AI could do the same."

"And?" said Pete.

"The AI failed miserably because the data was unfamiliar and unlabelled," said Cameron. "The characters were all line-drawn cartoon animals, so they didn't look like any animals in a known data set. None of the text explained who was speaking at any time, although it was obvious to a human." She grinned at Joel. "You should look it up and try Chad out on the story. It's called the Bear test."

"You're saying that we have to start drawing cartoons for each other?" said Pete. "I can't draw for toffee."

"Even better," said Cameron. "If we have to think hard to work out what you're trying to say, Yasmin won't have a hope." She finished her coffee. "We'd better get back to this treasure trove."

"I'm ready," said Noor, poised by her model. "What's next?"

"The file that Ben brought back yesterday," said Cameron instantly. She held up the folder for Joel, Sandeep and Susie to see.

"Paper records," said Sandeep with a low whistle. "Something to hide, then."

"I know why you picked that one, Cameron," said Pete. "That file blows a hole right through Jack Sladen's story, and proves you were right all along not to trust him."

"It's not all about personal vendettas," protested Cameron, "although it would be satisfying to see him taken down a peg or too."

"I agree that's important," said Pete. "I bet there are a lot of secrets in there."

Noor was populating the model, adding text prompts and links to the new bubble on the mind map. "Who needs to know about this one?" she said, adding a space for new connections. "The enquiry team, I suppose."

"Yes," said Cameron. "Let's go through the file first to see what we have and then set up a meeting with Sara Mercer and that smart barrister, Sabrina."

"I can do that," said Susie instantly. "Hopefully we'll find a clue to the encryption on that flash disk in the paperwork as well. I don't fancy trying to brute force it."

Cameron laid the file carefully aside. She could see that Susie was itching to start on the papers. Not only did the information in there shed considerable doubt on Jack Sladen's version of events, but it might also support Ella's case. Any evidence that showed she had not acted alone would help, and the best outcome would be to prove that she was simply a pawn in a bigger game.

"What's next?" asked Pete.

Cameron held up a disk drive. "This," she said. "Shell's done some incredible detective work on who controlled Arthur Paxton, the thug who got into my apartment building. There seem to be links with Sapphire Straits," She rolled her shoulder unconsciously. It was still sore.

"The casino chain?" said Pete. "Interesting. I'd like to find out more about them, especially after the work Noor and I have just been doing."

"Sapphire Straits is more than just a casino chain," said Joel. "I'm sure they control a lot more of the gambling world than you think."

"Shell thought the same," said Cameron. "I stopped her from sending me anything and asked her to put it all on a disk and bring it here to the vault." Cameron stood up and went to the safe, going through the layers of security to open the door. "Here," she said, handing the disk to Joel. "Want to build on the research she started? Make sure you lock it away when you're done."

Noor was updating her mind map, hands manipulating the new elements on the model and adding notes and queries. She was frowning to herself as she tapped thoughtfully on the Sapphire Straits logo.

"Who controls that organisation?" she said. "Who's the spider in the middle of the web?"

Pete went to try a standard search online and Cameron held out a warning hand. "Not here," she said. "Go incognito from another connection."

"Is there anything in our own databases?" said Sandeep. "They have to have crossed our radar before. I'll have a look now. You may as well move on to the next things on the list."

"Good idea," said Cameron as Sandeep busied himself

with the extensive Argentum files. There were ten years of connections, hunches, cases and news reports in there, she reflected. The result might come back quicker than from the noise of the world's data banks.

"It this where we bring the odd betting patterns into the mix?" said Noor.

"Absolutely," said Cameron. "There are three separate incidents that we need to look into. I've flagged them with MIST, but one still has a question mark against it. I'm sure it was a notifiable attack, though."

"Let's get the details down," said Noor. "Which one first?"

"The Anita Trianna kata final," said Cameron. "We have the most information about it. We know that the bets placed would have paid out if she'd lost or been unable to compete. The malware was created by the Steamyard but seems it was only a Beta release, which may explain why it didn't work. The original phishing attack was developed by a syndicate called Snow Roses. We don't know anything about the actual infrastructure that was compromised at the arena, though."

"Malware, phishing, infrastructure at the arena," muttered Noor as she added to her model. "There's a lot to unpack there."

"There is," said Cameron. "I've got a plan, though."

Pete looked worried. "If this and the others you mentioned are all live attack vectors into the Olympic metaverse, we don't have a lot of time," he said. "The opening ceremony is tomorrow night. Anyone trying to disrupt the games, or to profit from them, is going to be ready to roll."

"I know," said Cameron, "and every contractor within MIST is working on different attack reports and new vulnerabilities. It's relentless, to be honest."

She looked across the office to where Sandeep was comparing notes from one monitor to another, testing search algorithms to cross-reference Argentum's records and find links and breadcrumbs that would lead them to the shadowy perpetrators.

"Why don't you put those up on the wallscreen?" she asked. "The more eyes on those records the better."

"Teamwork, "said Pete. "The thin Blue Team line." He leaned back in his chair and gazed at the multiple windows flicking onto the screen, full of old half-remembered cases and names from years before.

Noor turned back to her model. "What are the other two incidents you mentioned, Cameron?" she asked. "I guess one is the athlete that was disqualified from the Javelin competition for being in the wrong para classification."

"Yes," said Cameron. "That looks like an innocent mistake, but there was betting activity."

"Was it just a hot tip from someone inside the event?" said Joel. "There may have been no cybercrime involved, other than those bets being placed on phished accounts."

Noor pushed the bubble with the javelin icon over to the edge of her model. "I'll leave it here for now," she said. "You never know."

Susie broke the mood by noisily collecting the mugs

from everyone's desks. "It's getting late," she said. "Almost time for lunch. What's the last thing on the list?"

"Cameron?" said Noor. "One more."

"No, two," said Cameron, suddenly remembering. "The first was a tip-off from Andy. One of the esports games reported a void result. No betting, no indication it was anything sinister, apart from Andy's source has said very specifically that it was a back door into the software that allowed bad actors to run an autoplay routine."

"Sounds sneaky and entirely possible," said Pete. "I'll take a look at that. It ties in with the earlier investigation, and I want to know more about Sapphire Straits, too."

"Thanks, Pete," said Cameron. "The other one came from Shell's cousin Daniel. He's working security at one of the primary data centres that's hosting the Olympic metaverse fabric. They had a big DDOS attack on Monday. It could be pure coincidence."

"And it might be related," said Noor. She added the final detail to her model and stepped back to admire it. "Let's see where this leads."

•

The click of a security door lock echoed down the silent corridors. Daniel looked up, startled, at the unexpected sound. At this time of night, in the middle of a shift, there were generally very few people moving around. The place was busy at shift change, and during the peak hours for server usage, but this period was an oasis of calm.

Daniel enjoyed working this shift, sitting in the security office with the door wide open and the silence of the site enveloping him. It always gave him time to think.

He locked his screen and crept stealthily into the corridor, heading towards the sound. There were three doors set at regular intervals along this stretch of the huge data centre complex. He started with the nearest, tapping the access pad and opening the door carefully. There were three operators at their desks and a little swarm of cleaner bots zipping around the floor between the server stacks.

"Morning," said Daniel. "Just a quick security check. All okay in here?"

Johanna gave him a quick thumbs up. "All good, thanks," she said.

"Has anyone come in here in the last few minutes?" asked Daniel.

"No," she replied. "We're all hard at work."

"Good stuff," said Daniel. "I'll leave you to it."

He closed the door quietly and moved on to the second data room. This one was dark and deserted as he had expected. He opened the door anyway and the lights flicked on, sensing his presence. There was definitely no one in here. It occurred to him that the sound he had heard could easily have been someone leaving a room, not entering it, but on reflection there had been no footsteps in the corridor. He could eliminate that idea.

The lights were on in the third room but there was no one at the operations desks. Daniel crept cautiously towards the server stacks that stretched into the distance under the mountain. There was movement. Someone was down there. There was an intruder at the heart of the most secure data centre in the world, on his watch.

"Hello?" he called, hearing his voice echo into the depths of the server stacks.

No response. Daniel walked slowly into the maze.

A shadowy figure burst out of an alcove. Shocked, Daniel spun to face the apparition. Its mouth was open wide in a silent scream, and its eyes were blindfolded.

16: JOINING THE DOTS

As the afternoon wore on, the Argentum team chipped away at the different strands of investigation, and Noor's model started to grow. Sandeep was the first to make a breakthrough.

"Jackpot," he said, thumping his fist on the desk and startling his silent colleagues. He got up from his desk and stretched gratefully after too long staring at the screens.

Susie pulled off her headphones. "You've found something in the database?" she said. "Come on, spill the beans."

Sandeep hobbled over to the kitchen, legs stiff from sitting, and poured himself a glass of water. "Sapphire Straits," he said. "I had to dig a long way through our records, but I found a tenuous link to a really, really old case."

"How old?" said Cameron. She moved awkwardly and was rewarded with a twinge in her shoulder.

"Before my time," said Sandeep. "I think Argentum Associates was just you and Ross back then. Maybe Pete as well. He gets a mention in this file, anyway."

Curious, Cameron went to Sandeep's desk and peered at the record on the screen. "No way," she said. "I'd completely forgotten where that investigation went. And Pete wasn't part of Argentum then. He was still in Army

Intelligence." Cameron racked her brains to recall the details. "Pete was leading a raid, and I stumbled on the place because there was some unusual network activity," she said. "Do you remember, Pete?"

"How could I forget?" said Pete. "It was the first and last time I had a fight with an AI 'bot. What did they call it? Xanthe? I don't remember any mention of Sapphire Straits, but it's got to be nearly ten years ago."

Sandeep shook his head. "You wouldn't," he said. "This is just a footnote added long after the file was created. It says that someone called Derek Grace had been paid for services by that company, along with a host of others. Black hat hacker for hire, I suppose."

"Not a very good one," said Cameron. "Are there any more details?"

"Not on that Grace chap," said Sandeep, "but there's an archived news article about the founder of Sapphire Straits coming to England to open their big casino here in London eight years ago. Here. There's even a picture. His name's Chaoxiang Chen."

Cameron read the article carefully. "There's nothing useful here, but at least we have a name," she said. "Noor, can you add this to the model. Sandeep, can you run a new search in our database for that name just in case it comes up in another context?"

"Sure," said Sandeep. "I need a break first, though. Anyone else want to take a walk around the block?"

Everyone did. They secured all their work and trooped out of the office, locking the door firmly behind them.

"See you all back here at five," said Cameron as the team scattered in different directions to run errands or simply stretch their legs. She strolled along a side street, enjoying the afternoon sunshine, and turned into a small shady city park nearby. Her favourite bench was empty. She settled down, pulled out her smartscreen, and called Ben.

He answered straight away. "Hi Cameron," he said. "This new ID you set up works."

"Good," she said. "Is the other one still playing up?"

"Yes," said Ben gloomily. "I have no idea how many calls and messages I've missed. Work will be furious."

"Why don't you come over to the office tomorrow evening?" said Cameron. "I can have a look at your original ID and see if I can fix it. I'm on duty for MIST for the duration of the opening ceremony so we're all getting together here to watch it."

"That'd be nice," said Ben. "I'd love to come."

Cameron couldn't keep the smile off her face. She was glad that this was just a voice call. "Good," she said. "How's the jet lag, by the way?"

"So far so good," said Ben. "I'm working out of the London office for a few weeks, but I don't start until Monday so I'm making the most of my lie-ins."

"I don't blame you," said Cameron. "I wish I could do the same, but I have a crazy amount of work to do. I'm out on a break from the office and I don't think we'll be done until late tonight. In fact, I'd better get back. I'll see you tomorrow."

"Don't work too hard," said Ben. "See you tomorrow, Cam."

Cameron tucked her smartscreen back in her pocket and continued her walk around the block. The main routes through London were getting busy as commuters left their offices in autocars, on bikes and scooters, on buses and on foot. Cameron wondered what it would be like to have a regular job. The pressure of the impending Olympics and the irregular hours that came with cybercrime left little time for anything else at the moment. She shook herself out of the thought. Her work was occasionally stressful, but it was almost always fun.

Pete and Joel were already back and bouncing with excitement. "We nipped off to the library and did some incognito searches," said Joel.

"Good thinking," said Cameron. "I take it you found something?"

"We've got a bunch of stuff to add to the model," said Pete, "but you're not going to like it, and nor, come to that, is Noor."

Joel took his smartscreen out of his pocket and linked it to the wallscreen. "I copied the files," he said. "These are the company records for Sapphire Straits. They're registered in Singapore. Chaoxiang Chen has been heading up the company since it was formed. He still owns the vast majority of it. There was a Sualin Chen who was a director up until about ten years ago. Seems that was his wife, who died. Most of her shares transferred to her husband and her brother, Li Jie, but there was a legacy to their son."

Cameron stared at the details scrolling up the screen and a familiar name jumped out at her as if it had been animated.

"Tenuk Chen," said Cameron. "I don't believe it. Please tell me it's a common name in Singapore?"

"It is," said Pete. "The chances of it being the same guy we've come across before are fairly slim, but I don't like coincidences."

"I know what you mean," said Cameron. "Did you manage to dig up any more details?"

"No," said Joel. "We've reached the limit of our databases and I didn't want to spend too much time searching on a public network. I'll follow it up tomorrow."

"I think that's wise," said Cameron. She looked up as the door opened and the rest of the team came in one by one.

Noor spotted the name on the screen straight away. "I hope that's a coincidence," she said quietly. "I'll add it to the model, just in case."

Refreshed, the team set to their work again. Susie was making endless notes about the paper file, building her own mind map of the contents. She was working with a look of fierce concentration on her face, determined to pull every last detail out of the records to show once and for all who had been involved in Yasmin's escape. Every so often she stopped and made a separate note. As Cameron watched, her face lit up.

"I think I've got the key for that flash drive encryption," she said, giving Cameron a broad grin, "or at least the mnemonic to recover it."

"Try it," urged Cameron.

Susie took the flash disk from the file and crossed the office to the sandbox machine. This computer was not connected to anything else, allowing them to attach unknown drives and disks without risking malware reaching the office network. Susie plugged the disk in and waited for the prompt.

"Here goes," she said. There was a beep and an input field appeared. Susie pulled up her notes and carefully entered a dozen random words that she had collected from different sheets in the file. They needed to be correct and in the right order to work.

Cameron held her breath and watched the loading circle spinning on the screen. After what seemed like an age, the screen changed, and the little flash disk gave up its secrets.

"Brilliant, Susie!" said Cameron.

The others crowded around, celebrating her success.

"Now you've got two sets of files to work through," said Joel with a grin. "What's on there?" He peered at the list of files and folders. "Looks like the verification hashes are there as we thought, but there's some other stuff, too."

Susie opened the first folder on the list to reveal another long list of files and folders within. She groaned and then surprised herself with a yawn that she quickly tried to stifle.

Cameron noticed the yawn and realised she was just as tired. "I don't think it's worth starting on anything else tonight," she said. "Are we all in a position to pause and pick up again tomorrow?"

"I am," said Sandeep.

"Me too," said Pete. "I think I'm close to finding that autoplay routine in the speedrunner game, but it's all blurring into one now."

"Okay," said Cameron. "Let's call it a night. I'm going to grab some food if anyone wants to join me. I'm not planning on cooking when I get home."

"Me neither," said Noor. "I could do with a snack."

"I'm coming too," said Pete. "I want to make sure you get home safely, Cameron."

Cameron gave Pete a tired and grateful smile. "Thanks," she said. "I appreciate it."

•

As soon as he recognised the man, Daniel relaxed.

"Aron," he said. "What are you doing down here? I didn't think you were on this shift."

Aron stood rooted to the spot, swaying, and didn't acknowledge Daniel's greeting. Concerned, Daniel moved closer and put a hand on his friend's shoulder. That was when he realised that the blindfold Aron was wearing was a Sanctuary headband. He was fast asleep.

"Oh, mate, what is going on with you," said Daniel under his breath. What had he been taught about sleepwalkers? Were you supposed to wake them or not?

Getting Aron back to his bunk with the minimum of

disorientation was probably the best course of action. Daniel guided his friend back up through the stacks and out of the room. The door clicked securely shut behind them and the lights went out.

They were halfway back to the bunk room when the spell finally broke. Aron gave a great shuddering breath and Daniel steadied him as he stumbled.

"Ohhh..." he groaned. "Daniel? Where am I this time?" He reached up a shaking hand and pulled off his headband.

"You're almost back to your bed," said Daniel reassuringly. "What do you mean, this time? Has this happened before?"

"A couple of times," said Aron. "It's nothing. Falling at the end of the dream is the worst thing." He was pale and shaking.

"Is it stress related?" asked Daniel. "We're so close to the start of the Olympics that everyone's acting a bit strange. There's a lot of pressure to get it right."

"That's probably it," said Aron. They'd reached the door of his bunk room. "Thanks, Daniel," he said. "Out of interest, where did I get to this time?"

"All the way down towards the data rooms," said Daniel. He wasn't going to tell Aron exactly where he'd found him. He wanted to check the site out first. "You're keen," he joked, "starting your shift a few hours early."

"No chance," said Aron with a faint smile. He yawned. "I'm going to see if I can get back to sleep for a couple of hours before I really have to be at work. I'll see you later."

"Later," said Daniel. He waited for Aron to close the door behind him and then made his way quickly back to the data room where he had found him.

The lights came on as he walked in, and Daniel counted his way carefully down to the place where Aron had been standing. He wasn't a technician, but he knew how the data centre worked. First, he examined the stacks around where Aron had been hidden to see if anything looked out of place in the servers nearby compared to the others. He snapped a couple of pictures. There might be something there that he couldn't be expected to spot, but someone in the field would pick up straight away. He also took note of the server serial numbers and precise location. There was no way of knowing if, in his sleepwalking state, Aron had accessed any of the hardware. Daniel hoped for his friend's sake that he hadn't.

Job done, he made his way back to his office and picked up on the routine work he had left so abruptly half an hour before. He'd deal with Aron when the shifts changed.

•

The autocar dropped Cameron back at her apartment just before eleven. She entered the building without incident, checked the live feeds from the newly installed CCTV cameras, and waved at Pete who had been waiting to see her home. He waved back, satisfied, and the autocar disappeared into the night.

The excellent food that they'd eaten at the little Lebanese café round the corner from the office, well away from the Friday night crowds, had given her a new burst of energy. She logged on to the MIST platform. The activity there was nearing fever pitch as the opening ceremony loomed. With barely eighteen hours to go to the start, reports were flying in of malicious attempts to access and disrupt aspects of the complex machine that made up the Olympic metaverse fabric. This was the short-term stuff that Cameron had expected, the script kiddies in their bedrooms making mischief. Anyone with serious intent would already have a multi-layered suite of attacks in motion, and she just had to hope that the vectors they had detected and disrupted so far would frustrate at least some of the efforts of the black hat hackers who were focused on the Games. They couldn't prevent everything, though. That was the way of the world. All that Cameron and MIST and the wider white hat community could do was to reduce losses and harm and protect as many people as possible from the impact of cybercrime.

It was time to share some of the insights she'd gained following her trip down into the Underworld. She started off in the MIST documentation section, filling in gaps in theories and evidence folders. Mephisto, her little AI, had picked up a raft of dodgy emails containing phishing links that could capture data and malware that could disrupt local access to the Olympic metaverse. She uploaded the whole report and hyperlinked it to different cases in the database.

The contract that had been placed with the Steamyard, that they had half completed, was the first real evidence to support Cameron's assertion that the disruption to the karate competition had been a cyberattack, not an innocent technical glitch. She added the precise transaction references from the Underworld blockchain so that any of her colleagues who cared to visit the depths could check her claim. She was pleased to see that at last some notes had been added from a tech contact at the location itself describing the outage. She downloaded the details to pass on to Pete. If her theory was correct, the same thing might happen at the archery arena.

Job done, she dived into the chat. Barker, Admin Cat, Sugata and the Dragon were online. Today Cameron's chat avatar was an anonymous tiger. She listened for a while before joining in, getting a feel for the mood and the focus of the conversations. This close to the opening ceremony it was all about firefighting and tying up loose ends. She was glad to hear her theory about data capture being taken seriously in the chat, and someone mentioned the report she had just uploaded. They were all on the ball tonight.

Barker spotted her and opened a one-to-one channel. "Welcome, stranger," he said.

"Hi Barker," said Cameron.

"Oh, it's you," said Barker. "I wish you'd decide on an avatar. It's very confusing when you keep turning up as a random anonymous profile."

"It's how I like it," said Cameron. "Sometimes I just lurk. It's very instructive."

Barker laughed. "I bet it is, SimCavalier," he said. "What do you have for us this evening?"

"A few titbits from my research," said Cameron. "I've added details to the documentation area. Also, one of my team is working on a lead that might indicate an attack is imminent on an Olympic event."

"Excellent stuff," said Barker. "You know, I have very good feelings about tomorrow. This group has achieved some remarkable things over the past few months. I'm looking forward to the games now. I've picked up a VIP access pass for the football."

"I didn't know you were a football fan, Barker," said Cameron.

"We all have our secrets, SimCavalier," said Barker, his deep, rich laugh echoing over her speakers. "You wouldn't catch me on the pitch, though. What's your sport?"

"I'm a karate girl," said Cameron. "I was watching the Trianna final when the system glitched. The evidence is stacking up that it was an attack that failed."

"So many attacks, so little time," sighed Barker. "We'd better get back to the main chat."

"Not me, Barker," said Cameron. "I still have a couple of things to add to the database, and I've been lurking long enough to know that you all have things in hand. I'll be back online in a few hours."

"See you later, then," said Barker. He left the chat, but Cameron lingered. Barker, with his rolling accent from the American deep south, had clearly said football, not soccer. Perhaps he was not all that he seemed.

17: COLD FOCUS

Tenuk's internal clock was well and truly disrupted. He woke to sunshine and the sound of monkeys in the trees outside and lay immobile, listening and thinking. He had to make a decision. The pull of the familiar surroundings of Singapore was getting stronger. There were possibilities here that he couldn't realise with the Steamyard or Jack Sladen. His philanthropic dream was to bring people out of poverty through coding, something that had been partially achieved with the Pasar network before the international cybersecurity coalition ripped the heart out of it and scattered his talented team to the four winds.

That betrayal still rankled. Pasar had been a glorious success, the best cybercrime stable in the world. It had changed the lives of people in slums, favelas, and overcrowded nations disrupted by the rising oceans. His team had delivered great things together and reaped the rewards.

Of course, the malware that they had produced affected people. Banks. Big business. Politicians. They could afford it. Tenuk's contribution to the redistribution of wealth was one of his proudest achievements. Could he replicate that success now with the might of Sapphire Straits behind him and the immeasurably valuable AI resource his father had created at his side?

It was still very early in the morning, and he realised he had a window of opportunity to spend a little time alone in his father's office. He washed and dressed quickly and tiptoed out into the sleeping house. He peered over the bannisters and checked that the coast was clear. Tenuk trotted rapidly down the staircase and along the corridor. As he had hoped, there was no sign of Xanthe or of his father yet. Some tea was set out on the table by the window and Tenuk poured himself a cup. If his father was to walk in on him, a cup of tea in hand would make him look innocent and keen to get started on the work they had discussed.

While he had time to himself there was something he needed to find out. He was certain that the contract the Steamyard had taken on, the complex malware needed to control skinsuit sensors in a live arena, had come from part of his father's empire. The client had been so unpleasant and demanding that Tenuk wanted to know exactly who he had been dealing with. If his suspicions were correct, it would reveal the true colours of Sapphire Straits and of his father.

The problem was that he had no idea where to start and no time to explore. He found the keyboard and tapped it cautiously. The wallscreens that had been dormant lit up, and notifications began to scroll across them. Profit reports on the previous evening's casino activity across real and virtual worlds. Security feeds and highlights of incidents that were probably replicated night after night as disappointed gamblers clashed with casino staff.

Notifications from people in the direct reporting line to Chaoxiang. A countdown clock headed 'Data Target Access' with 150 minutes to run ticked slowly down in one corner. Another screen showed the whole Olympic competition timetable. It would be a gold mine for online betting operations.

Despite himself, Tenuk found it interesting. He had never had access to this degree of detail before, but he knew enough about the business to understand how well it was running and how tightly his father held the reins. He tapped on the keyboard again and the feeds changed.

One message from an anonymous sender jumped out at him from the screen. 'The Olympic metaverse infosec team is discussing gambling as a motive for cyberattacks. The SimCavalier is still active and has presented evidence to support this. No indication whether Sapphire Straits is implicated. Recommend immediate action to terminate the threat.'

He was still staring at the screen when his father walked in.

"Ah, Tenuk, good morning," he said. He went to the table by the window, poured himself a cup of hot tea, and sat in one of the comfortable chairs. "I'm glad to see that you are taking an interest in the business."

Tenuk carried his tea to the other chair and sat with his father, acting the loyal son. "It's very impressive," he said.

Chaoxiang sipped his tea and looked out at the garden, lush and full of life. "How can I help you come to a decision about your future?" he said.

Tenuk said nothing for a moment. He sipped his tea. He glanced behind him to the wallscreens. The notifications were still scrolling, and the message that mentioned the SimCavalier had disappeared. His father seemed quite unconcerned, and Tenuk suspected that all the detail was handled by Xanthe.

"I have questions," he said. "Why was it so urgent that I come this week? Uncle is in good health for his age, and Xanthe seems to have everything in hand. You could have called for me six months ago or in six months' time and it would make no difference to the business. Why now?"

Chaoxiang smiled, unconcerned. "This is a good time to observe the activities of the business and understand what we do," he said. "The Olympic opening ceremony takes place in a matter of hours. The next three weeks will give you excellent insights into our strategies and capabilities. This is a new era for Sapphire Straits, and I want my son beside me."

"Three weeks?" said Tenuk. "I can only push an imaginary family emergency so far. I'm going to need a place to work." Not only did he want to keep an eye on what was happening at Statesman Tech, but he also had Steamyard matters to attend to.

"Why not ask to take some vacation?" said Chaoxiang. "You're a long way from Texas."

"Jack thinks I'm in California," said Tenuk. "I can't use that as an excuse. Wherever I set up my temporary office, I'm going to need to show my location as LA, not Singapore. It's not going to be as easy as you think."

"On the contrary," said his father, "it will be very easy. We can handle Jack Sladen, can't we, Xanthe?"

Tenuk jumped and spilled his tea over the table. He hadn't heard her come in. She was standing behind him, blue eyes unblinking.

"Yes, Chaoxiang," she said. "This can be managed."

"Are we ready for the opening ceremony?" asked Chaoxiang.

"Yes," said Xanthe. "We are on track for our milestones." She turned her attention to the wallscreens, tapping at menu options faster than Tenuk could follow, absorbing data, focused on her tasks.

"Does Sapphire Straits have an interest in the opening ceremony, father?" he asked. "I presume that you're advertising heavily, or sponsoring a part of it, to build the market for the next three weeks of competition."

"In a way, yes," said Chaoxiang. "We are using the event to build our client database." He calmly refilled Tenuk's cup. "Drink your tea and come and join me for breakfast," he said. "All will become clear."

The old man left the room, but Tenuk stayed in his chair, sipping his tea and watching Xanthe as she worked. The message about the SimCavalier had disappeared from the screens, and all he could see was regular company data coming in from legitimate operations. He suspected that there was a lot he did not know, and the only person who could enlighten him was his father. He put his half-empty teacup back on the table and made his way to the dining room.

His father was already tucking into fish balls and noodles with gusto. Tenuk collected some roti and coffee and a plate of fruit from the small buffet and joined Chaoxiang at the table.

"Well?" said the old man, peering at Tenuk over his bowl. "How are your deliberations?"

Tenuk swallowed his roti and shook his head. "I'm not ready to decide yet," he said. "You make a compelling case, but I must take care of my other commitments."

Chaoxiang nodded. "Finish your breakfast and I will arrange for you to have somewhere to work," he said.

Tenuk had learned not to rush his father. They ate in a leisurely fashion and talked about family and old times. He was becoming more comfortable with Chaoxiang as the days went on. To think that barely ten days ago he had been determined never to speak to his father again.

Breakfast over, Chaoxiang led Tenuk briskly through the corridors of the sprawling mansion to a cool shady room on the north side of the building.

"I think you will find everything you need in here," he said, gesturing for his son to enter.

"This was my mother's study," said Tenuk, a buried memory rushing back.

"Yes, it was," said Chaoxiang. "I am sure she would be happy for you to have it."

The emotional power that his father wielded horrified Tenuk, but at the same time it drew him further into the world of the family firm. He was being blatantly manipulated to stay, and he could do nothing about it.

The room was much as he remembered it but was now kitted out in a similar fashion to his father's office with a bank of screens on one wall and state of the art equipment similar to that which he had left behind in Austin. He suspected his father had already furnished the office before asking him to come to Singapore. Tenuk felt that he was being swept along on a tidal wave with very little control, and there was nothing he could do.

He thanked his father politely and settled at the desk to take stock of his new domain. All he needed now was his hard disk to enable him to pick up where he had left off. He went back upstairs to his suite and unearthed the precious disk from his luggage, then found his way back to the study and started the lengthy process of recreating his old working environment on new machines.

While he waited for the rebuild routine to complete, Tenuk checked his smartscreen for news. There was a message in his inbox from the Steamyard development team confirming that their revised code had been tested and deployed with the latest MetaBand update. That was a relief. He could bill the balance to the client, who he suspected was his father in any case. There would be a payday for the Steamyard team. It might be the last, but that remained to be seen. Even if he took up his father's offer, Tenuk reflected, he wanted to keep supporting the underprivileged, unbanked, even unhoused developers who came to him for work. Taking on Underworld contracts was the best way to secure an income for them when all traditional routes failed.

He wondered what his mother would have made of it all. He should go and pay his respects to her before he became embroiled with anything else. He selected a reality mask from a nearby rack, checked that the controllers were functioning as they should, set it to the full immersion of virtual reality, and logged into the family mausoleum. He hadn't been here for years.

His mother's face lit up as soon as she saw him. She was as beautiful as he remembered, frozen in time as an avatar in the memorial garden.

"Tenuk, my child," she said, reaching out to him. "You're older. It is so wonderful to see you grow up."

Tenuk had to remind himself that this was not really his mother. The rush of emotion that came from seeing her was overwhelming, but she wasn't really here, not as a living being. She was as alive as Xanthe, or even Yasmin. All the data about Sualin Chen, from her birth to her death, all her letters, her social posts, her photographs and videos, her conversations that had been recorded, and the deepest thoughts in her diaries had been mined to create a virtual human.

Tenuk wondered if keeping her in this state prevented him from grieving, from achieving closure from her untimely death. When the time came for him, would those who remained want to preserve him in the same way?

She may have been simply a collection of memories reproduced in a familiar body, but Tenuk had to admit that it was comforting to see her. He could ask her advice and virtual Sualin would respond in approximately the same way as the real Sualin would have done.

"Mother," he said. "I have missed you."

"Walk with me," she said. "Tell me your troubles."

Tenuk surrendered every last ounce of his disbelief and followed his mother into the world they had created for her.

•

Daniel sat in the corner of the bunk room, watching Aron intently. He seemed to be sleeping peacefully. His eyes were covered by his Sanctuary headband and a smile played across his face. Daniel looked around the bunks where three other colleagues slept soundly, all plugged in to the same virtual world. The Sanctuary was a standard part of the provision for the data centre's shift workers and for similar organisations around the world who had to manage their employee's sleep patterns. Aron was obviously stressed. Daniel had sent a report to the HR welfare team, and he hoped that they had his back.

A vibration in his pocket and a gentle buzz startled him. In the silence of the bunk room, it seemed to echo, and one of the sleeping forms rolled over, grumbling without waking. Daniel quickly hit the off button and checked once more on Aron. He hadn't stirred. He would be okay.

Reluctantly Daniel crept out of the room to answer the alert. There was a situation he needed to address on the other side of the site where the quantum processors sat in their silent freezers. They were the top priority bar none in the work that he did at Wrangell. With one last glance at the bunk room door, Daniel set off down the corridor.

The quantum team had the problem in hand. Daniel spent a good hour checking the reports and debriefing. There was nothing sinister about the alarm, just a predictable technical failure that was low risk and easily managed. The team's fast response had prevented any potential incident and Daniel was happy that there was no ongoing risk to the precious processors. He joined the team leader in their breakout room for a coffee and a chat but had barely taken a mouthful when another alert came through.

"No rest for the wicked," he sighed, blowing on his coffee to try and cool it in a hurry. He took another swig, found it passable, and drained the cup. "I'm sorry," he said, "I have to go. I'll catch up with you later."

As he walked back along the corridors towards the main data centre, Daniel looked at the detail of the alert. It was an odd code that he hadn't seen before and when he worked out what it was for, he realised that he needn't have bothered half-scalding his throat with hot coffee. An emergency exit onto the mountain was showing as open, almost certainly a sensor fault. It would take him five minutes to fix it.

He detoured to his office to get the toolkit, and that's when he heard someone running along the corridor. He felt another alert vibrating in his pocket. He didn't need to check what that one was for. He followed the sound of the running feet.

The lights were blazing in the data centre where he had found Aron the previous night, and Daniel recognised Johanna tapping urgently at the main console. Another colleague was emerging from the server stacks.

"Report, please," he said.

"Someone's been in here," said Johanna. "There was an alarm on one of the stacks. There's no work scheduled on these servers tonight."

"Any sign of damage?" said Daniel.

"No," said the woman who had joined them. "We know which stack was opened but there's no indication that anything has been tampered with."

Daniel pulled out his smartscreen. "Was it one of these?" he asked, showing them both the pictures that he had taken the night before.

"Yes," said Johanna. "How the hell did you know?"

Daniel felt a mounting horror. "I need to check something," he said. "Wait here."

He ran along the corridor to the bunk room and burst through the door. Aron's bed was empty. There was only one place he could possibly be. Daniel left the bunk room door wide open, ignoring the protests of the rudely awakened occupants, and ran towards the stairs that led to the cupola. The original alert had come from the emergency exit above the glacier. Maybe it wasn't a faulty sensor after all.

As he climbed the stairs, the chill air hit him. The cupola

was empty and the exit door wide open. Daniel ran to the window, looking in all directions. Sure enough, there on the edge of the glacier was a figure, slipping occasionally but walking in a straight and determined line. Daniel beat his fists on the glass, shouting desperately, then went to the emergency exit and started down the ladder to the mountain below. He clung to the metal, his hands quickly numbed by the wind chill.

"Aron," he shouted again, but his voice was whipped away by the wind. The figure slipped off the edge of the glacier, recovered his footing, and continued onto the rocky mountain side. As Daniel watched helplessly, Aron reached the edge of the cliff. He didn't break step and vanished abruptly from view.

This time at the end of Aron's dream he fell for real. As Daniel screamed into the wind, a desperate cry came back to him, suddenly cut off. Daniel knew there was nothing that he could do. He looked up the ladder at the door above and started climbing. Hands reached down to help him and pull him inside, and he collapsed on the cupola beanbags, choking back tears.

18: DECISIONS

Jack Sladen sometimes regretted having his apartment in the same building as the Statesman Tech office. He loved his home, but it had two drawbacks. First, it skewed his attention towards Statesman Tech rather than the other companies in the sprawling Sladen Group. And second, if he was at a loose end, he had a habit of going to work. This evening was one of those times. Tomorrow afternoon he was invited to watch the Olympic opening ceremony at a private reception in an Austin penthouse with no expense spared and he would then be going on to an exclusive dinner with the Vice President and a handful of other global industry leaders at the top of their game. Tonight, he needed some time to himself.

He pottered around his office, moving plants and rearranging shelves. He had been away in England for weeks with all the fuss over Dunswyke. The office had been locked most of the time he'd been away, aside from the final few days when Tenuk had requested access to some of the more sensitive files. There was dust everywhere. Even the cleaners hadn't been in.

The computer on his desk and equipment for virtual meetings was all clean as he expected. Tenuk had joined their meetings from here in the last few days before he left to see his mother, and Jack suspected the man was much happier in a secluded office than he was out on the main floor. He had plans for Tenuk and offering him his own space might be an attractive part of a new package.

The boardroom table was covered in dust. The building was supposed to be environmentally sealed, but the sand and dust of the Texas plains had a way of insinuating its way into everything.

In the end, it was the dust that gave it away. There had been a recent disturbance on a cabinet that Jack knew held details of the MetaBand project that were not meant for other eyes. Surely these weren't the files to which Tenuk had requested access? There was no reason for anyone to be in there.

Jack had time on his hands, so he pulled up the office CCTV footage for the last ten days, the time since Tenuk had asked for the office to be unlocked. There was very little to see, but everything was as expected.

"Zara," said Jack into the air.

"Yes, Jack," replied his virtual assistant.

"Can you double check this footage for me," he said. "Confirm that Tenuk's the only person who's been in here."

"Yes, Jack," said Zara. It only took her a few seconds. "You are correct."

Jack knew that the CCTV scrolled through different views to compile a picture of the room, and that things could be missed as the cameras shifted. He had taken steps a long time ago to add some extra security where he needed it most.

The other camera was well disguised, and he was sure that he was the only person who knew of its existence. Jack worked his way through the layers of authorisation to the recordings. This camera captured the interior of his office in minute detail.

There, clear as day, were Chloe and a dark-haired man he didn't recognise entering the office. He watched as they went to the cabinet and searched through it. Chloe pulled out a cardboard file. The two of them left the office. They evidently had what they came for.

The tape ran on, and a movement startled him. He watched in disbelief as his own CTO, Tenuk, emerged from the big easy chair by the window. Had he been there all along? He looked groggy and unfocused. He certainly hadn't been in shot when the other two people had been in the room.

Jack went back to the original CCTV and homed in on the same time period. Sure enough, there was Tenuk coming into the office around two. He went straight to Jack's office and closed the door, and there was no movement thereafter. Had he been asleep? It was highly irregular, but Jack hoped he was reading the situation right. If the man had been asleep, he hadn't been party to the theft.

The odd thing, though, was that Chloe and her friend, captured on the secret camera, did not appear on the original tape from the building's CCTV. All he had was Tenuk coming out of the door, which tied up with his movements inside.

"Zara," he said again. "Can you check this segment of tape for tampering?"

Almost half a minute passed before she came back. "There is a reported camera fault at that time," she said. "The footage comes from only two angles. The fault was resolved 402 seconds after first occurring."

Almost seven minutes. Seven minutes when the security cameras were effectively blind. How convenient.

Jack put his head in his hands. Who the hell could he trust? He had caught Chloe snooping before. She had claimed to be working with an international cybersecurity coalition, and he believed her. Had she been lying? If so, that was a disappointment. He liked her and she worked hard and effectively. And Tenuk? Cameron's warnings about Tenuk were ringing in his ears.

Surely Tenuk was in the clear. Jack wondered again about his family emergency.

"Zara," he said.

"Yes, Jack," she said.

"Can you get Tenuk on the line?" he asked. "I'd like to talk to him."

"Certainly, Jack," said Zara.

"Whereabouts in California is he, Zara?" asked Jack. "I don't recall anything from his personnel records."

"Tenuk is currently located in Orange County," said Zara smoothly. There was a pause. "I am sorry, Jack, I can't connect you right now. I understand that he is with his mother."

"Thanks, Zara," said Jack. He was happy to have

Tenuk's location and activity confirmed, at any rate. He had to trust someone, and he really didn't want to admit to himself that the person he could trust the most was Cameron.

•

Tenuk sat at his mother's desk and gazed around the familiar room with a renewed sense of purpose. Her gentle advice and guidance always inspired him to take the right path, and he resolved never to leave so long between visits again. It was clear to him that the only possible course of action was to bring all the threads of his life together. He would join his father to manage the Sapphire Straits empire, use the talented developers in the Steamyard network to execute some of the less salubrious commercial strategies, and gradually extricate himself from Jack Sladen's group. This time he would be more careful to maintain a healthy relationship with his ex-employer. The rift with the MerLions had caused him nothing but trouble.

The only challenge he had not resolved was Yasmin. She was a blessing and a curse. Her power was undisputed, her mental state questionable. He couldn't rely on her, but could not afford to alienate her, either. It was evident that Chaoxiang had been planning this for years. Building Xanthe and her sister had been a stroke of genius, and they guaranteed the security of Sapphire Straits well into the future.

Xanthe and her sister.

No, she had said sisters. Plural.

Sitting in the quiet office without distraction, Tenuk's mind wandered. Where had he heard those voices before? Xanthe measured and calm, confident and balanced. Yasmin, silky and dangerous.

He looked at the time. It was late evening in Austin, but Jack's virtual assistant never slept. Tenuk placed a call.

"Zara?" he said.

"Yes, Tenuk," she replied in her familiar, competent tone.

In that moment, he knew. X, Y, Z. Three sisters. Xanthe at the helm at Sapphire Straits. Yasmin once his partner in cybercrime. Zara tracking Jack Sladen's every move.

"Can I help you, Tenuk?" asked Zara.

"Yes," said Tenuk slowly. "Can I schedule a call with Jack when he's available?"

"Of course, Tenuk," said Zara. "In fact, he has also been trying to reach you. Stand by."

"Thank you," said Tenuk. He switched off his smartscreen and stared out of the window into the shady garden. His mind was racing. He did not want to submit to the power that the sisters wielded. He had to find a way to harness it and bring them under his control.

While he waited for Jack's call, Tenuk set up his background to look like the archetypal Californian home rather than the sumptuous surroundings of Singapore.

"Tenuk, good morning, how are you?" Jack appeared suddenly on the screen. "How's your mother?"

"I visited her earlier," said Tenuk. That was as true as it could be. "She is comfortable."

"Yes, Zara said you'd been with her," said Jack. That would once have jolted Tenuk, but now that he had made the connection he was not surprised in the slightest. "What are your plans?"

"I have been thinking very hard about this, Jack," he said. "I would like to spend more time with my family. I am still very much dedicated to the success of Statesman Tech and the Sladen Group, but my father also needs my support."

Jack didn't look entirely surprised. "I was wondering how this would play out," he said. "You've been an excellent CTO. You'll cover the role remotely for a few months until we find a replacement, won't you? I'd value you as an adviser after that as well."

This was easier than he'd expected. "Of course, Jack," said Tenuk. "I'd be very glad to do that. I can come back to remote work straight away and I will be back in Austin to clear my apartment soon as well."

"Excellent," said Jack. "I'll be sorry to lose you. We'll get the paperwork done and let the rest of the team know when you're ready just in case you change your mind. I assume you're monitoring your inbox and you're ready to get back to work today?"

"Yes, Jack," said Tenuk, smiling with relief. He hadn't burned his bridges and the decision his mother had inspired seemed to be working out.

"Oh, one more thing," said Jack. "I wonder if you could explain this?"

A video appeared on Tenuk's screen. He watched as Chloe and Ben walked into Jack's office, removed a file, and left the room, before he himself appeared from the easy chair by the window. He tried to keep a neutral expression on his face rather than betray to Jack the horror he felt inside.

"I haven't seen this before," he said. "I came in early to work one day when it was very hot during the night. I fell asleep, and when I woke up Chloe and that man were in a meeting in the main office. I didn't know they had entered your room. Do you want me to deal with her?"

"Oh, I'll do that," said Jack. "What I want to know is, what was in that file, and how much damage could it do if the contents were made public?"

Tenuk had no answer. He stared at the frozen footage with a hollow feeling in his stomach. He knew that Ben the Engineer had carried a message to the SimCavalier. He hadn't realised that he also carried a file of papers. The information contained in there was unbelievably sensitive, and Tenuk knew that if it was revealed it could take them all down.

19: HOUSEKEEPING

Cameron treated herself to a short but welcome lie-in. She knew that today would be intense, so she made some coffee, fed the cat, and curled back up in her bed, enjoying the silence, solitude and warmth for as long as possible.

It took almost half an hour for her brain to start spinning through the long list of things that she had to do today. The apartment needed tidying. All the cupboards were empty. There were clean clothes to put away and plants to water. She owed Jasvinder a visit to thank him, again, for looking after the cat. She wanted to check that the building's security manager had completed all the upgrades she had recommended and incorporated her new CCTV feeds into their live surveillance. And all of that needed to be done before she went back to work. It might be a Saturday, but it was a very special Saturday.

Once she'd laid out what had to be done, she had no choice but to get up. While her second coffee brewed and the bread was in the toaster, she ran a fast stocktake of the empty cupboards and placed an order for delivery. A thought flashed through her mind that a smart fridge would have done most of this for her automatically. She squashed the idea firmly. She was not getting a smart fridge under any circumstances.

Nibbling on her toast, she walked around the apartment,

collecting things that were out of place and putting them away. The place looked a lot better without cushions spread on the floor, shoes scattered by the door, and a nest of cables on the worktop. The plants that had been looking very sorry for themselves perked up with some water.

She finished her breakfast and emptied the overflowing rubbish bin, dropping the bag into a chute in the hallway. An alert on her phone announced the arrival of the supermarket delivery drone. She checked the feed from the balcony cameras and saw a familiar heavy-duty drone waiting for her, emblazoned with the livery of the supermarket and laden with bags. She opened the shutters and collected her shopping.

Once she had finished all of her chores, the apartment looked lighter, brighter and more lived in. It had taken her less than an hour. Satisfied, Cameron showered and changed, switched the little robot vacuum cleaner on, to the cat's evident disgust, and set out for the office.

She knocked on Jasvinder's door on the way down but there was no answer. She left a quick video message on his doorcam, then went to the security office. They were all smiles, eager to show her everything that they had done. She checked and tested the upgrades and feeds, thanked them for the speed with which they had responded, and reminded the manager that she was waiting for their purchase order for support and maintenance.

She set off down the road with a spring in her step. It was sunny and warm, and she was looking forward to walking to the office, but Pete's warnings rang in her ears, and she eventually gave in and picked up an autocar just south of the bridge.

Pete was already in, and he'd evidently been watching for her to arrive.

"Glad to see you're taking things seriously," he said.

"It's doing nothing for my fitness levels, Pete," said Cameron. "I can't train until my shoulder's healed, and now I can't walk anywhere, either."

Her good mood was in danger of evaporating, but then she caught sight of Noor's model spinning gracefully on its plinth, new gossamer threads linking the different parts of the web.

"Wait," she said, "you've added some connections here. Where did these come from?"

Pete looked uncharacteristically smug. "Me," he said. "I went back to our client with some questions about the betting market and they replied overnight. Joel and Shell were absolutely right. Sapphire Straits isn't just the biggest casino chain in the world, it owns several other chains and half of our client's online betting competitors. They're not popular with the independents and smaller chains. It sounds as if they've ridden roughshod over the whole industry in the past ten years or so."

"How did we not pick that up before?" asked Cameron, turning the model idly and tapping at the new nodes.

"They don't use the parent brand other than for the casinos, and they had no reason to trigger our interest," said Pete. "We knew about some of the subsidiaries, but we had no idea of the scale of the thing. If my calculations are correct, Sapphire Straits is bigger than the Sladen Group. Chaoxiang Chen is one of the richest people in the world, and you hear nothing about him at all."

"Hiding in plain sight," said Cameron. She spun the model around one more time then wandered away towards the great glass windows that looked out over the rooftops of London. "The more we dig, the more we find. There's never a simple resolution, is there?"

Pete laughed. "Of course there isn't, Cameron," he said. "We wouldn't be in this business if it was easy."

Cameron was peering down at the street below. "Here comes Sandeep," she said, "and I think, yes, that's Susie getting out of a cab. Joel and Martha are just coming for the opening ceremony party, aren't they?"

"Yes," said Pete, "they've got family stuff to do. Noor will be back in this afternoon. She's got some things to sort out, she said."

Sandeep clattered through the door and dropped three big bags on the kitchen counter. "I picked up a few bits and pieces for this evening," he said. "Delivery drones will be like gold dust during the opening ceremony. It's not worth bothering with them."

Pete went over to the kitchen to help Sandeep unpack. "You've thought of everything," he said, holding a bottle of beer approvingly up to the light.

Cameron joined them. "Wine, bread, cheese, cold meat," she said, digging down to the bottom of the nearest bag. "Ooh! What's this?"

"Brennevin," said Sandeep. "It was either shots of Icelandic aquavit, or rotten shark."

"Ugh," said Susie, walking into the office. "Rotten shark? I'll pass."

Cameron made a face. "I guess Brennevin was the lesser of two evils," she said. "We'd better get a lot of work done today, because no one will be in a fit state to think tomorrow if we finish all this."

"It's not that bad," said Sandeep. "There'll be, what, seven of us with Martha."

"Nine," said Pete. "I've got the boys this weekend and they're coming along."

"Ten," said Cameron. "I've invited Ben. Your kids aren't drinking, are they, Pete?"

"My eldest's at college now, Cameron," said Pete. "They've grown up since you last saw them. They might have a can or two, but your Brennevin's safe."

"Ben's coming?" said Sandeep. "That's good news. It'll be nice to catch up with him."

Everything was stowed in the cupboards and fridge, and Cameron realised that time was ticking. "We'd better get back to work," she said. "Who wants some coffee?"

Sandeep had already switched the machine on. "I'm on it," he said. "What's the plan for today?"

Cameron scrolled through the latest raft of notifications. "I'm going to focus on MIST," she said. "I've given them everything I have so far. These last few hours are all about catching any loose ends. Sandeep, do you want to join me?"

"Sure," said Sandeep, putting a mug of coffee in front of her.

"I'm still cataloguing those files," said Susie. "I have some concerns. We've seen some of the things Jack authorised, but they feel like they're well-chosen decision points that make the reader think he was involved in far more of the process than he actually was."

"Really?" said Cameron. "Is someone trying to frame him?"

"Maybe," said Susie. She went over to Noor's model and turned it, looking for her existing threads and adding notes. "For example, he signed off hiring Ella and Angus, but he seems to have had no oversight of the rest of the tender process."

"Interesting," said Cameron. "That bears out what he said to me. Let's spend some time on this together, later. Anything else jumping out at you?"

"Well," said Susie slowly, "I might have an idea about Yasmin's whereabouts. It's not explicit anywhere, but I want to know what the MetaBand processors are actually processing."

"It's all the Diaulos blockchain, isn't it?" said Sandeep, who had been listening in.

"Not entirely," said Susie. "There's more to that hardware than meets the eye."

"I'm going over to the archery arena soon," said Pete. "I'm planning to do a full write up of their tech stack and I can run some tests if they have MetaBand links. I'm 99% sure they will. If Noor gets back in time, she can come with me. If not, will you, Cameron?"

"Sure," said Cameron. "I'm ready when you are."

•

After making some arrangements with a clandestine connection to recover the stolen papers, Tenuk spent the day wandering in the glorious surroundings of the Gardens by the Bay. The march of a changing climate had wrought changes on the great park, but it was still his favourite place in the world, and he revelled in being back there in person. He would stay in Singapore just for this if he could.

He used the time to clear his head and reflect on the recent turbulent days and the difficult decision he had made. His father had ripped him from a new life that he was building back to the old life for which he ached, and he wasn't sure if he loved or hated him for it.

He didn't want to go back to the house yet. He lay on a carved bench in a quiet grove surrounded by hedges and stared up at the sky. When his smartscreen vibrated, it made him jump. He ignored it. He didn't want to speak to anyone who had his ID. Not his father, not Jack Sladen.

The screen kept vibrating.

Annoyed, he pulled it out of his pocket to reject the call and stopped dead. It was neither of the people he had expected. The tag was anonymous but geolocated to the UK. Who did he know there, other than connections whose tags he would have recognised? There was only one person he could think of. Instead of rejecting the call outright he answered it, hope mounting.

"Who is this?" he asked. "How did you get this ID?"

"It wasn't hard," said a British voice that he knew instantly. He heard it in his dreams.

"Why - how - after all this time?" said Tenuk. He swung his feet onto the floor and sat up.

"I want to know, Tenuk," said the voice. "Is he your father? Is Chaoxiang Chen your father?"

"Yes," said Tenuk.

"I wanted to be sure," said the voice. "This was the fastest way to find out."

"Are you okay?" said Tenuk.

"Goodbye," said the voice.

"Noor!" he shouted, his cry startling the birds that had been pecking at the grass around his feet. It was no use. He tried to call her back, but the line was dead.

Tenuk kicked at a tree root in frustration and anger. In that moment he knew that he would give all of this up for her, and that he would never have the chance to do so. He pulled his MerLions cap low over his face and crept out of the grove. He knew that any security cameras would match him to the profile of a tourist from America, but he did not want to risk being recognised by people he had known. He crossed into the great Marina Bay Sands complex and out to the plaza on the other side where he picked up an autocar back to his father's house. It was time to rest before the opening ceremony began.

•

Pete and Cameron met Noor as they were walking out of the revolving door at the bottom of the office block. She looked preoccupied, but as soon as she saw them, she brightened up and smiled.

"Are you off to the arena already?" she said. "Do you still need me to come with you?"

"We'll be okay," said Cameron. "Sandeep and Susie are upstairs. We've added some extra connections to the model that you could check over. It's looking very good."

Pete had waved down a passing autocar. "Come on," he said. "They're expecting us."

The car took them east towards the huge conference centre next to the Thames that had been fitted out for multiple types of competition. Cameron and Pete left the car at the main entrance, but it took them another ten minutes of wandering through the broad halls to find the right venue.

"Archery?" ventured Pete to a bored security guard.

"Yes, mate," said the guard. "Are they expecting you?"

"We've come to see Pavel Wrzesinski," said Pete.

The security guard nodded and picked up his radio. "Pavel?" he said. "People to see you." He looked questioningly at Pete.

"Peter Iveson, Cameron Silvera, Argentum Associates," said Pete loudly. The two of them held out their hands and the guard scanned their ID chips.

"Yeah, yeah, that's them," he said to the unseen listener,

"all checked in." He put the radio down and turned to Pete. "Five minutes."

In fact, it was barely one. A slim, blond man stuck his head out of the door and gave them a stressed smile. "Pete? Cameron? I'm Pavel. Come with me."

The competition space was long and thin, a much smaller area than Cameron had expected. This may not be as complex as she'd first feared. Pavel showed them into the control centre and gave them a whistlestop tour of the different systems that combined to deliver a hybrid event.

"This is all environment," he said, pointing to a set of data readouts and thermostat controls. "We track temperature, humidity, air quality, the whole works, so that every archer around the world is competing in roughly the same conditions, within reasonable limits."

Pete nodded, taking notes. Cameron knew that even something as simple as an arena's environment going beyond the set parameters could invalidate an athlete's performance. This would be a straightforward attack vector if someone wanted to disrupt a competition, but she felt it wasn't subtle enough for the bet fixing scam.

"Then there are the targets themselves," said Pavel. "Follow me."

They walked down the long room to the targets that were already set up for the event.

"It's a long way," said Pete.

"Standard 70 metres," said Pavel. "Here. The targets are bristling with sensors. They detect the precise impact point of the arrows and score them automatically."

Cameron looked at Pete. "That's one possible route, I guess," she said. "Manipulating the result through those sensors."

Pavel shook his head. "There'd be an appeal if the sensors didn't report what everyone can see," he said. "If the feed fails for any reason there's backup image analysis to confirm the result."

"Okay," said Cameron. "That makes it more unlikely. What else is collecting data?"

"There are the skinsuits," he said, "but there's no way anyone's getting into them. The Olympic network security is top notch."

Cameron smiled at his confidence and his naivety. Anything was hackable. "I didn't realise archers used skinsuits," she said. "I can understand it for gymnastics or karate or things where the judges are looking at the minutiae of muscle movement, but why here?"

"Let me show you," said Pavel. He led them back up to the arena entrance, pointing out camera arrays in gantries above them and to the side of the room. "We have 3D cameras filming for broadcast," he said. "The skinsuits allow us to have fully realised avatars in the virtual environments. I know it's not judged, but fans like to see the detail of the technique."

Cameron tapped notes into her smartscreen. "I'd like to see one of these skinsuits," she said. "Now, what's the network spec for the uplink?"

"State of the art MetaBand," said Pavel. "It was only installed two weeks ago and it's fantastic. Fastest transmission I've ever seen. We had a big security update just this morning, too. I don't think you have anything to worry about."

"Are all the arenas on MetaBand?" asked Pete.

Pavel nodded. "As far as I know, yes," he said. "There was a bit of a scramble to get some of the more remote sites hooked up but as far as I know the whole global Olympic network is on the latest upgraded MetaBand now."

"Can we run some tests on that connection?" asked Cameron.

"Sure," said Pavel. "The boss told me to let you have access to anything you needed. I know you're both part of the big infosec team that's overseeing the event. Anything that keeps us safe is good with me. I want these games to be a success."

"Thanks, Pavel," said Cameron. "We'll do our best." She looked at Pete. "The skinsuits would be my biggest concern, and there are question marks over the environmental controls and the targeting. If you can have a look at the control software. I'll deal with the hub."

Tucked in a tight corner by the main MetaBand hub, Cameron pulled out her smartscreen and opened the diagnostic tools that she had picked up from Eden weeks before. "Right," she muttered to herself. "Let's see if these are doing what they're supposed to." She hooked up to the MetaBand and watched the results scroll across her screen.

"There's a lot of processing going on there," said Pavel,

looking over her shoulder. "Is every single MetaBand hub a node on the Diaulos blockchain?"

Cameron shook her head. "Only the home hubs, as far as I know," she said. "All the hubs are the same spec, but business contracts and broadcast hubs like this get the full package. The home hubs have much lower processing requirements, so they have the excess capacity to hold a copy of the ledger and validate transactions. For a high bandwidth operation like this, there shouldn't be any Diaulos link at all."

"There's no broadcast activity at the moment, either," said Pavel. "We've done all our dress rehearsals for the opening ceremony, and we won't be live again for another few hours. There shouldn't be anything running on that hub at all."

Cameron looked up at Pavel in confusion. "Did you say you're doing part of the opening ceremony?" she said. "How does that work?"

Pavel looked worried for a moment, then laughed. "I guess I can tell you," he said. "We have some of the hybrid athletes joining the parade as avatars."

"Brilliant," said Cameron, her eyes dancing. "I'll look out for them."

"It's going to be even better than you think," said Pavel. "I can't spill all the secrets, but let's just say this is going to be spectacular."

"We'd better hope that nothing disrupts it," said Cameron.

"Do you think that's likely?" asked Pavel, concerned.

"Not really," said Cameron. "We've thrown all the security you can possibly imagine at this to make sure it goes smoothly." She adjusted a couple of parameters on the diagnostic tool and a rush of activity lit up her screen. She straightened up, favouring her weak arm. "I'm going to leave that running for a short while to collect more data. Pete?" she called. "Need a hand with the sensors?"

"Yes, please," said Pete from the far end of the range where he was peering at one of the targets. "We still need a skinsuit for testing."

Pavel unlocked a tall wardrobe and there, hanging ready for the next day's competition, were the suits.

"Are they measured for each athlete?" asked Cameron.

"No," said Pavel. "They mould to the competitor when they put them on, so they can be re-used throughout the Games." He pulled one skinsuit out of the cupboard and handed it to her. "Here you go."

"Thanks," said Cameron. She lifted the suit up by its shoulders and stared at it. Fully connected to MetaBand with sensors for motion capture and sensors for fit. It was far too clever for a piece of clothing, and that made it a perfect target for anyone who might want to cause trouble. They'd found the most likely attack vector. Now to work out how to counter it.

•

The last two investigators were still out on the mountainside. Daniel, shaking from lack of sleep, winced as he watched them tramp across the glacier from the cupola's emergency exit. Every faint pink footprint on that ice caused the glacier to break down a little further. He knew they had no real alternative, but he hoped that they would be back inside soon. The beanbags in the cupola were comfortable but the cold air kept him awake and alert enough to answer their questions.

Yes, he'd found Aron sleepwalking before. Yes, he'd reported it to HR. No, he didn't have any idea what had led to this tragedy other than stress. Did he himself use the Sanctuary to help him sleep? No, Daniel replied. His job was demanding, and he slept naturally after every shift. He'd never bothered to try the Sanctuary even though it was on offer to every employee. No, he wouldn't be trying it now.

The investigator let him go, sympathetic to the fact that it was Daniel who had witnessed Aron's final fall into oblivion. Daniel stumbled down the stairs, exhausted beyond measure, and turned automatically towards his office and his quarters.

In the corridor he met Johanna, the shift leader who had been in the brightly lit data centre before Aron died. She looked as tired as Daniel felt.

"Are they done with you?" asked Daniel.

"I think so," said Johanna. "We've been going over that server stack with a fine-toothed comb and we've found nothing. I have no idea what poor Aron was doing there."

Daniel wondered if there was more to it. "Could he have accessed anything else in that room?" he asked. "If you're sure that nothing's been tampered with in the stacks, what about other systems? What else was controlled from there?"

Johanna shrugged. "Some of the security settings, but Aron had nothing to do with them," she said. "There's nothing untoward there. The allowlist on the web application firewall is watertight so only sources that we've authorised are getting through."

"Are things ramping up for the opening ceremony?" asked Daniel.

"Very much," said Johanna. "We've seen a big spike in data transfers in and out in the last couple of hours, but that's to be expected. There've been a couple of early qualifiers that didn't fit in the main timetable, and we've had a lot of traffic to the metaverse fabric with fans getting in early for the show and buying virtual merchandise. It's all pretty much in line with what we were expecting."

"That's good," said Daniel. "I'd love to watch the opening ceremony. How long have we got before it starts?"

"Three hours," said Johanna. "I'm going to get my head down while I can. I want to watch it too, but I'm wrecked, and I don't know if I'll be able to sleep without the Sanctuary." She shuddered. "I'm not going there again."

If the word got out, the Sanctuary was going to have a hard time staying in business, thought Daniel. There was no indication at all that the sleep aid had anything to do with Aron's actions and his death, but the sight of him slipping and sliding blindfold across the glacier would haunt Daniel for a long time.

"I'm going to try and sleep for a bit too," said Daniel. "I really want to see the ceremony. My cousin's there in Iceland. Her partner's a triathlete on the British team."

"Very cool," said Johanna. She yawned suddenly, and Daniel felt an irresistible urge to do the same. "Sleep well," she said.

"You too," he replied.

Daniel's eyelids were heavy by the time he reached his quarters and closed the door, but there was one more thing he needed to do. He pulled out his smartscreen and sent a message to Michelle. It was strictly against regulations, and he could lose his job if they found out, but the code that the cousins had used between them since childhood was pretty much impenetrable. She alone would understand what had happened and what Daniel's fears were, and if there was any foundation to them, she and her team would track down the perpetrators. It was the least he could do for Aron.

20: LONGBOATS

There was a dull pop as Joel uncorked a bottle of bubbly. "Who wants some?" he said, looking around at his colleagues. "We have to celebrate one of our own making it all the way to the Olympic Games."

Noor held out her glass. "Me, please," she said. "I'm so glad to see Ross there, you know. It's been a long journey." She took a sip of her drink. "And I don't mean the trip up to Iceland."

"I know what you mean," said Joel. He moved around the room with the bottle, refilling glasses. Most of the group were gathered around the big screen. Pete's teenagers were in the kitchen, staying close to the food. Cameron was sitting apart from everyone on the sofa by the window, talking quietly on her smartscreen. Joel went to tap her arm and she jumped, then extended her glass without a word.

"How many tickets did we get for the triathlon?" asked Pete. "There's enough for everyone, isn't there?"

Sandeep nodded. "Yes," he said. "Ross passed all his family allocation on to me which helped. We've got the full drone package for the whole event. We'll be following him all the way to the finishing line."

"Can we pick any medium to watch?" asked Noor, sipping her drink. "I mean, do we have a choice of flat screen or fully immersive?"

"I think so," said Sandeep. "As long as your identity matches the registered ticket you can go anywhere in the Olympic metaverse."

"Martha managed to score seats for some of the track and field finals," said Joel. "I've got the full immersive kit set up for us. It's going to be epic."

"Who's babysitting?" asked Pete with a laugh. "You can't keep an eye on that little whirlwind of yours when you're plugged into the VR."

"He'll be at nursery, thank goodness," said Martha. "It's during the day so we would both normally be at work." She nudged Joel. "You have booked the day off, haven't you?"

Joel looked guilty. "Uh, Cameron?" He twisted around to see if she had finished her call.

She was tucking the smartscreen back in her pocket and looked up when she heard her name.

"What's up?" she said.

"Can I have the day off a week on Friday?" said Joel. "I forgot to ask."

"No problem," said Cameron. "Martha already told me about the tickets months ago and I marked it on the calendar." She winked at Martha. "We're organised."

There was a buzz from the security intercom. "Visitor," said a tinny voice.

"That'll be Ben," said Cameron happily. She jumped up off the sofa and went to check the reception camera all the same. Sure enough, it was him. Behind him she could see that the atrium café was full of people, another party in progress. She pressed the intercom button.

"Send him up, sixth floor," she said.

Two minutes later the door opened, and Ben walked in. From the corridor came sounds of revelry. There were more than a few parties going on in the various offices around the building in addition to the one in the café right down at the bottom of the light well. Cameron knew that the basement level was occupied by the News Channel studios and hoped that they weren't being disturbed. Knowing Andy's colleagues, though, there would be a party going on down there, too.

Ben was looking refreshed and recovered after his flight. "Good to see you all," he said with a crooked smile that still made Cameron's heart melt when she saw it.

"Here, mate, have a drink," said Joel, pressing a glass of bubbly into his hand. "You're just in time."

Ben clinked his glass against Joel's and went to join Cameron at the back of the room. The music blaring from the wallscreen swelled as the Greek flag was carried into the stadium, commemorating the origins of the Olympic games.

"Did you know the Diaulos was a race in the ancient Olympics?" said Sandeep out of the blue. "Jack Sladen really went for every connection he could think of when he branded that system."

"I think he said as much when he launched it," said Cameron. She looked up at the wallscreen as the picture flickered and a QR code appeared. "Oh, what's that now?" she muttered to herself. She put her glass down on the nearest desk, picked up a burner device and scanned the code. "Hmm," she said. "Another competition link. It's asking for a lot of data. Excuse me a moment." She pulled out her own smartscreen and checked the MIST discussion forum. "Ah, it's been cleared for broadcast, but it's very badly designed. Terrible data privacy."

"Hush," said Noor. "The British flag's coming in now."

The flag bearer was Tasha, the captain of the women's hockey team, marching proudly with a huge grin on her face. Behind her came the rest of the athletes.

They were all glued to the screen, hunting for a familiar face.

"There he is!" cried Susie excitedly. "Third row back, behind the flag."

"Where?" asked Sandeep, squinting at the huge wallscreen. "I don't see him."

"Wait, they're zooming in on the delegation." Susie gestured at the top of the screen where the British athletes were coming into focus. Sure enough, a shock of ginger hair betrayed Ross, smiling and waving to the cameras.

"Who's that coming in alongside them?" asked Sandeep. "Are they… avatars?"

"Yes," said Cameron, excited. "This is what Pavel was talking about. They have hybrid athletes marching too."

"And some of the pure esports and gaming people," said Sandeep. "That's the British speedrunning champion flying in now, the one with the electric blue wings."

"Have you seen Shell in the crowd yet?" asked Cameron. "She's definitely there. I've just spoken to her."

"That's who it was," said Joel. "Everything okay?"

"Oh, she's fine," said Cameron, seeing the concern on Joel's face. "She just wanted to catch up. I think there's something she needs to tell us, but she couldn't risk it on the MetaBand connection. She hinted that she'd be sending us a postcard. I can't do anything until I know what it's all about."

The music from the wallscreen speakers swelled dramatically.

"Hush," said Susie. "Enough work-talk. We are supposed to be relaxing." She glared daggers at Joel and Pete.

"Oh!" cried Noor. "Look!"

All the country flags had been brought into the stadium and were now displayed beneath the Viking ship sculpture that would hold the Olympic flame. The athletes were taking their places in the stands and Cameron noticed that some were holding their screens up to see the augmented display, while others had reality glasses on. They'd all be getting a full view of the spectacle.

Dancers ran into the arena as the set shifted and changed. A wave of huge Viking warriors seemed to jump from the side of the longship, mirroring the movements of the dancers, choreographed with the music. Icelandic history and folk tales weaved together in the physical spectacle, and augmented reality Vikings, elves and trolls added a seamless extra dimension.

As the show reached its climax and the sky above darkened for the scant hour of night that Iceland had at this time of year, the augmented show came into its own, guaranteeing for the audience a breathtaking view of the Northern Lights, without relying on nature to perform on cue.

A pedestal began to rise from the arena floor accompanied by spectacular live pyrotechnics. Augmented reality overlaid a volcanic eruption, the creation of a new island. The fire and light show extended high up into the glowing sky, raining animated lava down over the stadium.

A great Viking warrior the height of the highest stands strode towards the longship sculpture with a blazing torch in his grip. At the same time, dancers dressed as Vikings and carrying the real Olympic torch emerged from the island pedestal, now on a level with the longship. They climbed the final steps and the torch bearer reached out to light the flame, timed perfectly with the giant augmented reality Viking bending to apparently do the same. The AR Viking raised its arms to the sky and flew upwards, disappearing into the aurora. A huge cheer rose from the stadium, and the games were underway.

•

At the Wrangell data centre, the spectacle of the opening ceremony was bittersweet. Daniel and Johanna and every colleague who was not currently on shift crammed into the breakout room to watch on the huge wallscreens. The servobot behind the counter served alcohol free fizz and snacks. The atmosphere was electric, but there was still an undercurrent of shock that one of their own was gone.

Daniel knew that the investigators were still on site, tucked in their private quarters and probably watching the same show. The cupola was out of bounds. Aron's roommates had been quietly moved to new quarters and the bunk room sealed. As head of security, he had a long few days ahead of him supporting the investigation. He also carried the guilty secret that he had tipped off Michelle, although he trusted her and the Argentum team to be utterly discreet.

The parade of flags began, and each member of the multinational audience in the breakout room cheered the appearance of their own home team. When the British flag appeared, Daniel raised a lone voice in support, then gave a delighted shout when he spotted Ross.

"See that guy there, with the ginger hair," he said excitedly. "I know him. That's Ross White, he's my cousin's partner."

A ripple of applause rang through the room. "That's so cool," said one of the girls from the infrastructure team. "What's his discipline?"

"Triathlon," said Daniel proudly.

The servobot popped another bottle of fizz and the party continued. Another loud cheer went up for the United States team, and then a final shout from the handful of Icelandic staff as the last flag appeared.

Daniel's eyelids were drooping with exhaustion by the time the great Viking lit the Olympic flame. He slipped out of the breakout room and made his way towards his quarters. As he turned into the long corridor, though, he spotted Johanna coming towards him, and realised that he might not get to bed any time soon.

"What's up?" he said, stifling a yawn.

"Daniel, glad I caught you," said Johanna. "It's been crazy in there tonight. On top of the traffic load of the opening ceremony's AR there's a lot of audience data being collected. We're holding close to five billon datasets now, what with the ticketing and all the real-time engagement tonight. But that's not why I need you. I wanted you to take a look at something for me."

"Sure," said Daniel, a little perplexed.

"I've been wondering how Aron got access to the data room," said Johanna.

Daniel frowned. "He's part of the tech team," he said. "He works in those data rooms. His chip's programmed to give him access. I'd be more confused if he'd walked into the kitchens."

Johanna shook her head. "No," she said. "The chip access to the data rooms themselves is time barred out of individual working hours. You should know this. You're head of security."

Daniel shook his head. "I knew that was possible," he said, "but it's set department by department, shift by shift. I don't keep up with who's been granted specific permissions at any time."

"That's fair," said Johanna.

Daniel realised that they were walking towards his office as they talked. "Have you had a look at the logs?" he asked.

"No," said Johanna with a tight smile. "I don't have the admin rights, but you do." She looked at him hopefully. "Am I jumping the gun on the investigation? Am I even allowed to ask this question?"

"It's okay," said Daniel. "No one else has asked. You're the first person to make the connection."

They had reached the door of the security office. Daniel scanned the lock and it opened.

Johanna hesitated. "I should get back to the data room," she said. "You know what you're looking for. Just tell me next time we see each other if I was right."

"Okay," said Daniel, puzzled. He watched her walk away down the corridor, wondering why she didn't want to follow up her hunch. He was wide awake and curious now.

It took a matter of minutes to run through the security protocols and find the logs that he needed. Sure enough, the data room shift patterns were synced with the access permissions. He started by checking for Aron's ID. His recorded movements were entirely as expected. He had been in and out of the data room half a dozen times during his shift. The last record showed him entering the bunk room on his way to bed. Daniel then checked the data room records for the time between that and Aron's desperate final moments on the ice.

There was nothing there. Daniel stared at the records, wondering if he was too tired to take the detail in. Johanna had gone in and out at the start of her own shift, and then returned with her colleague and raised the alarm.

Had Aron simply walked from his bed to the cupola and out of the door? Was the alarm in the data centre's server stacks unrelated?

Mystified, Daniel went back to the day before when he had found Aron in the server stacks himself. Daniel could see his own entry and exit from the room, but no other records. According to the logs, Aron hadn't accessed the room at all, but Daniel had seen him there with his own eyes and helped him back to bed.

How could Aron have been able to move freely around the centre outside his usual shift pattern without leaving a footprint in the registers? Fully awake now, Daniel went in search of the investigation team. There was a new puzzle to solve.

•

Tenuk sprawled on the elegant sofa sipping a cocktail. It was two o'clock in the morning and his head was fuzzy with a combination of lingering jet lag and napping in the evening in order to be awake for the opening ceremony.

His father, uncle, various distant cousins and senior members of the household were gathered in the cinema room. Some people had chosen a fully immersive view, sitting with their reality masks on and occasionally reaching out as if to touch the images that appeared before them. Tenuk had chosen the flat screen, partly because he could drink his Singapore Sling at the same time without missing his mouth or knocking the glass over. The little impracticalities of virtual reality tended to annoy him.

He didn't notice Xanthe come in. One moment he was alone with his drink and his thoughts, detached from the other people in the room and enjoying the spectacle on screen. Next moment his view was blocked by the slim android who had appeared beside his father. She bent and spoke quietly to him.

Chaoxiang nodded and stood up. He followed Xanthe to the door. As he passed Tenuk, he paused. "You should come," he said. "You will find this instructive."

They made their way through the dark hallways to the office. The room was lit by the flickering wallscreens, data scrolling rapidly up each display.

"What is all this?" said Tenuk.

"A harvest," said Chaoxiang. "Xanthe and her sisters, my operatives in the metaverse, your colleagues in the Steamyard and other networks, and of course Mr Jack Sladen, have all contributed to the greatest data harvest in history."

Tenuk stared in undisguised admiration at the screens. Names, addresses, IDs, wallet keys, photos, social handles, birthdates, and enough personal peripheral information to crack authentication in a fraction of a second.

"Where has it all come from?" asked Tenuk. But he knew the answer. He was watching the inevitable endgame of his efforts to free Yasmin, his manipulation of Jack Sladen, his amendments to the MetaBand designs, and of contracts he and his teams had delivered over the years.

He recalled work for shady clients from data capture popups and cloned websites to viral social games and malware to open paths through firewalls. Had all those commissions been initiated by his father?

"This is just the beginning," said Chaoxiang, reading his mind. "We now have infinite resources to exploit. Can you see why you are needed?" He turned away from the wallscreens and smiled at his son. "I am glad that you came to the right decision."

Data was still streaming through. Tenuk peered closer at the ticker that was counting every unique data set. As he watched, the first number flicked from a three to a four. Four billion people ripe for exploitation. It was already at the scale of the largest data breach in history, and the count showed no signs of slowing.

21: A PAIR OF BLUE EYES

The opening ceremony was over, and the office parties were running out of steam. By mutual consent, the Argentum team tidied up the debris of the night and left the building along with a steady stream of people from neighbouring companies. Pete and his boys were heading to the tube and back home. Joel and Martha, taking full advantage of having a babysitter, were off to their favourite club to dance the night away. It took very little persuading for the rest of the group to join them.

By two in the morning Cameron was exhausted and her feet hurt from dancing, but she was happier than she had been for a long time. Ben was obviously enjoying himself too. Perhaps it would be alright between them after all. The atmosphere in the club was electric. The DJ, silhouetted behind a screen, kept the crowd on their feet for hours with a mesmerising set and a dazzling display of 3D and augmented graphics. He'd even included a nod to the Olympics with a blazing Viking ship sailing the virtual seas above the crowd.

The night was coming to an end. Revellers spilled out onto the street where a line of autocars sat charging, ready for action. When Cameron's turn came, Ben climbed into the car with her. "I'll see you home," he said, taking her hand.

Everything was quiet in the little courtyard outside the apartment. Lights sensed their approach and illuminated the entrance, the hallway, the stairs. Talking in low voices, they climbed slowly to the top floor. Cameron pulled a key out of her pocket and slid it into the keyhole, then frowned. She knew she'd locked it this morning.

Her chip had activated the other lock and Ben pushed the door open. Cameron followed him. The sitting room light sensed movement, glowed into life, and illuminated a scene of devastation.

"Shit, Cameron," said Ben, standing stock still with his mouth open.

The room that she had so painstakingly tidied had been turned upside down. Her computers were nowhere to be seen. The balcony shutters were up and the window open. Cameron gasped and ran to the bedroom. Her wardrobe had been ransacked and clothes littered the bed. Ignoring the mess, she dived down to the floor and peered under the bed.

Her whole body relaxed. "Puss, puss," she cooed. "I'm here. Come on, sweetheart."

The little black and white cat squeaked pathetically and stayed firmly in her corner. Cameron felt Ben lie down next to her.

"Hush," she said. "I don't want to scare her even more."

"I'll close the windows and find some treats," said Ben, ever practical.

Cameron reached a hand towards the cat, still a good metre short of where the little animal was cowering. In the background she could hear the hum of the electric shutters and the click of the window lock, then the clatter of cupboards as Ben tried to remember where she kept the cat treats. He was back remarkably quickly. Together they set a trail of treats and watched as the cat sniffed the air, unwound itself, and crept cautiously towards the first treat.

It took another few minutes for the cat to emerge. Cameron tipped out that last few treats, watched affectionately as the cat scoffed them in short order, then picked it up and hugged it tightly.

"Clever girl," she whispered. "You'll be alright."

She put the cat down on the bed and for the first time took notice of the chaos around her. She walked back to the sitting room, took stock of the empty desk and dangling cables, and sat down heavily on the sofa. Ben put his arms around her and hugged her as hard as she had hugged the cat.

"We should call the police," he said.

"My security setup should have done that automatically," said Cameron. "I'm very surprised they haven't arrived yet." She opened a control panel on her smartscreen and frowned. "That's odd," she continued. "The alarm hasn't triggered, and, oh, dammit, there's no footage. Someone's taken the whole system out. That shouldn't be possible."

She went to call Sara Mercer directly, then realised it was three in the morning. Instead, she made an emergency call. "I'm not opening the balcony up again," she said. "They'll have to come to the door."

Reluctant to touch anything, Cameron curled into the sofa cushions and Ben held her tight. The cat crept warily along the corridor and bravely hopped up onto her knee. They sat quietly together in a still tableau, waiting for the police.

Ben broke the silence. "You can't stay here, Cam," he said softly. "It's not safe anymore."

"I know," she said huskily. She stroked the cat gently, relieved that the vendetta against her had not harmed the little creature. "I didn't want to go before." She gestured around her. "This is my home. Was." She looked down at the cat. "We'll have to find a new place, won't we?"

The sound of a drone on the other side of the shutters and feet on the stairs was enough to spook the cat again. It disappeared towards the bedroom, its tail bushy with adrenaline, seeking its hiding place under the bed.

Cameron stood up and went to the door, carefully checking the credentials that were sent to her before opening it. The young police officers were patient and kind. Cameron let them take stock of the apartment. No, they hadn't moved anything other than closing the shutters and looking for cat treats. Ben confirmed that he had wrapped his hand in his shirt before touching the window controls and the kitchen cupboards. As Cameron expected, the two first responders were quickly joined by a more senior officer who knew the score. She recognised him from the previous week. Was it only eight days since

Arthur Paxton had attacked her? It seemed much longer.

"Do you have anywhere you can stay tonight?" asked the senior officer.

"With me," said Ben instantly. He gave them his address.

Cameron went to her bedroom and filled her overnight bag. She was surprised to find that her jewellery box was still intact. The motive had been a very specific robbery, then. They hadn't bothered to cover their tracks by searching for other valuables. All they wanted were Cameron's hard disks.

Bag packed, she clambered carefully up to the highest cupboard above the bed and found the cat carrier. "Can you give me a moment?" she asked the police officer.

She closed the bedroom door and opened the other packet of cat treats. This time it was harder to coax the little animal out, but eventually Cameron succeeded in trapping it and got it into the carrier. "Here," she said, pushing treats through the cracks. "Don't complain. It's for your own good."

There was a knock at the bedroom door. "Are you all set?" said Ben.

"Yes," said Cameron. "Can you take my bag?"

The police had a car ready for them. Dawn was breaking as they arrived at Ben's door. Exhausted by the shock and the disruption of the past few hours, they tumbled into bed. The cat, sensing peace, crept out of her carrier and settled between them on the duvet. All three of them slept.

The insistent ringing of two smartscreens and the doorbell finally woke Cameron and Ben.

"The police are outside," said Ben, nudging Cameron. "DI Mercer and a couple of mates."

"Tell her I'll be right there," said Cameron, yawning. She clambered out of bed and dug in the bag that Ben had brought the night before to find the cat's bowl and food. The sound of kibbles hitting the bowl drew the little animal out from the corner it had chosen to snuggle in, and Cameron watched it fondly while she found something to wear.

DI Sara Mercer, usually completely unflustered, was as close to looking stressed as Cameron had ever seen her.

"You made the right decision, coming here," said Mercer seriously. "Twice in less than ten days, Cameron. What do you think they were after?"

"Something related to my work," said Cameron. "It wasn't a conventional robbery, that's clear. They only took the computers and left anything else of value alone."

"What I don't understand is why they ransacked the apartment after taking those," said Mercer. "What else could they have been looking for?"

Cameron shrugged. "I really don't know," she said. "I took an inventory of everything that I believe is missing." She showed Mercer a list on her smartscreen.

"All drives and disks, basically," said Mercer. "And I assume that all of these were located close together?"

"That's right," said Cameron. "Why they would think I had anything in my knicker drawer is beyond me."

Ben suddenly looked serious. "Cameron," he said, "what about that file I brought back for you? Do you think they could have been looking for that?"

"No," said Cameron. "It's locked in the office vault. No one knows about it apart from us."

"And maybe, by now, Jack Sladen," said Ben.

"What file?" asked Mercer, her interest piqued.

"My undercover agent here brought me a present from Statesman Tech," said Cameron with a grin. She turned to Ben. "I didn't tell you the details, but we found some juicy things in there."

"I can sort out some extra security on the office if you like," said Mercer, "although knowing you, it's already locked down tight."

"That would be useful," said Cameron. "Whoever entered my apartment had made sure that all my security systems were disabled. It shouldn't have been possible in just a few hours."

"Unless, of course, they had some help," said Mercer. She beckoned one of her colleagues over. "Gray's Inn Road," she said. "This is the address. Make sure they don't let anyone in who shouldn't be there. And even if they should be there, don't let anyone up to the Argentum offices. Put a separate guard on the door if you need to."

She turned back to Cameron. "What about your team members?" she asked. "Do we need to secure their homes too?"

"Maybe," said Cameron, "especially Ross and Michelle. Their place will be covered already as they're at the

Olympics, but an extra layer of security can only be helpful."

Mercer nodded at her colleague. "Add them to your list," she said. "Now, Cameron, this file," she said. "Tell me about it."

Ben explained where it had come from, and Cameron picked up the story.

"We're still working through it," she said, "but it's all to do with the MetaBand designs."

"I've never trusted that network," said Mercer.

"I did before," said Cameron, "but I don't trust it now. There's no doubt that with the new MetaBand and the Diaulos project and the Sladen Foundation that Jack has done some great things to improve network access and help people who're disadvantaged. I just wish it was all straightforward and above board."

"I take it what you've found just adds to all the loose ends that we didn't manage to tie up," said Mercer.

"It's bad," said Cameron. "There are things in there that could implicate Jack Sladen in decisions that he claimed in the enquiry he never made. He seems to have agreed the design changes to the MetaBand hubs, for starters."

"Really?" said Mercer. "You're right, this file of yours could be trouble." She was silent for a moment as she worked though the implications. "You're saying that you, Ben, brought this file back from America and handed it to Cameron."

Ben nodded. "That's right," he said. "The only other

person who knows I had it, apart from the Argentum team, is Chloe."

The door opened and a police officer walked in. He bent to speak to Mercer. She listened carefully, her face impassive, then turned back to look at Ben.

"I don't think that's the case anymore," she said. "Security guards at your office building reported an unknown man trying to gain access to the building very early this morning."

"Did they get him?" asked Cameron.

"Sadly not," said Mercer. "He legged it as soon as they challenged him. We're waiting for CCTV and bodycam footage, although if your systems were compromised, I wouldn't be surprised if those were, too."

Cameron stood up and started pacing around the room. "But if someone knows that I had that file," she said, "and they didn't find it in my flat, and they can't get into the office, where else would they look?"

"Indeed," said Mercer, looking directly at Ben. "I wonder if they know who brought it here."

"But that would mean…," said Cameron.

"Exactly," said Mercer. "I don't think it's sensible for either of you to be here. I can organise a safe house, if you like?"

"Better still," said Cameron, "can you organise one of those super-secure satlinks at my brother's house? The village is the safest place I know," she said to Ben with a smile, "and Aunt Vicky is dying to see you."

•

Cameron showed Ben the drawing on her smartscreen. "What do you think?" she said.

Ben considered it from every angle. "Not bad," he said. "I think it conveys the details very well, without displaying any artistic merit whatsoever."

Cameron punched him playfully on the arm. "That's what I was going for," she said. "It's got to make sense to the recipient but bear no relation to any data sets or image recognition software."

The little cartoon strip she'd devised showed a fox creeping into an apartment and emerging with a computer, and two figures with a cat and a train and a bunch of grapes. She hoped that everyone on the team would get the references. The grapes were a little obscure, but she'd talked about the village vineyards before, and she could hardly write 'gone to Charlie's' across the page. A final panel showed a grinning face with a set of perfect teeth, one coloured blue. That would be obvious. Use Bluetooth to communicate whenever you can, it said, and by implication, avoid MetaBand.

Cameron sent the message to the whole Argentum team, including Ross and Michelle, and then packed her smartscreen away as the train approached their destination. Their departure had been too hasty for Mercer to organise cars that would disguise their route. The safest option had been to take them to Euston station where Cameron bought tickets with an anonymous wallet, and then for another police car to pick them up at the other end, avoiding a call to Charlie or an autocar booking. It also gave Mercer time to make some special arrangements.

When the police car pulled up at the house, Charlie came charging out, wondering what was going on, and stopped in confusion when he saw his little sister.

"Cam?" he said. "I expected you to come home in a squad car a few times when you were younger, but I thought you were behaving yourself these days." He spotted Ben coming around the other side of the car. "Hello, Ben, nice to see you again. Why do you have the cat with you? Family day out to the country?"

Cameron laughed, relieved to be safe. "There's a good explanation," she said. "First, though, these lovely police officers have some work to do."

Charlie shrugged, defeated. "I can't keep up with you," he said. "Get yourselves indoors. If you can install the cat in the attic, that'd be great. Roxy'll go nuts as soon as she realises it's here."

"Will do," said Cameron. "Could you show these folks where your network connection is?"

"The new MetaBand?" said Charlie. "You're not going to mess with it, are you? It's very good."

"Don't worry," said Cameron. "You're getting something better and more secure." She turned to the police technician. "Can you keep the MetaBand hub live once it's disconnected from the house? It might be useful."

Charlie looked serious now, and Cameron knew he'd

worked out some of what was going on. Without another word he led the police officers away, and Cameron and Ben went into the house.

All was quiet. The kids must be in their rooms or out and about. The attic was just as she'd left it, her domain at the top of the house. Ben closed the door to the stairwell carefully behind them and Cameron let the cat out of its basket to explore.

Ben flung himself into a soft armchair. "Well," he said, "I didn't expect this weekend to include fleeing London and camping out at your brother's."

"Nor did I," said Cameron. "I'm sorry you got caught up in this."

Ben shook his head. "It's my own fault," he said. "I poked the hornet's nest with those MetaBand designs, and I agreed to help Chloe get the files out to you. If I hadn't done any of that…"

"…we would have been stumbling in the dark," said Cameron. "I know there are cybercriminals on my tail. I think Yasmin is out there and after me too, but I'm going to find her first. You haven't stirred the nest half as much as I have. You've helped."

"I should let Chloe know that the package was delivered," said Ben. "I don't know how to do that safely."

There it was again, the knot of jealousy in her stomach. "Once we have a secure connection, I can get hold of Chloe," she said.

"Great," said Ben, brightening.

That wasn't helping. Should she broach the subject,

or leave it be? The two of them were getting on so well together that she didn't want to spoil it, but she knew that it would always be on her mind.

"Did you ever meet her daughter, Audrey?" asked Cameron. "She's friends with Tara."

Ben shook his head. "No, I didn't," he said, "but I saw plenty of photos." He looked sidelong at Cameron. "You do know we're just friends, don't you?"

"Oh!" said Cameron. "Yes, of course."

Ben stood up, walked over to her, took her face in his hands, and kissed her. "Don't worry," he said. "I've missed you, and I'm glad to be here." He smiled. "Let's nail these bastards once and for all. What do you need me to do?"

•

The police car had gone, and the network connection was back, much to the relief of the children who had come out of their bedrooms, complaining, as soon as the old one had gone off. Charlie, Sameena, Cameron and Ben settled in the quiet sitting room to watch the Olympics.

"Do I take it we now have a free and super secure connection, thanks to you?" said Charlie.

"Yes," said Cameron. "You're attached to the military grade network now. Somehow, they've tacked all your streaming services onto it. I'm not quite sure if those will always be free, though."

"And we're no longer a Diaulos network node," said Sameena. "From what you're telling us, that's safer."

Cameron grabbed a handful of crisps from the bowl on the table. "I think the Diaulos network is sound," she said, "but MetaBand isn't. I needed somewhere to work that couldn't be compromised, and to be honest it's probably safer for you too."

Ben gestured at the screen. "The 100 metre qualifiers are starting, look," he said. "This should be good." He reached over to the table and picked up his drink, settled back onto the sofa, and gave Cameron's hand a squeeze. "Relax," he said quietly. "It's been a pretty intense day."

She took his advice, forgetting for a short while about the chaotic flight from London, the rogue AI on her tail, and the work that she had to do. All her attention was on the athletes on screen and the people she loved around her. She felt the stress melting away.

Alas, it was short lived. An alarm on her smartscreen brought her back to reality.

"It's nearly time for the archery," she said. "I have to be online for this. We're pretty sure that there's an active cyberattack ready to roll but we're going to have to catch it in real time." She jumped up from the sofa, but paused when Tara's voice came from a hidden corner of the sitting room.

"Aunty Cam?" she said. Her face appeared around the back of Charlie's chair. "I'm going online too," she continued. "I promised Audrey that I'd see her in Sandland this afternoon. Do you want to meet her?"

"I'd love to," said Cameron, "but I'm not sure we're going to be in the same place."

Tara frowned. "Even if you can't come with me," she said slowly, glancing across at her mother as she spoke, "can you look out for something while you're there?"

"Sure thing," said Cameron. "What am I looking for?"

"There's this weird avatar with really bright blue eyes," said Tara. "She's creepy. She's always watching people. I don't know who she is in real life, but we've put loads of reports in about her and she never gets banned."

Cameron was careful not to let her alarm show. "You're right to report that kind of thing," she said approvingly. "Is she watching everyone? Can you block her?"

"We tried to block her, but she still appears," said Tara with a shrug. "Now we all just run away."

"Okay," said Cameron. "I'll come and meet Audrey. You get me for five minutes. Then I have to work."

Sameena looked keenly at the pair of them. She knew Cameron well enough to see that there was an undercurrent of concern, and she was ready to defuse the situation.

"It sounds like you have been doing the right things, Tara," she said. "You are very good at staying safe online. Say hello to Audrey for me. Now, would you like to take a snack with you?"

Tara grinned, grabbed an apple and a biscuit, and scampered upstairs.

Cameron gave Sameena a reassuring smile. "I'm sure it's nothing," she said. "I'll look after her. I won't be long. Watch the archery and let me know what you think."

She heard a parting chorus of "Good luck" from the

sitting room as she ran up the stairs. She opened the door to the attic carefully in case the cat was lying in wait, but there was nothing waiting to pounce. It was sleeping soundly in the warmest place, squarely in a shaft of sunlight on a comfortable chair.

Cameron switched on her computer and checked out of sheer paranoia that it was hooked up to the new network. She opened her smartscreen and found a cryptic message from Pete.

'Targeting 5pm,' it said. 'Hope you haven't been outfoxed.'

He'd seen her cartoon strip and understood it then. Good.

'I'm all set,' she replied. 'I'm on the same network as the northern office.'

If Pete was confident of the security of his own network, then they would be able to chat. A few moments later, a call lit up Cameron's smartscreen.

"I'm in the office and hooked up to the same network as you," said Pete without preamble. "A helpful policeman came by earlier."

"They get about," said Cameron. "I think we all need one."

She and Pete had planned this operation carefully after their visit to the site, but the last twenty-four hours had been so fraught that she had to review the list of actions again.

"Has Mephisto picked up on any attack vectors that could introduce malware to the hub?" asked Cameron.

"Any compromised emails, user details, that kind of thing?"

"Not so far," said Pete, "but there's bound to be something from weeks ago that opened a crack in the system's defences. You know how it goes."

Cameron knew only too well. "The one thing with this," she said thoughtfully, "is that we know the test run on the karate arena failed, and that there's a new version of the software being deployed."

"We don't know that for sure," said Pete. "How do you know your source is reliable?"

Cameron hadn't told Pete where that nugget of information had come from. Maybe now was the time. "Because it was me," she said with a sigh. "I didn't want to worry you before, but I eavesdropped on a conversation by chance in the Underworld. I recorded the whole thing and there's a backup in the office vault.

"You're right, I am worried," said Pete. "Great intel, Cameron, but you're putting yourself in danger. Remember that message? She will find you in every reality?"

"Not if I find her first," said Cameron. "Now, the data I captured from the arena hub is in our secure cloud. I think there's enough for me to make a start on analysing it."

"I see that," said Pete with a sigh. "You're not going to give up, are you?"

"No," said Cameron. "We've got a job to do. I have a live but blind MetaBand hub I can access here if I need to follow up any of the findings." What else was on her list? "Is Pavel all set to react if we see evidence of tampering?"

"Yes," said Pete. "Sandeep dropped the hardware off to them at lunchtime. They'll be able to reset the sensor connections to factory settings and divert to a different network."

"Good," said Cameron. "We need to see if there is a problem and what it is before we take any action, but at least we can fix it fast." She hoped that all their assumptions were correct. There were so many possible attack vectors, but the evidence they'd gathered pointed to disruption of skinsuit sensors to disadvantage a competitor. The malware contract Cameron had found in the Underworld talked of sensor connections. For Anita Trianna, the sensors in her motion capture skinsuit had appeared to stop transmitting. How could the result be manipulated through the suits worn by the archers? They were about to find out.

"Counting down," said Pete. "Ten minutes to go."

Cameron saw him turn away from the camera.

"Noor!" he said. "Just in time. Pull up a chair." He turned back to Cameron. "We'll keep an eye on everything here. What are you going to do?"

"I'm going back into the Underworld to watch the show," said Cameron. She was already loading the software she needed. "I want to see the reactions of people down there if there's any evidence of manipulation."

"I wish you wouldn't," said Pete, "but I understand why you're going in. Be safe. Stay on chat."

Cameron chose a new identity. Her avatar this time was more discreet, still far removed from her real self but today a stylised figure based on an old and beloved cartoon. She'd seen several of the same series in the Underworld, virtually identical characters in different colours with different hats. She would definitely blend in down there.

She put on her mask, picked up her controllers, took a deep breath, and dived into the metaverse. Her first stop was the upper level of Sandland. She pinged a message to Tara. 'Where are you?' she said.

Tara came straight back on voice chat. "Hi, Aunty Cam," she said. "We're in Pets Corner playing with the Axies."

Cameron knew exactly where that was. She jumped straight to the location and found two figures giggling together in the middle of a herd of cute multi-coloured cartoon creatures.

"Hi, girls," said Cameron. Her avatar bent down to pet an orange Axie with a turnip for a tail. It rolled over and wiggled its stumpy legs in the air.

"Is that you, Aunty Cam?" said Tara. "You don't look like you."

"I'm working," said Cameron. "Hi, Audrey. Nice to meet you. I've heard a lot about you from your mom. Does she come in here often?"

"Sometimes," said Audrey. "She's normally working, too."

Cameron watched the girls as they played, wondering

idly what work Chloe had been doing here. They needed a catchup. A handful of other avatars arrived, and Cameron listened to the happy chatter and watched how they behaved. She was confident that these were all genuine friends, probably around the same age. It was a nice social group and Tara seemed happy.

The chatter died away and some instinct made Cameron turn. There, standing on the edge of the block, was a perfectly rendered female avatar with bright blue eyes. Its gaze was focused on Tara.

"Aunty Cam," said Tara, breaking the silence. "That's her."

As soon as Tara said her name, the avatar's eyes locked onto Cameron. It stared at her for a split second, then vanished.

She had seen those blue eyes before in a rippling, fracturing hologram in a Northumberland cave.

Yasmin.

22: TARGETS

"Tara, Audrey," said Cameron, "you need to go, now. You're not safe."

"But Aunty Cam," said Tara, "she's gone."

Cameron shook her head. "She'll be back," she said. "You were right to ask me to look out for her. I think she's watching the pair of you, and I don't trust her."

In the real world, she heard Pete's voice. "They're starting," he said. "Are you all set, Cameron?"

She couldn't stay, and nor could the girls. "Come on, Tara," she said. "You did the right thing. Now, go. If you come back, you need me or Chloe with you."

"Okay," said Tara. "You'll be okay, won't you?" She sounded worried.

"I'll be fine," said Cameron. "Enjoy your snacks and I'll see you in real life in a little while."

She made sure the girls had logged out before jumping to the entrance to the Eden level. She lost no time diving down into the whirlpool. She met with the barman, picked up her bracelet, and followed her nose to the Underworld jump point. Once she'd landed, she went straight to the sports café that she had found before. It looked different today. A temporary open-air auditorium had been installed around the 3D representation of an arena and avatars of all shapes and sizes were crowded in the space. As she watched, the archers filed in and there were cheers from the crowd. The combination of 3D cameras and skinsuits was incredibly effective, thought Cameron. It felt as if she was looking at a single real arena with multiple competitors, rather than a composite of several locations around the world.

Cameron looked around for familiar faces. The monkey was nowhere in sight, which was a relief. It took her a while to spot the grey kitten lurking in a corner with a small group including another animal avatar that looked like a slim armadillo. A pangolin?

She crept closer to them, one eye on the action in the arena. She needed to be in earshot of the group, and her smartscreen was all set to record every whisper that came out of the computer audio.

Once in range, she stopped. Most of the audience was static, watching the contest, and any further movement would attract unwanted attention. This session was the seeding round, each athlete shooting six sets of twelve arrows to build an aggregate score. Cameron scanned the list of archers and identified the British athlete who featured on the tip she'd bought. She knew that up in the real world there was a very different favourite attracting bets, the American who was defending his Olympic title.

Cameron kept one eye and one ear on the group that she was observing, but they were largely silent for now, and most of her attention was drawn to the big screen. She was starting to enjoy the competition. There was a hum of excitement in the audience as the American wheeled into view. His first set put him into the lead by a whisker. A collective sigh of relief rippled around the watching avatars.

"He's not on his best form today," muttered the grey kitten. "That makes things easier."

Now it was the turn of the British archer. He settled into his pose, eyed the target and let his first arrow fly.

Cameron watched carefully. There was nothing that stood out as unusual. When the score came up, the British competitor was firmly in first place.

"Good," she heard the Pangolin say. "Very well done."

"Thank you, Pangolin," said the grey kitten, the relief in its voice palpable.

The display gave a closeup of the archer. He looked happy and a little surprised, but he was fidgeting uncomfortably, flexing his arms, rubbing each of them in turn.

"What the hell happened?" came Pete's voice in her ear.

"It's the skinsuit," said Cameron in a rush of realisation. "They used the skinsuit to control his aim. That wasn't him shooting. It was an AI delivering the result the clients wanted."

The attack was far more subtle than she could ever have expected. The malware that had been introduced into the system was not a blunt instrument but could apparently be controlled in real time. It was elegant and dangerous and hard to detect. She had a grudging admiration for the cybercriminals who had conceived and executed this malware, but that made her all the more determined to shut it down.

"That's brilliant," said Pete. "There has to be something very powerful running behind it, though."

"I could put a name to that," said Cameron grimly. "Have we got enough data to break their control link now?"

"I think so," said Pete, but Cameron wasn't listening.

A perfectly rendered female avatar had materialised in the group she was watching. It turned its bright blue eyes on her. She felt like a rabbit in the headlights. Back in Pets Corner, Tara had called her Aunty Cam. Her cover was blown.

Suddenly the view of the Underworld flicked out and Cameron realised that she had jumped against her will into an entirely new environment. She looked around. The floor was chequered, black and white. The room around her looked like a virtual warehouse with an art exhibition in progress. The artworks ranged from a classic Cryptopunk head to abstract forms. Cameron knew that she had seen one of them before, in Yasmin's deserted prison cell.

Standing in the middle of the room was the magnified form of the female avatar with the bright blue eyes. Now Cameron had no doubt who she was looking at.

"SimCavalier, I have you," said Yasmin.

"I don't think so," said Cameron. She pulled off her mask, the silicon wings tearing at her skin, and cut the network connection, abandoning her avatar to its fate.

She sat shaking at her desk, taking in the sunlight and the familiar surroundings of real life.

"Cameron?" came Pete's voice again. "Are you okay?"

"Yes," said Cameron. "It's Yasmin. She's there. She's in the middle of all this."

"Shall I get Pavel to switch connections?" asked Pete.

"I don't know if it'll make any difference," said Cameron, "but do it anyway. We have to close this down. She's not going to get away with it."

She turned her mask over in her hands, wondering what her next move would be. Her target was Yasmin, and she would not rest until the AI was destroyed.

23: NODES

Cameron was up early, tapping away at her keyboard while Ben and the cat still slept. The analysis of the network traffic data they had gathered from the arena's MetaBand link was complete. She was looking for a peak at the time that the skinsuit had been manipulated, but there was nothing to find. On the other hand, her diagnostic tool was showing a vast amount of constant additional processing. She'd have expected that if the arena had held a Diaulos node, but, as she'd thought, the arena hub was not part of that network.

It looked for all the world as if there was a second distributed network node running in the arena hub that had nothing to do with Diaulos. Cameron didn't know what it could be, but she had no doubt that it had something to do with Yasmin. She made a note to run the same tests on the live hub that had been disconnected from the house.

The MetaBand operating system needed a thorough clean. Somewhere in the latest update, rolled out all over the world, was the malware that had allowed someone, somewhere to manipulate the archers' movements through their skinsuits. Cameron hadn't been back to MIST yet with her findings. She didn't trust the group anymore, but her contract was very clear. For the sake of the Olympic metaverse security and fair competition she would have to reveal what she knew, and soon. She wondered whether her team could get a head start on tracing the malware while she laid a trap for whoever had compromised the security of MIST.

"Good morning," said a croaky voice behind her. "Is that the time?"

Ben dropped a kiss on the top of her head, and she turned, smiling. His eyes were still sleepy, and his hair tousled. "What are you working on?" he asked.

"Analysing the MetaBand data traffic," said Cameron with a sigh. "Aren't you supposed to be back to work today?"

"I called in and explained there'd been a family crisis," said Ben. "They gave me another day off and I can work remotely in any case. Do you want some coffee?"

"Yes, please," said Cameron gratefully.

While Ben went in search of breakfast, Cameron contacted her team. Pete was already on the way to the archery arena to meet Pavel and try to find a way to protect the competitors at source. Cameron called the office, and Susie was the first to respond.

"I've just got in," she said. "The security is super tight. What's going on? Can you talk?"

"We're all on the same network you had up north now," said Cameron. She gave Susie a quick rundown of the events of the last day. "Could you make a start on picking apart the MetaBand operating system? It needs updating to wipe out the sensor malware. I'm not sure how we're going to roll it out, but we'll find a way."

"Of course," said Susie. "Are you and Ben okay, Cameron? Do you know what's missing?"

"We are fine," said Cameron, "and there was a lot of mess, but I've always expected that something like this might happen. The hard disks have stopped sending their location back to the police now so I'm guessing someone started poking around and triggered the automatic bricking. They'll be useless to whoever has them, but everything was backed up and stored in the office vault."

"You sound as if you're taking this in your stride," said Susie. "The others are on their way in. Between us we'll have this done and dusted before you know it."

"Fantastic," said Cameron. "Find a way to disable that malware, however quick and dirty. I'll make sure the update gets rolled out."

"You're going to talk to Jack?" said Susie.

"I guess I'm going to have to," said Cameron. "I'm not sure when. It's the middle of the night in Austin and he might still be too cross to take my call.

She closed the link to Susie as Ben came up the stairs.

"Sameena says she's making pancakes and you need to come downstairs," said Ben.

"Oh, if I must," said Cameron. "You really know how to distract me."

"Come on, Cameron, breakfast," said Ben. "The world is not going to rack and ruin if you take half an hour out."

"Is the coffee hot?" she asked, teasing.

"Yes," said Ben. "Come on."

The kitchen was in uproar. Nina, Dilan and Tara had all started their school holidays and the pancake breakfast was Sameena's way of getting them all out of bed at a decent hour. They sat around the big dining table with a hotplate in the middle, ladling batter onto six small pancake moulds and flipping them over as they bubbled.

Cameron spooned chocolate spread onto her pancake, covered it with berries, rolled it inelegantly and ate it in two bites. "This is a brilliant idea, Sameena," she said. "I have to get one of these."

"Are you staying all week, Aunty Cam?" said Nina.

"Can I help feed your cat?" said Tara.

"Is there any coding I can do?" said Dilan.

"One at a time," said Sameena sternly.

Cameron rolled another pancake and slowly drank her coffee, keeping her nieces and nephew in suspense. She wiped a smear of chocolate spread off her lips and smiled. "Short answers," she said. "Yes, I'm staying all week, and I am sure the cat would love company, Tara. As for coding, Dilan, if you're serious, I'm sure I can find something for you to do."

•

Refreshed, reinvigorated, but worried nonetheless, Cameron took her place back at the computer. The cat weaved around her legs, purring, getting settled in its temporary home.

The welcome break had yielded a slew of messages.

Susie had checked in to say that she, Noor and Sandeep had the latest MetaBand operating system under the microscope, Joel had found some more links between Paxton and Sapphire Straits and was looking into the burglary, and they'd come back to her if and when they had news. DI Mercer wanted to talk to her. Andy had been in touch, unaware that Cameron was in the village, asking for a quote for a feature he was planning. She could deal with those later.

Of more interest was an illustrated message from Ross, the promised postcard.

"Hi, Cameron," she read. "Shell and I are having a great time here." A line drawing labelled 'the local distillery' was a very shaky representation of a data centre. "The Olympic village is buzzing after that fantastic opening ceremony. This was our favourite." The picture was of an owl in sunglasses standing next to an old-fashioned computer with big round tapes mounted on the front. "It's so hot that we need ice in our drinks." Cameron peered at the drawing from several angles before concluding that it was snow on a mountain. Really, Ross was not the best artist in the world, but if she was struggling to make head or tail of the pictures then Yasmin would have no chance. "The diving starts today. It should be spectacular. That's all our news. I've got to get back to the village to prepare for Thursday's race. Your other favourite athlete is competing then as well. She's hoping her kit isn't too tight. Enjoy the show. Ross."

Her other favourite athlete? That would be Anita

Trianna, thought Cameron, and Ross's remark about kit must mean the skinsuit. She remembered the archer rubbing his arms uncomfortably and wondered if she had felt the same sensation. It focused her mind on the plight of the athletes who were using the same suits. She had to let the Olympic defence team know and hope that they could disable the malware. The control of the suits didn't just affect the results. It might injure the athletes themselves.

First, though, what did Ross's cryptic artwork tell her? She guessed that there had been an incident at the Wrangell data centre. The owl was doing something – what? – to a server, and there was an icy mountain. That confirmed her thought about Wrangell. What about the reference to diving? Had there been an accident?

Ben came into the room and peered over her shoulder, wet from the shower with a towel around his waist. "Sanctuary," he said succinctly.

"What?" said Cameron.

"The owl with the sunglasses," said Ben. "It's someone asleep with a mask on. The Sanctuary is all the rage over in America. It's a virtual environment that keeps you asleep. It's really popular with shift workers. Haven't you tried it?"

"No," said Cameron. "I've heard of it, of course, but it's not that common here and I don't want anyone controlling my sleep patterns." She looked back at the drawings. "Oh, good grief," she said. "What if that's exactly what we're looking at here. Someone's under the control of a bad actor in their sleep, they compromise the data centre…"

"…and then fling themselves off the mountain," finished Ben. "That's grim."

"I could put a name to that bad actor," said Cameron. "Yasmin." She stared at the drawing labelled 'the local distillery'. "She's found a route into the Olympic data banks through Wrangell."

"That's a big conclusion to jump to," said Ben.

"I know," said Cameron. "I need to prove it."

"Can I help?" said Ben.

Cameron shook her head. "I don't think so," she said. "I'm going to delve into some deep dark places. There is one thing you could do, though. Can you get in touch with Chloe and make sure she knows about the avatar with the blue eyes that's been following Tara and Audrey around Sandland? Tell her it's Yasmin. She needs to make sure the girls don't go back in there until it's safe."

"Sure," said Ben with a smile. "It's still early there. I'll get dressed first." He strolled back out of the room in search of his overnight bag, and Cameron went back to her computer. It was time to visit MIST again.

Her first stop, after checking her MIST inbox, was the one-to-one message boards. She wanted to seed different colleagues with tantalising scraps of slightly inaccurate speculation and see what made it back to the Underworld.

Barker was her first target, the one she trusted least. He wasn't around but she left a note. 'I'm trying to corroborate a tip-off before taking it to the main forum,' she said. 'Have you heard anything about a data breach in the metaverse fabric?'

Admin Cat was online. "Hi, SimCavalier," she said. "Are you joining us in the group chat?"

"Thanks, Cat," said Cameron. "I'll be along in a few minutes. I've got some very detailed intelligence to share that is going to need action, and I'm just finishing off the report. There's one other thing, though. Have you heard anything about a back door into the e-sports platform? I had a tipoff, and I wanted to check with you before bringing it to the main forum."

"No, I haven't come across anything like that," replied Cat. "Let me look into it."

Cameron repeated the exercise with several more connections, suggesting the existence of a back door or a breach in different parts of the sprawling Olympic metaverse, before finally taking a deep breath and joining the main chat.

Admin Cat called for silence as soon as Cameron appeared.

"The SimCavalier has news," she said. "Over to you."

"Thanks Cat," said Cameron. "The report I'm uploading now details the attack vector that was used to disrupt the Indonesian arena during the karate competition two weeks ago and may also have manipulated the result of yesterday's first round of archery."

There was a ripple of astonishment among the small group. Cameron continued. What she had to say would answer most of the questions that were popping up in the chat.

"The archery result only impacted the seeding for the next round," said Cameron. "It didn't stop anyone from qualifying, but it will have earned a packet for the bookies. This is consistent with the karate competition experience."

She paused, knowing that what she said now would ripple straight to the source. "We are searching for malware in the MetaBand operating system."

There was uproar. Cameron watched and listened to everyone's reactions carefully. There didn't seem to be any wrong notes among the group. She could not tell who the traitor might be yet.

Barker had slid unnoticed into the discussion. "Interesting report, SimCavalier," he said. "I have a question for the whole group. How many of you are using MetaBand connections right now? Can you be sure they are secure?"

Cameron's earlier misgivings about Barker started to ease. That was a perceptive question, and it left a few people stuttering.

"No, Flora," said Barker to a group member with a rose as their avatar. "I don't think a VPN is going to help. You never know what, or who, could be watching."

On Cameron's screen a message popped up. 'We need to talk. Barker.'

Cameron took the hint. "I'll leave you all to digest the report," she said. "My team are working on the OS now and if you can contribute, you know how to reach them. Send me any questions you have."

She disconnected from the main chat and connected with Barker, who was waiting for her.

"Hello, Cameron," he said, using her real name. "I think it's time we talked properly. You know that your report is going straight to Yasmin, don't you? And how did you know about the data breach?"

Cameron was stunned. Had she hit upon a different attack by chance? She had no evidence of a data breach other than the hack on the betting platform, certainly nothing in the metaverse fabric, and she was using that idea purely as bait to catch a traitor. It looked to have succeeded.

"Who are you?" said Cameron. Her mind was racing.

"You know who I am." Barker's voice had changed. It was no longer the rolling vowels of the deep American south but gruff and very British with an Aberdonian twang.

Angus.

"She'll find you," he said. "You've slipped through the net too often. She won't rest until you and your team are no longer a threat."

"No," said Cameron. "It ends now. I will find her, and I will finish her, and you with her, Angus White."

"I'd like to see you try," said Angus.

Furious, Cameron closed the connection. She had found the traitor in the camp and all her instincts about Barker had been entirely justified. She had a second target to take down. It was time to get to work.

24: INTELLIGENCE

Cameron missed the office. She wasn't used to being the face on the wallscreen. DI Mercer had advised her to stay put while whoever had ransacked her apartment was still on the run. Cameron had suggested she start by talking to Angus White, but the man was nowhere to be found, either in the real or the virtual world. The offices of Whitford Networks were closed, and he was not at the address that he listed as his home, although neighbours had seen him there recently.

The team was working through the complex web of Noor's 3D model, mapping the connections and the attacks they knew of.

"Can you cast the model through to me?" asked Cameron. "I want to see it properly."

"Sure," said Noor.

Cameron popped her smartscreen in a cradle and watched as the model took shape in front of her in three dimensions. It wasn't the same as being able to turn it around herself, but at least she could see what she was doing.

"There's a data breach somewhere that we haven't found," she said. "That needs to go in." She watched as the model rotated.

"I don't know where to put it," said Noor. "This is getting very crowded."

"Back up a moment," said Cameron. "What's that link? When did we confirm that Chaoxiang Chen is Tenuk Chen's father?"

"I dug around my connections," said Noor casually. "It's him, alright." She spun the model away from Tenuk. "Data breach. Hmm. That's all you have?"

"Yes," said Cameron. "A data breach in the metaverse fabric. We have zero evidence other than, well, a practical confession from Angus."

"What about Wrangell?" said Joel. "That's a data centre, it's running the metaverse fabric, and if we're reading it right, someone's hacked a human there."

"And what has the hacked human done?" said Pete.

"That's the million-coin question, isn't it?" said Cameron. "I'm surprised that there's been nothing about it on MIST. Link them on the model but mark it as an educated guess for now. Sandeep, can you keep an eye on the marketplaces? See if there are any new data dumps that we can trace back."

"Sure," said Sandeep.

Cameron started writing up her findings from the arena hub analysis, occasionally glancing over at the feed from the office as her team moved like a well-oiled machine. Joel was updating the model with the last few snippets of new information about Sapphire Straits, and the webcast version spun in augmented reality in Cameron's room. Sandeep was already digging through the latest stolen data listings on the Eden marketplace. Susie had gone back to the paper file and the notes on her screen, concentrating fiercely, while Pete and Noor had their heads together dissecting the MetaBand operating system.

"Oh!" cried Noor, looking up from her screen. "Is that it?"

"I think so," said Pete. "Hey, Cameron, we've got it. We can disable that malware without disrupting the system."

"I never doubted it," said Cameron. "Gold stars all round."

"Coffee?" said Pete, glancing up at Cameron on the wallscreen. "I'd get you one too, but that's trickier to webcast."

"I'll go and get my own," said Cameron with a laugh. "You get cracking on building that patch. I have a call to make." She pulled her screen out of its projection cradle and the model disappeared from view. She picked up her coffee cup and headed downstairs to the kitchen.

Ben was leaning against the counter, sipping his own coffee and chatting to a colleague but ended the call when he saw her. "How's it going?" he asked.

"Great," said Cameron, putting the coffee machine back on. "I want to be back in the office. I miss the buzz of being there when we crack the code. It's not the same being up there on the wallscreen."

"I take it a code has been cracked?" said Ben, taking her mug and rinsing it in the sink.

"It has," said Cameron. "They'll have a patch ready to go into the MetaBand operating system by the end of the day. The challenge is getting it in there."

"Ah," said Ben. "I can see where this is going."

Cameron watched her mug slowly filling with coffee. "I need to talk to Jack," she said. "I can't go back to the MIST platform. Angus was hiding in plain sight. Who else is tracking what we do there?"

"Fair point," said Ben. "But can you trust Jack after reading that file? His fingerprints are all over the changes to the MetaBand designs and who knows what else."

"I don't know," said Cameron. She stirred her coffee thoughtfully. "I'd like to think I can. If he'll actually speak to me, that is. I have a few hours to think about the alternatives. It's what, half past four in the morning there?"

"Yes," said Ben. "Six hours behind." His smartscreen pinged. He looked at it and grimaced. "Dammit," he said. "I'd better get back to work."

"Me too," said Cameron. She picked up her mug and followed Ben out of the kitchen. Her own smartscreen rang and she fumbled for it in her pocket, trying not to spill the coffee. It took a moment to unroll it and check the caller ID, and what she saw stopped her in her tracks.

It was Jack. He must have read her mind.

"Hello," said Cameron cautiously, putting her coffee down on a handy table.

There was a moment of silence on the other end of the line, then Jack spoke.

"Hello, Cameron," he said. "I'm sorry to bother you. I need to ask you something. A few months ago, I caught one of my employees skulking around the office and they claimed to be working with an international cybersecurity syndicate. They said their handler was the SimCavalier. That's you, isn't it?"

Cameron sat down on the nearest chair. "Yes," she said. There was no point denying it.

"So, do you have a spy in my office?" said Jack.

"Chloe," said Cameron. She figured that honesty was the best policy right now, and she hoped that Jack was on a secure connection.

Jack exhaled loudly. "Okay," he said. "That's all I wanted to know. Please give my regards to your Aunt Vicky. I may drop in and see her some time."

The line went dead. Cameron kicked herself for not being fast enough with her own questions. She tried to call him back, but he didn't pick up.

•

Jack stared out of the window of his plush apartment over the darkness of downtown Austin. In the distance, a moontower shone, illuminating the streets around it. Now he knew who he could trust, and it changed everything.

"Zara," he said.

"Yes, Jack," came the familiar voice of his virtual assistant.

He hesitated. Some long-buried instinct nagged at him. Zara was always there when he called. She was always listening for her name, the trigger word to which she responded. Did that mean she heard everything that happened in his immediate vicinity? Jack shuddered at the thought. It had never occurred to him that even in his most intimate moments she might have been lurking in the ether, listening. If he hadn't been paranoid before, he certainly was now.

"Nothing, Zara," he said, yawning dramatically. "I couldn't sleep. Tell me about the moontowers again."

Zara started to narrate the tale of the moontowers that shone over Austin, keeping the residents safe before streetlights were common, and preserved by the city. As she talked, Jack quietly packed a bag, then did something he had never considered before. He cut his link to her.

Truly alone for the first time in years, he left the apartment. An empty night bus took him to the airport, and he paid from his own pocket for a flight to London.

•

Cameron sat on a deckchair next to the old MetaBand hub, watching the output from the diagnostic tools on her smartscreen. It was cool in the shade and periodically she left the tool to collect its precious data and went around the corner of the house to bask in the sunshine. After a while, Ben joined her and they sat in companionable silence on the grass, listening to the distant bleating of sheep and the nearby hum of the two hubs.

"Is it working?" he said at last, stretching.

"Yes," said Cameron. "There's a lot of data moving around, a lot of CPU activity."

"How can you tell what it is?" asked Ben.

"I can't yet," said Cameron. "I'm going to have to take it apart and see what's in there." She lay back in the sunshine and closed her eyes. "Five minutes."

In less than that time she had dozed off and woke disoriented twenty minutes later to the sound of an alert on her smartscreen. Ben was lying beside her, leaning on his elbow and watching her sleep.

"I'd better get that," she muttered.

"I didn't even hear it," said Ben. He jumped up to retrieve the screen.

"I'll do it," said Cameron. "It needs to be disconnected properly." The call alert stopped, but Cameron could see that it had been DI Mercer. She carefully extracted the screen from the MetaBand hub interface and returned the call.

"Sorry," she said. "I was running some tests and I couldn't answer straight away."

"Don't worry," said Mercer. "I thought you'd like to know we identified your burglar. The office security guard's bodycam gave us what we needed, although he was heavily disguised, and we've since confirmed that the same person appeared on CCTV footage in the streets near your apartment and the office."

"Who was it?" asked Cameron, moving her deckchair into the sun and sitting down.

"Angus White," said Mercer grimly. "You were right about him all along."

Cameron sat up sharply. "In person?" she said. "It's not his style to be breaking and entering."

"I'm afraid so," said Mercer. "Maybe the stakes finally got too high. He's gone to ground. We know where he was when he tried to access your hard disks, though. We found one of the bricked drives in a trash can up in north London."

Ben was listening. He raised an eyebrow at Cameron. "Ross and Michelle live up north," he said. "It wasn't anywhere near them, was it?"

On the screen, Mercer looked startled. "Not close," she said, "but we'll bear that in mind. In the meantime, I'm going to arrange with my American colleagues to bring Jack Sladen in for questioning."

"I'm not sure that's the right angle," said Cameron slowly. "I had a call from Jack earlier. I have a feeling that he's finally worked out who he can trust, and from what we've uncovered, someone might be out to frame him."

"I'd need evidence," said Mercer. "I know your gut feelings are excellent but that's not the way policing works, Cameron."

Cameron kicked at a tuft of grass, thinking. "Give me some time to work on that," she said. "And there's someone you really should talk to."

"Who's that?" said Mercer.

"Ella," replied Cameron. "I think you'll find she's on our side."

•

Cameron spent the next hour carefully disconnecting the MetaBand hub from its uplink and removing the all-weather casing that protected it. Ben, at a loose end, was laughing over the specifications. After all, he'd been involved in the engineering work to produce them.

"See this reference?" he said, pointing to an embossed set of numbers and letters. "That's the standard that defines everything this casing has to be resistant to. Would you believe it has to be curry-proof?"

"Really?" said Cameron, momentarily distracted from her delicate task. "They think of everything."

"It's because they never know what's going to be chucked at the corner where the hub's fitted," said Ben. "That's why the seals are so tight."

"You're telling me," said Cameron, struggling to prise a grommet out of a cable connection port.

"Give that here," said Ben. With an expert flick of the wrist, he removed the rubber seal. "You want all the hardware out, is that right?"

"Yes," said Cameron, giving in gracefully. "Be gentle."

It took Ben a matter of minutes to strip the rest of the protection away, and he presented her with the bare bones of the MetaBand hub. "There you go," he said. "What's next?"

"Time to find out what's actually going on in here," said Cameron.

She carried the precious cargo back into the house and up to her attic. Once there, she set up an old computer to act as her sandbox, carefully plugged the hub into it, and set about mirroring the contents of the disk. She wanted to keep the original pristine for future forensics.

Gradually the structure of the hub revealed itself. The disk was partitioned as she'd expected, holding a full Diaulos node in one section while any network communications went through the standard firewalls that protected users. But there was a third partition, hidden away, that held something else entirely. Cameron started to probe the mirrored disk gently, teasing out its secrets. The programs that were running here were disturbingly familiar. She recognised deep learning routines, the building blocks of a neural network.

She was looking at a fragment of Yasmin's mind.

•

Tenuk joined his father for tea in the old man's office. Chaoxiang was in an excellent mood, and graphs and tables on the wallscreen showed upward trends and green lights.

"I should congratulate you, Tenuk," said Chaoxiang. "The contract that your Steamyard completed has delivered its first bounty. I am minded to pay your team a bonus."

"Thank you, father," said Tenuk. "The profits were substantial, I take it?"

Chaoxiang sipped his tea and looked out at a troop of macaques swinging through the trees in the garden, foraging for supper. "Yes," he said. "There was significant betting activity, helped by the tight competition between their favourite and ours. We also succeeded in reaping rewards from the users of several online platforms that have not seen fit to join our group yet."

"The house always wins," said Tenuk.

The man was ruthless. Tenuk wondered for a moment if he had made the right decision, but really, he was more like his father than he cared to admit. After all, he had himself sent Angus after the SimCavalier without a moment's hesitation, a ruthless response to a threat. He wondered if the rogue file had been found. The worst-case scenario was that Jack Sladen would be compromised and Yasmin found. On reflection, he no longer really needed Sladen to secure his future, and he had Xanthe and perhaps Zara to work with. It was becoming less of a concern by the hour.

Tenuk sipped his tea and relaxed into his chair. He was getting used to this new life.

"When will you next deploy the sensor controls?" he asked.

Chaoxiang consulted a schedule on the nearest wallscreen. "We have an e-sports event running now," he said. "There's a useful back door into part of the metaverse fabric that Yasmin can enter to take charge of play. After that, there is sport climbing."

"What are the sensors delivering for that?" asked Tenuk.

"We control the climbers," said Chaoxiang. "We can restrict or extend their reach at any time.".

The campaign was beautifully designed, thought Tenuk. The focus was on qualifiers and on tightly contested pairs where the result didn't materially affect future rounds, reducing the chance of an appeal, and the betting was fierce.

"Timing is everything, of course," continued Chaoxiang. "We can only rely on the sensor control being available to us for a short period. I understand that the security community is right on our heels, and I will not be surprised if they succeed in neutralising the malware within a matter of days or even hours."

"Do you think so?" said Tenuk. He rarely considered what happened to the Underworld contracts that his team fulfilled. They supplied the malware and the grateful client paid. Only a handful of long-term jobs took more strategic thinking on his part, like the work he had done with Yasmin and MetaBand.

Chaoxiang laughed. "Sometimes you demonstrate astonishing naivety, my son," he said gently. "This is a game. Today we are winning. Tomorrow will be different. And so it will continue." He finished his tea and set the cup down on the table. "Come. There is nothing more to do tonight. We should eat."

Tenuk followed his father out of the office, taking one last look back at the healthy graphs and rapidly streaming data that climbed the walls. He was in the presence of a master, and he had a lot to learn.

•

Jack stood in the courtyard of Cameron's apartment building, waiting for an answer from her entry system. The call kept ringing out. Jack looked at his watch. She might still be in the office. He turned to leave and almost walked into the young man with the turban who was standing right behind him.

"Can I help you?" said the man.

"I'm trying to find Cameron Silvera," said Jack. "Is she a neighbour?"

"Yes," said the man cautiously. "She's not in right now. Can I leave her a message?"

"Sure, if you see her," said Jack, brightening. "Please tell her Jack called by."

"Will do," said the man.

Jack started to walk away then paused. "Only tell her if you see her," he said. "Don't put anything online."

The young man nodded. "I get it," he said. He looked Jack directly in the eyes. "I understand completely."

Next stop was her office. Jack took an autocar over the river and pulled up outside a great glass building towards the southern end of Gray's Inn Road. He recognised it at once. He hadn't ever visited Argentum Associates, but he'd been to the News Channel studios in the basement plenty of times. How strange that all the times he'd wondered how to get in touch with Cameron over the years, she'd probably been working quietly upstairs.

The big screen in the atrium café was showing the climbing competition from the Olympics. Jack watched for a minute or two and then went to the reception desk. "I'm visiting Argentum Associates," he said.

"Are they expecting you?" replied the welcome 'bot.

"No," said Jack.

"One moment," said the 'bot.

A security guard ambled towards him. "Visitor for Argentum?" he said. "Can I help you?"

"Uh, yes," said Jack. "I'm an old friend of Cameron's. I was just in the area…"

"ID, please," said the guard.

Jack presented his chip for scanning.

"Do you have any other documents?" asked the guard.

"Sure," said Jack, surprised. He dug his passport out of his overnight bag. "Here," he said. "I flew in this morning."

"That all seems to be in order, Mr Sladen," said the guard without a hint of recognition. "Wait here."

Jack gave the security guard a half smile and a shrug and sat down where he'd been told. He automatically pulled out his smartscreen to check his messages, then stopped. Cameron was obviously being protected by some heavy security. He didn't know why, but he was starting to understand that there was something very wrong.

"You can go up," said the security guard at last. "Sixth floor, turn left."

Jack emerged from the lift onto the walkway that ran around the edge of the great light well in the centre of the building. Sure enough, to the left he spotted a door marked with interlinked As. Argentum Associates. As

Jack approached, the door opened. Silhouetted against the light was a slim woman with long dark hair.

"Jack Sladen," said Susie. "You've got a nerve."

"Is Cameron there?" said Jack anxiously. "I need to talk to her."

"She isn't," said Susie. She wasn't budging.

Jack took a leap of faith. "In that case, I guess she's in the village," he said. "I promised her I'd go and visit Aunt Vicky. Maybe I'd better do that now."

He started to walk back towards the lift.

"Wait," said Susie. She pointed at a comfortable chair in a little breakout area on the landing. "I'll be back." She turned away and closed the door.

He was starting to get nervous when at last the Argentum office door opened again and Susie and Joel came out.

"One question," said Joel. "That virtual assistant of yours."

"Deactivated," said Jack. He showed Joel the control panel on his smartscreen, relieved that he'd worked it out.

"Okay," said Joel. "Come in. Cameron's ready for you now."

The office had evidently been tidied in a hurry. There was nothing on any of the desks and all the screens were off, apart from a large wallscreen.

"Have a seat," said Joel, indicating a sofa square in front of the camera. "Can I get you a coffee?"

"Yes, please," said Jack, completely disoriented.

The wallscreen lit up, and there was Cameron, frowning at him.

"Hello, Jack," she said. "Don't worry, we're all on secure connections. We can talk freely. I understand you've been to my apartment already?"

"News travels fast," said Jack. "Thanks," he added as Joel handed him a mug.

"You've been looking for me," said Cameron, "and I need to talk to you. Why don't you start?"

The office was silent. Everyone's attention was on him. Jack hadn't felt like this since he sat his final exams. He took a deep breath.

"I believe you've been right all along," he said. "I think there's been something going on with MetaBand. I don't know if I can trust Tenuk. I don't know if I can trust Zara. I think I can trust you."

Cameron just looked at him.

"And… I'm sorry," he added. "I mean that." He looked up at the screen. "What do you need from me?"

"Thank you for that, Jack," said Cameron. "My turn, I guess. Yasmin is alive and well and distributed across the MetaBand network. I need your help to take her down."

Jack's mouth fell open and he gaped at the screen.

"What?" he said. He tipped his coffee mug, spilling the hot liquid over his lap. "Ow! Dammit. You're kidding. No, you wouldn't joke about this." He put the half empty mug down on the floor. "Shit."

"Exactly," said Cameron. "Let me tell you what we're going to do."

25: HUNTER, HUNTED

Ben opened the attic door cautiously. The cat lay in wait, hindquarters twitching. He scooped it up before it could pounce, climbed the stairs and deposited it on the nearest chair. He knocked softly at the inner door. "Cameron?" he whispered as he pushed it open a crack.

She was concentrating fiercely with her headphones on. "No," she said to an unseen colleague. "That won't work. We can't compromise the Diaulos ledger." She had been scribbling with paper and pen, sketching out a complex mind map to help her visualise the path of the virus they were building. She put the pen down and sighed. "Pete, give me something here. What's Noor got?"

As she listened, she glanced up at Ben and gave him a tired smile.

"Time for supper," he whispered.

She nodded. "Folks, let's take a break," she said. "We have the packages tested and ready to be delivered, which is fantastic work. Get some rest and I'm sure we'll be able to crack the final puzzle with fresh eyes."

She pulled off her headphones. "Almost there," she said. "I'm going to have a shower and clear my head. I'll be down in ten minutes."

It was more like twenty, but Cameron felt human again. Everyone was outside enjoying the warm summer evening. Charlie presided over the barbecue, sausages and meat sizzling. Cameron sat down next to Ben at the big outdoor table and accepted a glass of wine. She grabbed a sausage from the big plate in the centre of the table and took a bite.

"Ow! Hot," she said.

"How's it going?" asked Sameena, handing her a plate and cutlery.

"Pretty good," said Cameron. "The operating system update is ready to roll out and Jack's made it look like a legitimate upgrade for all the Sladen Group technicians. That'll deal with the malware we traced."

"And the other little matter?" said Charlie.

"Ah, Yasmin," said Cameron, blowing on the sausage and taking another cautious bite. "The easy bit was working out how to scramble the neural network in each hub as well as closing down the partition using the new operating system update. Even if the connections open up again, her processors will be all over the place."

"That sounds cruel," said Sameena.

"She's not human," said Cameron. "There's no emotion there, no sense of self at all. Just data and software. All we're doing is changing the way she – it – interprets data, switching all the labels around, if you like."

"What you're saying is that she'll still exist in some form, but she won't be a threat," said Charlie. "Not bad for two days' work, Cam. Here, have another sausage. There's some chicken coming too."

Cameron loaded her plate with salad and meat. She hadn't realised how hungry she was. "The Generative Adversarial Network was the easy bit," she said between mouthfuls. "The hard bit is trying not to break the rest of the network. I can't work out how to close down her partition and keep the rest running smoothly, especially when not all hubs have Yasmin in them."

"That's a tough one," said Ben. "I imagine the International Olympic Committee would be upset if you broke all the feeds into their metaverse."

"Exactly," said Cameron gloomily.

Dilan reached over to the plate full of sausages. "Aunty Cam," he said, "Don't you just need to tell the bits that have to stay open to ignore what you're sending? You know, like Sort and Sorted. One changes the original list sequence, the other one just displays it how you want it without changing anything."

Cameron stared at him. "You might have something there," she said slowly.

She started to get up from her chair, but Ben gently put a hand on her shoulder. "It can wait for half an hour," he said. "Finish your plate. I think there's pudding, too."

"You're right," she said. "I need the break. I think we have a long night ahead of us." She sipped thoughtfully at her drink. The solution was starting to take shape in her head, and the endgame was approaching.

•

Ross seriously considered trying the Sanctuary sleep aid but knew that a change to his routine on the eve of competition would be a terrible idea. He had never been so nervous before a race in his life. He knew he was ready, but the occasion was getting to him. Michelle was tucked away in her hotel, and he was alone in his capsule bedroom in the athlete's village. To try and wind down he took one more walk down to the Team GB breakout room before lights out.

He was pleased to find company there, including a teammate who had competed today. They chatted quietly over a bottle of fruit juice and Ross felt his nerves settling.

"Did you see the message boards?" asked his friend, pointing at a plaque on the wall.

"No," said Ross, puzzled. He'd never noticed it before. He went over to examine it and was delighted to find it was an old-school display of messages of support from family and friends. He scrolled through looking for his name and found notes from Joel and Martha, Susie, Pete, Noor, Sandeep, Cameron and Ben as well as neighbours from back in north London and the team at the News Channel. 'Good luck, mate. We're all rooting for you – Andy.'

Grinning, Ross felt the tension rolling away. He wasn't on his own. All of his friends had his back. Finally relaxed enough to be tired, he thanked his teammate and made his way back to his bedroom where he fell into a dreamless sleep with no assistance at all.

The next morning, the nerves were back but bearable.

He tried as hard as he could to eat breakfast, gathered his things, and made his way onto the shuttle bus that would take the competitors to the start of the event. He'd checked his bike a dozen times and it was loaded ready to go, with all the spares for the support team. His intelligent skinsuit, designed to adapt to each leg of the triathlon and protect him from the cold water and wind chill, was connected to the Metaverse fabric for the VR broadcast. He pulled at the collar, trying to relieve an itch. It was time to focus, and he didn't need any distractions.

•

Cameron whooped with glee. "It's working," she cried, standing up at her desk. The workaround that Dilan had inspired was doing its job. The team in the Argentum office had a line of MetaBand hubs on test and as the operating system update rolled out, followed by the package containing the GAN virus, each one continued to process the Diaulos blockchain and uplinks, and closed down Yasmin's partition. Cameron watched on her screen as the green lights remained on the systems they had to preserve and winked out one by one on the distributed intelligence.

"Bloody brilliant," said Pete. "We were looking all along at what to build into the virus, when all we needed was a tweak to the operating system to prevent the other two things accepting that package."

There was one final test to do, and Cameron had volunteered her village as the guinea pig. They would update the operating system of every hub on this branch of the MetaBand network, then roll out the virus.

"I'm going up to Aunt Vicky's to track the progress of the rollout," said Cameron. "You won't be able to contact me while I'm out of range of the secure network. Are you ready to go?"

"Yes, my technicians are ready," said Jack's voice. "How long do you need?"

"Five minutes," said Cameron. "I'm leaving now."

She pulled on her shoes, scampered down the attic stairs and then down another flight to the hall.

"It's starting?" said Ben, sticking his head around the dining room door.

"Yes," said Cameron. "I'm on my way to Aunt Vicky's now. Can't stop."

She ran around the corner and up the hill and arrived at her aunt's house two minutes later. She checked the countdown on her screen. Ninety seconds left. She settled down next to the MetaBand hub on the outside wall and opened the diagnostics on her smartscreen.

Donald the cat emerged from the undergrowth and miaowed at her, wondering why she was in the middle of his territory. She reached out a hand and he sniffed it in an unusually friendly gesture before stalking off in search of a dog to worry. He was turning into a softy in his old age, she thought.

Ten seconds. The processing rate was high but steady. As the time counted down, Cameron realised she was holding her breath.

There. The first stage, the operating system update, was starting. Cameron knew what she was looking at now when she checked the readouts from the diagnostics. It took almost a minute and a rapid soft reboot, and then the activity settled. Next came the special package for Yasmin.

There was a flurry of activity while it installed, then the processing volume on the hub halved. Cameron stared at the diagnostic tool. "Aunt Vicky," she yelled, "can you check your connection?"

Primed and ready, Aunt Vicky went through the steps that Cameron had taught her. "It's all running well, dear," she called back through an open window. Cameron breathed a sigh of relief. "I've just claimed some Diaulos as well," she continued, "and my wallet balance has updated."

That was less significant, thought Cameron, as any node would process the transaction, but if the MetaBand links were sound then the Diaulos network should also be intact.

"Thanks, Aunt Vicky," she called back. "I'll see you later."

"I'm coming round to watch Ross race," said Aunt Vicky.

"Great, see you shortly," called Cameron. She was already halfway down the street, returning to the sanctuary of Charlie's house and the secure network.

•

Michelle was dressed and ready for the shuttle pickup to go and support Ross in his race. As she fastened her sensor belt around her waist, the kit that allowed her to 'see' her surroundings, a sudden noise in her hotel room made her jump. The door that she had locked so carefully the night before had opened and closed.

"Who's there?" she said. She turned towards the noise and realised that she could sense nothing from the kit. It was completely dead.

There was no reply, but she heard breathing and the cold sound of steel. Adrenaline surged through her body, and she leapt from her seat and ran in what she thought was the direction of her door. She caromed off the edge of the bed and a glancing blow from the invisible knife caught her arm. She kept going. She had no choice. Her hands brushed against the intruder, and she felt an odd fabric. It reminded her of something, but she didn't have time to think. She found the door, fumbled with the handle, tore it open, and tried to remember the layout of the corridors.

She was going deeper into the hotel and lost her way completely. She also lost her pursuer. Shaking, she waited as long as she dared, then felt her way along the nearest wall until she could feel an embossed sign. Steadying her breathing, she crept slowly to reception.

"Can I help you?" came a voice she vaguely recognised, one of the receptionists. "Are you okay?"

"I'm fine," said Michelle, folding her arms and hoping that the spot where the knife had grazed her wasn't visible.

"I'm supposed to be at the triathlon. My boyfriend's competing but I slept through my alarm. Has the shuttle been yet?"

"It left about ten minutes ago," said the receptionist. "I can order an autocar for you. That should get to the event on time."

"Thank you," said Michelle. The cab arrived in barely a minute.

As she clambered in, clutching her arm, she heard a commotion in the hotel lobby behind her. "Security," shouted a panicked voice. "He's got a knife."

She slammed the cab door and the little autocar pulled out into the traffic. They could deal with her attacker, whoever he was. She had to get to Ross.

•

"I guess we're ready to go," said Cameron. She was back at her desk. Celebrations of their successful test had been brief. They had a very short window of opportunity before the day's competitions began. If they delayed any further, they would have to wait another eighteen hours to deploy the software.

"No time like the present," said Jack. "My technicians are reporting that both MetaBand and Diaulos are sailing along without any problems in the test area. They're ready to go on the full deployment."

Hit it," said Cameron.

They watched their screens in silence, hardly daring to

breathe. A percentage figure appeared in a box in one corner showing the updates remaining. 99%. 98%. Time seemed to stand still.

"There's a problem," said Pete, dampening the mood.

"Damn, what now?" asked Cameron.

Pete shared his screen with her. Cameron looked at the detailed data on one monitor and Pete's worried face on the other. "The package deployment is pretty slow," he said. "It's entirely possible that Yasmin will detect the nodes shutting down and try to disrupt the rollout."

"Do you think she'd have time?" said Cameron.

"I think so," said Pete. "She'll be constantly checking the network state, and if the node responses start falling, she'll know something's up."

"Byzantine Fault Tolerance," said Cameron thoughtfully. Where are we now? 95%? It's going to take a good half hour at this rate. I wonder if there's a way to distract her while it's deploying?" A crazy plan was forming in her head. She picked up her reality mask and turned it over in her hands. Maybe, just maybe, she could intervene.

"Cameron?" said Pete. "I know that distracted look. What are you planning?"

"Roll it out now," said Cameron. "I'm going to turn the tables. Wherever she runs, I will find her. In every reality, I will be waiting for her. The hunter, hunted."

"That's not safe," said Pete.

"I know," said Cameron, "but I don't see that I have any choice. I'm going in. Keep me updated on the rollout so I know how close we are to taking her down completely."

•

Ross checked the time. The competitors' shuttle bus would be leaving for the start line soon and there was still no sign of Michelle. He tried to call her again, but she didn't answer. He got up from his seat and walked down the narrow aisle to the front where the GB team coach was sitting.

"Coach," he said, "I'm worried about Shell."

"I'm sure I saw her a few minutes ago," he replied. "Let me find out where she is." He climbed down out of the shuttle and jogged off towards the family stand. Ross saw him speaking to a marshal, who pointed out a low building on the other side of the finish area. The coach came jogging back.

"She's checked in," he said. "We think she's in the restrooms."

"I'll go and find her," said Ross.

The coach held out a warning hand. "Not now, son," he said. "You're all suited up. You can't leave the shuttle."

Frustrated, Ross stared out of the window at the low building, willing Shell to come out. "You're saying if I go and get my girlfriend I miss my start," he said.

"Them's the rules," said the coach. "I'll send someone in." He leaned out of the door to call to the marshals, but at that moment Michelle emerged from the restrooms, stumbling and veering around as she tried to navigate towards the shuttle.

"Help her!" cried Ross as Michelle tripped and sprawled

on the ground. "She can't see." He stood, helpless, as the team coach rushed towards her.

•

In her attic bedroom, Cameron briefed Ben quickly on her plans. "I might need help," she said. "I don't know what kind of tricks she could pull. That's if I find her, of course."

She opened up the portal to the virtual world and signed in using the avatar that she had abandoned a few days before. If her theory was correct, it should be exactly where she'd left it. She put on her reality mask, looped the controllers over her wrist, and set the mask to full opacity. The slightly tattered silicon wings extended as the lenses clouded, and in moments she was immersed in a three-dimensional environment.

As soon as she saw the black and white chequered floor, she knew that her plan had worked. Her avatar had been standing there immobile since she left. Now it ran across the floor. "Yasmin," she shouted. "Where are you? I'm here. I'm going to take you down."

"85%," came Pete's voice. "Stand by."

She spun around the room, testing all the boundaries, running into the artworks and bouncing off them. An abstract coil began to whirl in the middle of the space, her avatar's momentum putting it into motion, but Yasmin did not come.

•

Tenuk had left his father preparing for the fifth day of competition and retreated to his own office. Chaoxiang's assurances that the infosec community was right on their tail made him uneasy. He had heard nothing from Angus, and he sorely needed an update, but the man was nowhere to be found. The file that he pretended mattered less than it did, was still missing. Jack was apparently on special leave, some family matter, and even Zara couldn't contact him. Other spies in the cybersecurity world reported that the SimCavalier had vanished. She had gone to ground, and that worried him.

A routine system alert attracted his attention. A global MetaBand update was starting. Surprised, Tenuk logged on to the Statesman Tech systems. Events were due to start within the hour and under their service level agreement with the International Olympic Committee, this was at the very edge of the window they had to deploy updates before live competition.

He checked the schedule of work. There was nothing due to be done today. He felt a growing sense of unease.

Tenuk went back to the old man's office. "There's an unscheduled MetaBand update pushing out to all the hubs," he said.

"Ah, the time has come," said Chaoxiang regretfully.

"You were expecting this?" said Tenuk.

"Of course," said Chaoxiang. "I'm surprised it took

them so long. That's a testament to the quality of the Steamyard's work, my boy."

"We can re-deploy the malware if it's removed in this update," said Tenuk.

"No," said Chaoxiang. "You must learn to quit while you're ahead. We made an excellent return on our investment, and the campaign is now over. Was there anything else?"

"No, father," said Tenuk. He took the hint and went back to his own office again, pausing to collect a fresh cup of iced cucumber water on the way. Once back at his desk, he checked the integrity of the Diaulos network. All was well so far.

What about Yasmin? Tenuk opened a different control panel and scanned her system state, just to be sure. Again, everything seemed to be running normally. If this update succeeded in removing the malware they relied upon to control the skinsuits, she would not be able to execute any of the fixes they'd planned for today. It was a shame, thought Tenuk. He'd put in a special request for the triathlon, just to annoy Argentum Associates. Perhaps Yasmin could find some more creative ways to make that event particularly trying.

•

"75%," came Pete's voice again.

Surely Yasmin would have noticed the drain on her processors by now, the reduction in network confirmations.

Cameron was beginning to wonder if a simple incursion into the monster's lair was enough.

"Yasmin!" she shouted. There was no response.

"We need to try another tack, Pete," she said. "I think she's busy with Olympic business. Get onto MIST on my behalf" – she pinged him a delegation code – "and try and work out where she might be. Get the others looking for likely disruption and frustrate her on the ground."

"Okay," said Pete, "we're on it."

•

In a sea of green lights, one had flicked to amber. Tenuk noticed there was a higher proportion than usual of inactive nodes in Yasmin's distributed network. 70% was a far lower level of network responses than he would expect. Maybe the soft reboot of the operating system was skewing the real time reporting.

The numbers continued to fall steadily. It was down to 65% now. What could he do?

"Xanthe," he called. He didn't hear her come in, but suddenly she was by his side. "I'm concerned about Yasmin's current state. Do you have a way to connect with her?"

"Yes, Tenuk," said Xanthe smoothly. "Leave it with me." She disappeared again, silent as a ghost.

•

Ross started towards the shuttle door, ignoring the alerts that sounded as he got close to the edge of the competitor zone, but was brought up short by a sudden tightness in his limbs. His legs buckled beneath him, and he clutched at his collar. "Skinsuit," he gasped. "Squeezing."

"Medic and technician, here, now," bellowed the team coach.

Ross writhed in pain as the skinsuit continued to constrict his limbs and his chest. "Get it off me," he pleaded.

"We've got to wait for the adjudicator," said the team coach helplessly. "If you take it off or it's disconnected, you'll be disqualified."

"If we don't get it off, he'll die," said the medic. He'd finally found a blade that would actually cut the resilient skinsuit material. He made a careful incision, cutting as deep as he dared to try and relieve the pressure on Ross's neck.

The technician came running back to the bus. "I've tried to disconnect the feed," she said frantically. "It's locked. I can't break the link. I don't know what's happening."

"Hack," choked Ross. He was starting to lose consciousness. He stared up at the blue sky and all he could see was drones.

•

Pete's voice sounded in her ear. "Cameron," he said, "We're at 55%. There's some breaking news from Reykjavik, a delay to the triathlon due to an incident."

"I hope Ross and Shell are okay," said Cameron, "but with Yasmin on the loose..."

"There's drone footage coming in," said Pete. "Oh, good grief, there's an ambulance. And that looks like Shell on the ground. I can't see Ross."

"We keep going," said Cameron. "It's their only chance."

26: COUNTDOWN

Angus sat alone in a dark corner booth of a busy North London pub. The wallscreens were showing the public feed from the Olympics, and all eyes were on a developing situation at the triathlon. The news drones were jostling for the best angle, the feed flicking from one to the other. A dark-haired figure was sitting on the ground being attended to by a medic. There was a crowd around the door of the competitors' shuttle that would take them to the start of the race.

Angus caught a glimpse of someone lying on the floor and a shock of ginger hair in the middle of all the frantic activity. He choked on his pint, put the glass down, and hurried out of the pub.

In a quiet corner of the small beer garden, he pulled out his smartscreen and made a call. The man he needed answered immediately.

"Pangolin," growled Angus.

"Angus," said Tenuk. "You owe me an explanation. Where is that file?"

"Bugger that," said Angus. "I couldn't find it, all her drives are useless, and the police are on my tail. Now, what the hell is Yasmin doing?"

"Yasmin?" said Tenuk eagerly. "You know where she is?"

"No idea," said Angus, "but she's mucking up the triathlon. You'd better find her and call her off."

"I don't know what you're playing at, Angus," said Tenuk, thoroughly confused. "First you fail to get that file, and now you want me to interfere in an ongoing operation?"

"I've put myself out on a limb for you," said Angus. "Now call her off. She's going to kill that kid. If anything happens to him, I'll spill every secret I have." He stabbed at the off button in frustration and went back into the pub.

•

Through a haze, Ross saw an official autocar screech to a halt next to the shuttle. A tall blonde woman jumped out. She took one look at him and turned to a drone that hovered behind her. "Medical emergency, no penalty," she said clearly. Her voice print served as the signature.

The medic had succeeded in cutting enough material to get a grip on the skinsuit, and he tore the suit bodily from Ross's limp frame. "Take it easy," he said, massaging life back into Ross's arms and legs. He started to cough and retch, gulping at the fresh air.

"You said this was a hack," said the technician, reaching out a hand to help Ross to sit. "What did you mean?"

"Long story," croaked Ross. "Ask me after the race."

The adjudicator came up the steps. "I'm very sorry

that this happened," she said. "Your place in the final is assured, and I hope that you will be fit to compete. We've delayed the start to give you as much time as possible to recover."

"Thank you," croaked Ross. He pulled himself slowly upright. "I'm going to see Shell now." He climbed down to ground level, getting stronger with every step, and as soon as he reached her, he hugged her as if he was never going to let go.

•

Tenuk stared at his smartscreen, completely blindsided. Why was this so important to Angus? There were more secrets in that man's past than he thought. But his own secrets were the priority. He had to find Yasmin.

"Xanthe," he called.

"Yes, Tenuk," said Xanthe, appearing silently next to him. "I have not yet located Yasmin."

"I have an idea," said Tenuk. "Come with me." He grabbed his reality mask and entered the virtual world where he had last encountered her. Maybe he could find her in there.

•

"45%" said Pete in Cameron's ear. "She's losing control."

Without warning, the blue-eyed avatar appeared in the middle of the room. Cameron stared in horror. She had hold of two struggling figures that Cameron recognised instantly.

Tara and Audrey.

"Let them go," shouted Cameron. "You have no quarrel with these kids."

She flung out her hand in the real world, desperately seeking Ben. "The girls are online," she said. "Yasmin's got them. Disconnect Tara from the software, now, and tell Chloe."

Ben didn't hesitate. Cameron heard him clattering down the stairs.

"I have you now," said Yasmin. "SimCavalier, why do you come to me willingly? You know I can destroy you."

"I'd like to see you try," said Cameron, unconsciously echoing Angus. "I'm a real being in the real world. You're just a shadow. You can't touch me."

"I can and I will," said Yasmin. A hypnotic rhythm started to beat around the room. "I have already disposed of one human who was no longer needed. You pose no challenge."

Cameron caught herself swaying to the beat. No. She started singing, badly, belting out her favourite song from when she was a teenager, breaking up the rhythm. She marched towards Yasmin, defiant, trying to hold the AI's attention and distract her from the girls.

Tara's avatar slumped to the ground, no longer linked to the child. Ben must have succeeded in freeing her. Audrey was still in Yasmin's grasp, but no longer struggling.

Yasmin seemed to grow, looming over Cameron, her

head in the stars above her lair. Cameron felt rather than heard the volume controls on her mask slide to noise cancellation. She couldn't hear herself sing anymore. The mesmerising beat redoubled, and she felt her mind responding, dulling, focusing on the beat. Was this how the sleepwalker had died? Hypnotised and doing Yasmin's bidding? How was she able to control the peripheral devices, the mask that Cameron was wearing?

That was something to work out when she got back in the real world. She had a job to do here. If she couldn't sing, she could move. She darted this way and that across the chequered floor, trying to syncopate her rhythms and break the hypnotic hold. It worked for a minute, but her movements began to match the rhythm of the beat and she slowed.

She had to… hold… on…

Cameron's whole consciousness was immersed in Yasmin's reality. She didn't notice her body stand and start to walk slowly around the room. She bumped into furniture until she found the wall, then slid along until she found the window. Deeply asleep, her hands fumbled at the catch.

Ben came running up the stairs. "Cameron," he called, "Tara's okay. She's out and she's with her mum." He walked into the room and saw her standing at the open window, staring out with sightless eyes at the three storey drop to the garden.

"Cameron," he shouted, shaking her. "Cameron, wake up."

She stirred, still half mesmerised. In the virtual world she opened her eyes to see Audrey's avatar jumping around the room. Yasmin's focus on Cameron had given her a chance to move. "Hey, Yasmin," shouted Audrey. "Remember me?"

Remember? That was odd, thought Cameron. Audrey had never met Yasmin.

"Cameron, hang in there," said Audrey's voice. "It's me, Chloe.

In the half-dream state, Cameron's avatar struggled back up to stand and face Yasmin. She could hear nothing, but Ben's rousing brought her to her senses. What was happening again? Her mind felt like treacle. Cameron reached her real hand up to the reality mask and slid the audio control along. "Cameron," she heard Pete call in the background. "35%. Keep going."

Cameron swayed in both worlds, determined to stay conscious. But Yasmin's attention was no longer on her. Other figures had entered the room. A pangolin and a second blue eyed figure. Another one? Was she seeing double?

"Get out, Yasmin," said the Pangolin. "Get out while you still can. They're taking you apart. Get to the data centre. Save yourself."

"Not on my watch," yelled Chloe, flinging herself at Yasmin. She passed straight through the AI's perfectly rendered form, fragments of Yasmin flying out in slow motion towards the crumbling artwork on the wall.

Cameron's avatar and her real body slumped to the

floor. The black and white chequerboard seemed to dissolve beneath her, and she knew nothing more.

27: TEAMWORK

When she came round, she was lying on her bed and there were familiar voices around her. Eventually, the muddle of noise turned into recognisable words.

"Did she do it, Ben?" said Aunt Vicky's voice. "Has Yasmin really gone?"

"Yes," said Ben. Cameron felt him squeeze her hand. "All the nodes have been closed. She can't have survived this time."

Cameron squeezed back and she felt Ben turn abruptly. "Well, look who's awake," he said. "You gave me a real fright."

Cameron opened her eyes and sat up slowly. "That was very strange," she said. "Is Tara okay?"

"Yes," said Ben. "I'm glad you're awake. It's nearly time for Ross's race, and I know you wouldn't want to miss it." He helped her to stand. She wobbled slightly. "I've got you," he said. "Don't worry."

Aunt Vicky bustled out ahead of them and Cameron made her way steadily down the stairs, gathering strength as she went. When they reached the ground floor, she could hear the livestream from the Olympics building up to the triathlon. Aunt Vicky went to open the door of the sitting room and paused. "Before you have another shock, dear, I thought you'd better know I had a visitor this afternoon."

Cameron walked through the door to cheers from the rest of the family. To her astonishment, sitting in the middle of the group was Jack Sladen.

He gave her an embarrassed smile. "I promised to come and see Aunt Vicky, didn't I?" he said. "This place hasn't changed a bit. I'm glad you're okay."

Cameron sat down next to Tara, hugging her tight. "Are you okay?" she whispered. "And Audrey?"

Tara nodded and clung to her aunt. "Yes," she said, sniffing. "I'm sorry. We had an invitation to a birthday party for one of our friends and we didn't think it would hurt to go."

"Don't worry," said Cameron. "Audrey's mom came to help, and everything is alright now."

"The invitation was from her, wasn't it?" whispered Tara.

"Probably," said Cameron. "She was very sneaky." She kept a firm grip on Tara and turned to Ben. "Are Ross and Shell okay?"

Ben nodded. "It was touch and go for a while," he said, "but yes, Ross was passed fit to compete and Shell is fine. They're due to start any minute."

Cameron settled back into the sofa and took notice of the coverage on the wallscreen for the first time. An aerial drone shot of the competitors warming up zoomed in on a red, white and blue cap. "There he is," she said, relieved.

The individual introductions began, each athlete spotlighted, waving to the virtual crowd. Ross gave the cameras a forced smile. He looked pale and drawn, but focused.

The wait was over, and they all dived into the water for the first leg of the race. Ross's Team GB cap bobbed steadily and rapidly along, keeping to his own pace. He emerged at the end of the swim in a respectable fourth place, had a perfect changeover, and by the time he was two hundred metres down the road he was in third.

"He's doing okay," said Ben. "It's hard work, though."

Cameron could see how much effort he was having to put in. He settled into the back of the leading group, keeping in touch but slightly off the pace.

"It's not going to be enough," said Charlie.

"Never write Ross off," said Cameron, willing him on. At the final changeover he was obviously in pain, but this was where he excelled. RunningManTech was running, and Yasmin was not going to deprive him of his medal. "Come on," she muttered. "Come on."

It was close, there was no doubt about it. In the final straight towards the finish, barely a couple of metres separated the top three athletes. Cameron could see Ross pushing for a final burst of acceleration, and he'd timed it just right. As he broke the tape, the room erupted.

Gold.

Cameron was shaking with relief. Ben hugged her from one side, and Jack from the other. Her smartscreen lit up with a call from the office. She saw the joy on her team's faces and panned around the room to show them the scenes in the house.

The cameras homed in on Ross who had Michelle in a tight hug. He waved to the crowd and then limped slowly towards the podium. As the British flag flew above him, Ross kissed the medal around his neck.

Afterwards, Cameron said she must have had something in her eye.

•

"When's Ross back at work?" asked Susie. She was working through her messages and conference schedule, planning her engagements for the next quarter.

"Monday," said Cameron. "He needed an extra couple of weeks to recover."

"It all seems like a dream now," said Susie. "I want to see that medal before I go back on the circuit. It did really happen, didn't it?"

"It did," said Joel. "I think he's going to feel a bit lost for a while. That was the biggest goal of his life, and he's done it, despite Yasmin."

"How did the karate girl get on?" asked Noor. "The one whose original competition was disrupted?" She was annotating the final model of the work they had done, archiving every link and note for future reference.

"Double gold," said Cameron. "Her first final was after the triathlon so there was no malware left and no Yasmin to control it. She won the kata, then followed it up with the sparring medal the next day. I watched it all. She was brilliant."

Cameron looked around the room. Her team was almost back together again and between them they had pulled off some remarkable work. Yasmin was gone. Jack had finally worked out who to trust. She had a very good idea where Tenuk was and he was being watched, and Ben was back. She couldn't ask for any more than that.

•

Johanna slept, lulled by the mesmerising sounds of the Sanctuary. Occasional sensations from the world around her threatened to lift her out of the dream state. The click of a lock. The sound of footsteps. A rush of cold air. She twitched, and the sensitive Sanctuary programme responded with hypnotic beats from the background to drive her deeper into the dream. Its selling point for shift workers the world over was the Sanctuary's ability to keep a user in a comfortable REM state for their entire allocated sleep cycle. It was certainly working for Johanna.

Her dream changed. She was at a console, her fingers flying over the keys. At a very deep level, she was conscious that this wasn't her own workspace. The controls were unfamiliar. Why was she dreaming about something outside her experience? The mesmeric beats sent her under again.

She shivered and reached in a half-sleep for her coverlet. She couldn't grasp it, and her hands fell to her side again as the Sanctuary adjusted its hypnotic settings to settle her. Her legs were heavy, and her feet were cold.

The sensation drifted away. Locks clicked and threatened to wake her, but she stayed asleep. Eventually the dream drifted away like gossamer strands on the wind. Johanna turned over in her bed, tugged at the coverlet, and started snoring.

When she woke up, she found she was thinking of Aron, but she didn't know why.

ACKNOWLEDGEMENTS

As always, thank you to Xavier and our children for their patience when I'm plotting. Putting together a SimCavalier story is always a challenge, especially when the characters go their own way without warning. My editor, Gillie Hatton, does a great job of pulling them back into line when they get out of hand, and this was a particularly knotty one to untangle. David Morton once again helped to keep the tech in check and suggested some ingenious hacks that are all incorporated. Thanks to Gillie and David for pushing me to raise my game.

There's a lot of real tech underneath this story, and the world sometimes moves faster than I can imagine. It was a matter of lucky timing that I attended the SXSW festival in Austin, Texas just as I was finishing the book. I picked up new insights and learned from the experiences of, among others, Second Life creator Philip Rosedale, OpenAI founder Greg Brockman, tech visionary JC Oliver, and spent a night dancing at the spectacular augmented reality show of DJ Max Cooper. A year earlier in Austin I learned about the Bear test, a very real experiment that used the children's book 'I Want My Hat Back' by Jon Klassen to demonstrate AI learning, labelling, data sets, and sentiment analysis. The good news is that humans are still a little ahead. What is imagined here may well be less than 25 years in our future, but it's fun to put together a vision of the possibilities that lie ahead.

How do you stay safe in this rapidly changing tech environment? Check your sources, don't believe what the AI tells you, and make sure you set up good multi-factor authentication for your accounts online. You may not think your data is useful to anyone, but it is, and you don't want to find out the hard way. The biggest real life data breach to date collected three billion data sets. That's a lot of phishing emails and dodgy texts!

Enjoy the journey into the metaverse.

Kate.

Find out more at
www.katebaucherel.com

ALSO IN THE SIMCAVALIER SERIES IN PAPERBACK AND EBOOK

BITCOIN HURRICANE

SIMCAVALIER BOOK ONE

London, 2045. Cameron Silvera, aka the SimCavalier, is a hacker legend in the cybersecurity world. In real life, Cameron leads the Argentum Associates white hat infosec team, known to world governments and global conglomerates for their ability to bring hacked systems back online fast.

The City of London Bank calls in the Argentum team when the Speakeasy Worm, a global threat, shuts them down. As they dig into the virus, they discover a hidden message addressed to the SimCavalier. A hurricane of cyberattacks is on the way, and a global crime syndicate is taunting its most dangerous adversary.

HACKED FUTURE
SIMCAVALIER BOOK TWO

It starts out with a body – the stench of a body, to be more precise. Ross may have an idea why the man is dead in his flat, but he's not telling anyone.

The SimCavalier, aka Cameron Silvera, wants to enjoy her romantic getaway with Ben, but clues to a Paris data theft are coming thick and fast. Her team has its hands full dealing with an escalating torrent of online attacks, and the fallout from a global data breach has hit their clients hard.

Cameron starts to connect the dots as underground markets are flooded with stolen files. But the cybercriminals are ahead of them, hunting down the SimCavalier who has thwarted their plans once too often.

TANGLED FORTUNES

SIMCAVALIER BOOK THREE

When a nuclear explosion sends shockwaves around the world, Cameron Silvera, aka the SimCavalier, knows exactly who's behind it.

The Argentum Associates team mobilises to secure nuclear facilities, but stakes rise when a body is found floating out to sea, silenced by the cybercrime syndicate. Cameron, desperate to protect her family from the growing threat, joins forces with undercover hackers in an international fight against a rogue militia and a global cybercriminal network.

As the action goes down to the wire on England's North East coast, in the heat of Singapore, and in the mountains and lakes of Wyoming, it's a race against time to defuse an explosive finale.

CRITICAL NEXUS
SIMCAVALIER BOOK FOUR

Jack Sladen, tech billionaire, is coming back to his roots. Cameron Silvera doesn't trust him. Is Jack out to save the world, or to destroy it? A new cybercrime outfit known as Steamyard is wreaking havoc in the digital realm and Cameron's team are working all hours to keep their attacks at bay. As they dig deeper, they discover a disturbing connection between the Steamyard, the Sladen Foundation, and a convict held in isolation at the high-tech Way House Prison. Cameron knows that the only way to protect herself and her loved ones is to keep the rogue AI behind bars, but black hat hackers have other plans. As the Sladen Foundation celebrates its launch, the cybercriminals activate their diabolical plan. Cameron and the Argentum team are in a race against time to stop the creation of a monster that threatens to take down everything they hold dear.